Praise for

"… an impressive debut and a promising start to a smart new mystery series." — Kirkus Reviews

"If you've ever wondered what Stephanie Plum would be like with a little experience in life under her belt, Nanci Rathbun has the answer. … Her heroine is flawed and complex, her plot perfectly constructed to bring out all of the facets she's created. For mystery lovers, or fans of romantic suspense, Nanci Rathbun is one to watch." — Shelf Awareness, October 8, 2013

Praise for *CASH KILLS*

PI Angelina Bonaparte "reminded me at times of Parker's Spenser in her detecting, her sense of humor, and her flamboyant sartorial style. … *Cash Kills* is a first-rate mystery that combines police procedural with private detection and it features a compelling lead character and a marvelous cast. It's entertaining, fast-paced and suspenseful, and is highly recommended." — Reviewed By Jack Magnus for *Readers' Favorite*

"To find justice in the midst of lies and cover-ups, Angie must face her own fear of trusting another. Readers will relate to her humor, vulnerability and dedication to the truth." - IBPA Benjamin Franklin Silver Honoree for digital ebook excellence — September 2014

Praise for *HONOR KILLS*

"I found *Honor Kills* an extremely satisfying read. It ticks all the boxes of a good detective mystery, and the lead character Angie is extremely easy to empathize with. It's not often you come across a middle-aged PI hero, who is also female. The plot was intricate and full of twists and turns as befits such a mystery story. Having read *Honor Kills*, I am motivated to read the other books in Rathbun's series, which is probably as high a praise as a reviewer can give an author. – 5* Review by Grant Leishman for *Readers' Favorite*

"Nanci Rathbun takes the time to explore why her characters doggedly pursue their objectives; and this too makes *Honor Kills* a superior read in a genre that too often focuses on the 'whodunnit' over the 'why pursue this inquiry' question. The result is another spirited Angelina Bonaparte mystery that requires no special familiarity with predecessors in the series in order to prove satisfying to newcomers and prior fans alike." – Reviewed by Diane Donovan for *Midwest Book Review*, April 2018

TRUTH KILLS

Angelina Bonaparte Mysteries #1

Nanci Rathbun

Published by Dark Chocolate Press LLC
http://darkchocolatepress.com

This book is a work of fiction. All characters, events, and organizations portrayed in this novel are the product of the author's imagination or are used fictitiously. Any resemblance to actual events, locales or persons—living or dead—is entirely coincidental.

SECOND EDITION
ISBN: 978-1-9867626-2-5 (Print)
ISBN: 978-0-9987557-1-7 (Digital E-book)
Library of Congress Control Number: 2017903141
Rathbun, Nancianne.
Truth Kills / Nanci Rathbun
FICTION: Mystery/Suspense

Cover design by Nathaniel Dasco
http://BookCoverMall.com

Formatting by Polgarus Studio
http://www.polgarusstudio.com

Author photo by Michele Rene Chillook, Dubuque, Iowa

Published by Dark Chocolate Press LLC
http://darkchocolatepress.com

Acknowledgements

I wish to thank the following persons: Rev. Barry W. Szymanski, who read the draft from the point of view of a former police officer and provided me with valuable insights into police procedure and weapons use; Michael Giorgio, who taught me the basics of the mystery genre at AllWriters' and who also coached me through one of my many drafts; Robert McGee, who read the final draft and gave me valuable feedback; and all my fellow workshoppers at AllWriters'—I hesitate to name you lest I forget someone—who encouraged, critiqued and laughed with me. Any mistakes are my own.

Chapter 1

I'm a professional snoop and I'm good at it. While on the job, I can look like the senior partner of an accountancy firm in my pinstriped navy business suit, or the neighborhood white-haired old-lady gossip. Off the job, I'm a fifty-something hottie—white hair gelled back, dramatic eye make-up, toned body encased in designer duds. Gravity has taken a small toll, but who notices in candlelight?

As I rubbed potting soil into the cooking oil that I'd already smeared on my Salvation Army second-hand clothes, I examined myself in the mirror. A short, plain woman (five foot, three inches) with choppy white hair and no make-up, wearing dirty, baggy clothes, looked back at me. A homeless person. I nodded and headed down the fire stairs to the parking garage, trying to avoid meeting any of my neighbors.

The beauty of being a woman, as the French say, "of a certain age," is that I can be invisible. Young people, both men and women, look right through me, unless I make the effort to be noticed. Older men look past me, too, to gaze upon the tight, toned, tanned bodies that they wish they could possess. Only older women seem to notice me,

1

because they're judging me against some invisible standard and wondering how I measure up compared to them. It's not usually malicious, it's just how we were raised. Believe me, I do it myself. Is her ass tighter than mine? Are her boobs perkier? Any cellulite on those thighs? It's competition at the most primitive level, the female equivalent of two silver-backed gorillas thumping chests and roaring at each other.

Today, however, wasn't a hottie day. Elisa Morano, one of the aforementioned tight, toned and tanned, was suspected of playing house with my client's husband, Anthony Belloni, a.k.a. Tony Baloney. Tony's cellular phone bill listed lots of calls to Ms. Morano's apartment, coincidentally located in one of Tony's many real estate holdings. His credit card statement showed purchases of lingerie, perfume and a fur coat, stuff that his wife, Gracie, had yet to see. To top it off, Gracie was eight months pregnant with their fifth child and spitting mad. She hired me to find out whether Tony was indeed cheating with Elisa Morano.

Which brings me back to my bag lady persona. Dumpster diving is legal. Once the trash is on the curb, it's public property. The Supremes ruled on it, and I mean Scalia and company, not the group Diana Ross fronted. People like me make a good living, finding out stuff from the trash. The problem is getting to it. The super will stop an average Jane from digging through the garbage, but if he sees a bag lady, he'll likely turn the other way. No harm in recycling, right?

So on this hot Thursday morning in August, I parked my car a block away, shuffled up the drive to Elisa's building and jumped into the dumpster that squatted behind it. My short stature made it easy for me to hide in there, as I searched for something with her name on it. These people were upper class, everything was nicely bagged and I didn't think I'd have to worry about getting crap on my car seat when I was done.

It took about twenty minutes to find the bag, full of paper that was run through a shredder. I couldn't be sure until I put it all back together, but there was a piece with an "El" still intact. Maybe it was "Elisa." It was all I found that even remotely fit, so I tossed it over the side and heaved myself out, straight into the path of a hulk in a black suit.

"Watcha doin' there, lady?" Tony Baloney's bodyguard, Jimmy the Arm, asked as he grabbed me and pinned me to the side of the dumpster. Jimmy's sleeve-defying biceps compensate for his tiny mental gifts.

I realized that Jimmy didn't recognize me, despite having seen me on numerous occasions, both social and professional. My bag lady persona was my best defense. "Nothin.' I ain't doin' nothin.' Just lookin,'" I responded.

"For what?"

"Stuff ta sell. Clothes. Shoes. Books. Cans. These rich folks toss out good stuff." I pulled a face. "But not much today, one bag. Just my luck."

"Well, leave it and get goin' and don't come back to this building. Unnerstan?" He gave a little shove for good measure, not enough to hurt. His mama must have raised him well. Of course, he'd toss a rival into a cement mixer with no qualms. But I'm not averse to using whatever advantages come my way. I earned all the white on my head, and if it gets me out of a jam, it's just one of the perks of being slightly older.

I sloped off down the driveway, looking behind me as if scared that Jimmy was following. Actually, I was checking that the bag was still lying next to the dumpster. Sure enough, Jimmy ignored it and entered the building by the super's door. Guess Jimmy's mama never taught him to pick up trash. I scuttled back, grabbed the bag, and sprinted down the street to the lot where I left my car, to drive back to the office.

I share office space on Prospect Avenue, on Milwaukee's east side, with the firm of Neh Accountants. The "s" on the end is misleading. It's a one-person company run by Susan Neh, a third-generation Japanese-American. Susan and I met when we both worked for Jake Waterman. She conducted his financial investigations and I did his legwork—computer searches, tails, background checks. It didn't take Susan long to earn her CPA and go out on her own. I joined her when I got my P.I. license and needed a place to hang my shingle. Most of Susan's clientele are of Japanese descent, but lately, she's working with a few Hmong and Vietnamese. She kids me about my super-expressive Italians and Sicilians, and I jab her about her inscrutable Asians. I was glad to find that Susan was out on a client call today. It saved me from explaining my less than glamorous appearance.

It took me six hours of tedious, neck-straining, eyeball-screaming work to piece the shredded paper from the bag back together. Luckily, Elisa didn't have a cross-cut shredder, just the kind that produces long strips of paper. I can reassemble cross-cut, too, given enough time and motivation. The only way to be absolutely sure that no one can read your letters is to burn them and pulverize the ashes, or soak the paper in a pail of water mixed with a half-cup of bleach to destroy the ink. Then you can toss the blank paper with no worries.

Like most people, Elisa simply put a plastic bag into the can and shredded it into the bag. When she lifted it out and discarded it, the remains were in distinct layers, making it easier to separate and reassemble. It helped that the paper had different colors and textures. It's like working a jigsaw puzzle, without the picture on the box for a guide.

Six hours later, I had a pretty fair understanding of the woman—vain (online article about Botox, with list of local practitioners), fertile (Ortho-Provera drug interaction statement from a mail-order prescription company), savvy (year-old Vanguard mutual fund statement showing a 70K balance), cautious (no intact papers with her name in the dumpster, she apparently shredded everything).

I wasn't any closer, though, to discovering if Tony was indeed making it with the beauteous Ms. Morano, and my back was screaming from hours of bending over the office work table. My skin itched, even though I'd changed out of my clean dirty clothes, and it was already six o'clock. I made copies of the pieced-together papers, tossed them in my briefcase, and headed for home in my Black Cherry Miata convertible. There aren't enough top-down days in southeast Wisconsin, but this was one and I felt good, tooling down Lincoln Memorial Drive with the cool air of Lake Michigan on my skin. Heaven.

The Miata, like my condo, was a gift to myself following my divorce. The decree restored both my self-respect and my maiden name—Angelina Bonaparte, pronounced Boe-nah-par-tay, not Bo-nah-part. Napoleon was a Corsican-*cum*-French wannabe, so he left the last syllable off, but I'm one hundred percent Sicilian and I pronounce it the way it was meant to be pronounced.

I love my car. It symbolizes my post-marriage financial and emotional independence, and the sense of personal daring that I kept under tight wraps while I was Mrs. Bozo (I call him "your dad" when the kids are around, even though they're grown and have their own kids). I still shudder to think of twenty-five prime years spent trying to fit the pattern of wife, lover, mother, housekeeper. Picture June Cleaver wearing a sassy red thong under her demure shirtwaist dress.

Bozo started playing around when he turned fifty. Funny, whenever

I heard about some guy running around on his wife, I always told my best friend, Judy, that the door wouldn't hit my butt on the way out. When it happened to me, though, I decided that I owed a twenty-five year marriage at least one chance. Or two. Three was when I changed the locks, packed his clothes and put the suitcases on the front lawn. I reminded him of Papa's toast at our wedding—"There are no divorces in our family. There are widows, but no divorces." It scared him purple.

Of course, we did divorce and I did manage to dissuade Papa from having Bozo fitted for lead sneakers, or seeing to it that his body was made unfit for further nookie. The Miata was my first indulgence after the proceedings. I went down to the dealer with a check in hand that very day. Then I put the house on the market and signed the papers for my East side high-rise condo. I heard the whispers about "middle-aged crazy" and "trying to prove something," but I ignored them. This was me, the real me, not that convention that I'd tried to squeeze myself into all those years.

I stepped into my foyer and locked the door behind me. Shedding clothes as I walked, I tossed the dirty duds into my bedroom closet's built-in hamper and walked naked into the bathroom. If driving the Miata is car heaven, standing under a steam shower with five heads massaging from toes to crown is surely water heaven.

Thirty minutes later, moisturized, gelled, dressed in yoga pants and a tee shirt, I sipped a glass of Chardonnay and stared into the fridge. Then I glared at the goods in the freezer. Why is it that there's never anything to eat when you just want to stay in? It would have to be another deep dish Milwaukee special night—cheese, sausage, mushrooms, onions, the famous "SMO." I was either going to have to step up my exercise program and cut back on the fat, or buy a bigger wardrobe. While I love shopping for clothes, the second option didn't appeal. Bozo used to pinch my waist and smirk when he could get an inch between his fingers. I love to see him assess my figure now, when we attend family functions like birthdays and baptisms. There's no way I'm gaining back that inch, so I resolved to do some grocery shopping soon. Just for good measure, I did twenty minutes of yoga/Pilates while waiting for the pizza. A couple chapters of the latest Sue Grafton (I love that Kinsey, but, jeez, one black dress for her whole adult life?) and I was ready to pound the pillow. Solo.

It's been months since my last serious involvement. He thought I wouldn't find out about the bar-time pickups. "Honest, Angie, it doesn't mean a thing. I just like a little variety." Sometimes I wish I was a lesbian, it would make life so much easier. I hear they're more than ninety-percent faithful. What a concept!

I met Kevin, my current guy, four weeks ago. My neighbor Sally and her son, Joseph, introduced us. Joseph was diagnosed with Muscular Dystrophy at age six. Kevin is his physical therapist. Picture Harrison Ford as Han Solo in the first *Star Wars* movie—a little rough, killer body, redeeming lop-sided smile that gets him out of all sorts of trouble. He's thirty-eight, so, yes, he's a few years younger than I am. Given the actuarial tables and my energy level, that's good.

We've been doing that painful boy-girl dance ever since, the one we all first learned in adolescence. Is he available? Cute enough? Is she needy? Pretty enough? Will he want to go to bed right away? Do I want to? Should I? Add today's refinements —STDs? Last HIV test? Last lover? *Ad infinitum. Ad nauseum.* Even my best friend Judy is getting sick of me. "Just DO IT," she yelled at me last week.

"Can't," I responded. "You know me." She groaned. We've been through this a lot in the course of the five years since my divorce. I have this little hang-up. I won't deal with dishonesty on a personal basis. Go figure, someone in my line of work! So I operate on the assumption that everyone is hiding something. I run credit checks and criminal and civil court searches on the men who ask me out. I watch them for signs of fooling around—scents they don't normally wear, clothes changed in the middle of the day, long lunches when they can't be called, lots of little clues that mean nothing and everything. I'm not proud of it, but I won't be a fool again. I haven't figured a way out of the morass that women and men seem to sink into. Most nights, like tonight, I sleep alone.

Chapter 2

Murder is unique in that it abolishes the party it injures, so that society has to take the place of the victim and on his behalf demand atonement or grant forgiveness; it is the one crime in which society has a direct interest.

W. H. Auden

I woke, groggy and disoriented, to the sounds of buzzing and pounding. The digital clock read 4:48. Groaning, I pawed for the "off" button. Still, the sounds persisted. I sat up and listened more intently—telephone, doorbell, hammering on the entry door. *Good grief*, I thought, *has the world exploded?*

I picked up the phone with a raspy "Hello?" as I pulled on my robe and slid my feet into slippers.

"Angie, it's Bart Matthews. Listen closely, there isn't much time until the police get to you."

"I think they're already here, Bart," I responded, as I looked out the peephole at two men, one of whom I knew. "Joe Ignowski and another guy are pounding on my door."

"Okay, before you answer the door, I want to hire you on behalf of Anthony Belloni."

"Just a minute, I'm getting some clothes on," I yelled at the door, hoping to stifle them before all my neighbors heard. The pounding and buzzing stopped. *Why*, I thought, *would the infamous "Mafia attorney" (media phrase, not mine) be representing Tony? Adultery isn't illegal.* "Bart, I have a conflict of interest in that regard." I was trying not to name Gracie.

"I know, Gracie told me. She also told the police when they arrested Tony tonight for the murder of Elisa Morano. I don't want you talking to the cops without a briefing. If you're employed by me, you're covered by attorney-client privilege."

"Hang on, Bart, I'm thinking." I opened the door and motioned the detectives in. "Give me a minute," I told them.

"Hey, Angie," Joe whined, but I ignored him as I walked into my bedroom and shut and locked the door.

From the back of my walk-in closet, surrounded by sound-muffling clothing, I resumed my conversation with Bart. "Let me get this straight. Tony's in the slammer for killing Elisa and Gracie wants me to help him?"

"Right. She's in a 'Stand by Your Man' mood." He paused and I heard the click and the little explosion of butane flame, then the sucking sound as he took a drag. Bart weighs at least three hundred, smokes non-stop, and works eighty hours a week as legal counsel for the Family. I doubt he'll see forty.

Ignowski and partner were now pounding on my bedroom door. "Give me a minute, Bart." I exited the closet, opened the bedroom door and stood there, one hand brandishing the phone and the other on my hip. "You guys will have to wait. I'm talking to my attorney." Joe's partner started to protest, but I raised my hand and pointed. "Go press the Start button on the coffee-maker in the kitchen. It's loaded and ready. Pour yourselves a cup and I'll be out as soon as I can." Before either man could respond, I closed and locked the door and walked back into the closet.

"I can't say yes or no to the offer, Bart, until I know whether Tony did it. I won't protect him if he did."

"No way, Angie. He never touched her." Hoarse cough/laugh. "Well, at least he never touched her that way."

"But they were making it?"

"Yeah, they were. He's properly ashamed, believe me. He and Gracie had it out tonight, after she told him about hiring you. He broke down and confessed, told her he wanted to end it with Elisa, that he'd never cheated before. Then the police came to the door and she lost it and told them the whole story, how Tony couldn't have done it because he loved her and not Elisa. Silly twit just couldn't keep her yap shut."

"She's under a lot of pressure, Bart. Four little kids and another on the way, and a lying husband accused of murdering the girlfriend. I think you should cut her some slack."

He had the grace to apologize, and even sounded sheepish as he did. "Sorry, Angie, you're right. Gracie's got a lot to deal with. That's why she's begging you to help clear Tony." He let it lie there for a couple seconds. Every good lawyer or interrogator knows the technique. I use it myself. That doesn't make it easier to handle.

"Can you get me into the jail tomorrow? I want to talk to Tony in person."

"No problem. You can go in as part of my staff. You're taking the job, right?"

"For now. You're lucky, I didn't find anything incriminating on him, just the affair. Now I'd better get out there and talk to Iggy and his partner before they explode."

"Lucky draw, getting Iggy, huh? Could be worse. I'll call you first thing in the morning."

"It's already morning, dammit. Don't call me before ten." I hung up the phone and washed my face before joining the men, who were drinking coffee at my dining room table.

There's a lot of common ground between criminals and cops. Both savor power, thrills, control. The good cops know they're only a step or two away from the crooks they're arresting. Iggy is one of the good cops. I heard that Iggy's new license plates arrived in the mail one year with a little message scratched on the back from the prisoner who stuffed the envelopes—HI IGGY. Go figure.

Iggy introduced his partner to me. "Angie, this is Detective Ted Wukowski."

I extended my hand. "They call you Wookie?"

"Only once." He gave me a real Sergeant Friday look, no smile, no expression, all business.

Iggy coughed, a little embarrassed by Wukowski's manners. "Angie, we're here to talk to you about Tony Baloney, uh, I mean, Anthony Belloni."

"I know, Iggy. I was just on the phone with Bart." We both knew who I meant, and if Wukowski was in the dark, what did I care? "I'm on retainer to help him represent Belloni, so I can't talk to you."

Wukowski stood, looming over me as I sipped from my coffee. "You know the rules, lady. You can lose your license for withholding evidence of a crime."

"That's right, Detective. But the last I heard, running around on your wife isn't a crime. It's dishonest and lowdown and immoral, but if I had to report everyone I knew who cheated, the streets would be pretty empty." I gently set my cup down on the table, pushed back my chair and stood up. I knew I didn't hold the advantage, five-three to his six feet, dressed in slippers and robe, with my hair in its wild bed-head mode, while he wore a navy blue suit and his dark hair was perfectly combed and parted.

Nevertheless, I stuck out my chin and took a step toward him. He backed up. I graciously extended my hand toward the foyer. "If you gentlemen will excuse me, I have business to attend to. You may direct any further inquiries to Bart Matthews."

"That scum," Wukowski muttered under his breath.

Iggy grabbed his arm and pulled him to the door. "Ange, a woman is dead. We need to find out who did it."

"How'd she die, Iggy?" I asked.

He hesitated. "The coroner will have to decide. There was a gunshot to the chest, and a lot of cuts to the face and hands. It wasn't pretty."

After they left, I sank down on the couch and stared out at the panoramic view of Lake Michigan. Light was just breaking over the horizon. A new day, but not for Elisa Morano. I slowly recited the prayer for the dead that I learned as a child:

Eternal rest grant unto her, O Lord, and let perpetual light shine upon her. May her soul and all the souls of the faithful departed, through the mercy of God, rest in peace. Amen.

Considering her lifestyle, I wasn't sure that Elisa was one of the faithful, but I figured there was no harm in asking.

Chapter 3

The public have an insatiable curiosity to know everything. Except what is worth knowing. Journalism, conscious of this, and having tradesman-like habits, supplies their demands.

Oscar Wilde

Bart called on the dot of ten o'clock. "Angie, you up?" he asked.

"Yes, Bart, I'm up." My voice was edgy. I don't do well without my usual seven hours of sleep. "What's the story?"

"You can see Tony at one o'clock, at the county jail. You're listed as on my staff."

I heard the intake of yet another of Bart's cigarettes. "Bart, those things will kill you."

"Yeah, yeah. I've heard it all before. Read my bumper sticker—'Eat right, exercise, live healthy, die anyway.' I figure I might as well die from something I enjoy."

No sense arguing. My Aunt Teresa would say, "Save your breath to cool your soup." Switching gears, I took out a legal pad and started to make notes. "Did they charge him yet?"

"Nah, the DA is tap-dancing around it for the moment. It's all circumstantial."

"Tony still claims he's innocent, right?"

"Right." He hesitated. "The thing is, I believe him, Angie. And you know I'm no sucker for a story."

That made me pause. Bart had probably heard every low-life excuse there was, every alibi, every outright lie. I've seen him break a guy's story with just a raised eyebrow and a long silence. If he believed Tony, it carried weight with me. "What line do you want me to follow, Bart?"

"If Tony didn't do it, someone else did, right? She didn't shoot herself. Even disregarding the cuts, there was no gun at the scene. We need to find some other plausible suspect. We don't need to prove anything, but we need to cast doubt on the Tony angle. Dig into her past and see who might have had a beef with her. Let's sling a little mud."

He was right, in a crude way. I'm not saying Elisa deserved to be murdered, because I don't think anyone has the right to make that decision for another person. But she wasn't an innocent bystander who was gunned down on the street; she was a kept woman who was murdered in her own apartment. Somebody hated her pretty badly, or was so afraid of her that murder seemed the only way out. Either way, it didn't look like Elisa's reputation would be lily-white when we were done.

We ended the conversation with Bart promising to fax the police report to me. I dressed and headed for the office.

Susan was already hard at work when I got in. Looking up from her computer monitor, she raised an eyebrow and glanced at the clock. I'm generally in the office by eight, with a cup of Starbucks in hand, ready to lay out the day's work. "Bad night," I responded to her unspoken question.

"You and Kevin finally made it?" She grinned.

"No. But I did have three men vying for my attention at four this morning." I slipped behind my desk, uncapped the coffee and poured it into a ceramic mug. I hate drinking from Styrofoam or cardboard.

Susan lifted her ever-full teacup in a toast. "Way to go, girl."

I told her the real story, leaving out Tony's name. She just shook her head in wonderment as the details unfolded.

When her phone rang, I turned to my mail. The business side of my profession is not one that I can afford to ignore. Too many independents fold because they don't get their bills out on time. Most of it was junk mail, which I shredded anyway. I don't put any paper in the garbage, and I contract with a company that hauls my bags of shreds away and burns them. Even landfills are not secure. The city doesn't just roll the garbage truck in and randomly dump it. They have a systematic plan for what garbage goes where, based on the day, and a committed snoop with enough hands to help can usually find something that she knows was discarded on a particular day.

There was one envelope that I dreaded opening. The return address read "Marcy Wagner." Marcy hired me four years ago. Fifty-three months, to be exact. Every single month, I get a check in a letter from Marcy, asking if there's any news on her deadbeat husband, Hank. When he first ran off and left her high and dry, I spent time tracing his contacts and family members. I had Susan run forensic accounting programs on him. I did all the usual things, but every avenue ran dry and Marcy couldn't afford the charges for an intensive ongoing investigation. So we reached an agreement. For a small fee, I would continue to check the usual online sources each month—DMV records, credit reports, online court judgments, marriage licenses, even death certificates.

I logged on and did my monthly search. Still no luck. I sure wanted to find that creep. He'd cleaned out their bank account and left Marcy with three kids to raise. She worked two jobs while her mom watched the kids, and still found a way to get to school conferences and scout meetings. In my mind, women like Marcy are the saints of this world. I composed a short note telling her that I still hadn't traced Hank, wrote VOID across her check, tucked the note and check into an envelope and sent them back to her.

Next, I called Gracie Belloni. She answered on the first ring. "Gracie, it's Angie Bonaparte."

"Angie, thank God it's you. I don't know what to do. The TV crews are camped outside the driveway, and the phone's been ringing nonstop with reporters. I'm so scared for Tony."

"Try to stay calm. This will be a three-day wonder. They'll disappear as soon as they realize they're not going to get an interview with you. I need to talk to you about our contract, but I don't want to say too much on the phone. Bart Matthews told me that you want me to work on Tony's case. I just want to be sure you understand that I can't represent both of you at the same time, due to the possibility of conflict of interest. In the course of my investigation for Bart, I might find out something that I can't tell you without Tony's permission. You hired me, though, and if you want, I'll turn down Tony's case."

"No, don't do that. I understand about your representing Tony, and right now, that's the best thing for me and the family. I'll deal with the other issues when Tony's free."

"Then with your permission, I'll put the original case on hold and I won't issue a report until after Tony's cleared." Although I had no idea if Tony would be cleared or not, I couldn't send Gracie into a panic. "I'm going to see Tony this afternoon and I'll call you later. Bart's on it and he's the best. Now take a deep breath." I heard her inhale. "Let it out real slow, Gracie, kind of like the breathing you use in early labor."

That drew a shaky laugh. "If there's one thing I can do, it's labor."

"Good girl," I said. "Are you on a cordless phone right now?"

"No, I'm using the regular phone in the bedroom."

"That's at the back of the house, right?"

"Right."

"Now, I don't want you to get upset, but I need to give you some instructions so the press won't hound you to death. Here's what I want you to do. Don't answer the phone, let it go to voice mail. If it's someone you want to talk to, you can always call back. Don't talk to anyone you don't already know. Don't use a cell phone or a cordless, they're not secure. Anyone with half a brain will call you to tell you they're coming over, so unless you're expecting someone, don't answer the doorbell. Keep the shades down and the drapes drawn, so no one can photograph you or the kids through the glass. Keep the kids indoors for the day. Don't have a conversation about anything confidential while you're in a room with a window or a patio door. With the right equipment, you can actually pick up conversations through the glass. Got all that?"

Gracie made a low groan. "We can't live like this. What are we gonna do?"

"It's just for a little while. After I talk to Tony, I'll be over to see you. Then we can discuss options. Meanwhile, just keep a low profile and don't let them get to you. You've got four little kids to think of, and Tony. You can't fall apart now. You can do this, I know you can. It's no harder than running a house, right?"

"Right." Her voice sounded strained. "Angie, is it okay if I call Father Martin? He's our parish priest. I'd like to talk to him about Elisa."

"If you're thinking about a separation or a divorce, I have to tell you that it couldn't come at a worse time for Tony's defense."

"No, that's not it." There was a long pause. "I just need to get some things off my chest. I guess I always thought of myself as a good Catholic, a good person, but right now, I'm all mixed up. I love Tony, but I hate him, too, for what this is doing to our family and to me. And I'm sorry that girl was killed, but in a way, I'm glad. Now Tony can't be tempted."

Did she really think that Elisa was the cause? Did she really believe that with Elisa gone, Tony would never look at another woman? Of course, I couldn't challenge any of that. Let her live in her fool's paradise for now.

"I'm sure that what you're feeling is pretty normal, kind of like feeling relieved when your teacher is sick on the day of the big math test." She giggled a little. "Ask your priest if he can meet with you at home. If not, just follow the rules when you talk to him, use a landline and maybe drag the phone into the closet or the bathroom, just to be safe."

"Okay. I'll see you later?"

"It's a promise."

I hung up, worried about Gracie and the kids and madder than hell at Tony. Once I showed up at the Belloni home, the press would surround me like hungry sharks circling a bleeding swimmer, but I couldn't see any way to avoid it and still keep my word to Gracie. Crap.

Chapter 4

In jail a man has no personality. He is a minor disposal problem and a few entries on reports. Nobody cares who loves or hates him, what he looks like, what he did with his life. Nobody reacts to him unless he gives trouble. Nobody abuses him. All that is asked of him is that he go quietly to the right cell and remain quiet when he gets there.
—Raymond Chandler, The Long Goodbye

At noon, I drove over to the Milwaukee County Criminal Justice Facility—the jail. In my experience, those who wear uniforms respect others in uniform, so I wore my best business attire—green pinstriped navy blue skirted Nine West suit, plain white button-up blouse, plain hosiery, low-heeled navy pumps. After seeing a female attorney humiliated by having to remove her bra in order to pass through the metal detector, I now took care to only wear a sports bra for jail visits, one with no metal hooks, eyes or underwires. I waited for Tony in one of several interrogation rooms. I'm not really intuitive, except where my kids are concerned, but these rooms always evoked feelings of desperation, fear and anger. The smell of bodily secretions was palpable.

I stood when the door opened and Tony entered, escorted by a jail deputy. Tony still wore the clothes he'd hustled into when the cops came to the house in the middle of the night, and his hands were handcuffed behind his back. The deputy unlocked the handcuffs and gestured Tony toward a chair. "Ring when you're ready to leave," she told me, and pulled the door closed as she left.

I gestured at a chair across from me, and Tony slumped into it. "Do you remember me, Tony? Angelina Bonaparte?"

"Yeah, I know you. Your old man runs Bonaparte's Fruits and Vegetables, right?"

"Right. I'm a P.I." Bart had told me that Tony and Gracie had a heart-to-heart last night, before the arrest, so I thought I might as well lay my cards on the table. "Gracie hired me to find out if you'd been cheating on her after she found the credit card items. I've done some work for Bart Matthews in the past, so when the cops showed up at your door, Gracie and Bart agreed to hire me to help clear you."

He just stared at me. The cops had picked him up and booked him at about two in the morning. He'd been parked in one of the forty-eight bed "housing pods" for ten hours. His hair was sticking up at crazy angles, his eyes were bloodshot, his beard was a shadow of stubble, black mixed with gray. In short, he looked like hell. I waited.

"Can I call you Angie?" he finally asked.

"Sure."

"Angie, I didn't do this thing." He leaned across the table, put his right hand on his chest and held my gaze. "I swear, I didn't kill her. We hadn't even seen each other for three days."

"But you were making it, right?"

"Yeah." He ran his hands through his hair. "But that doesn't mean I killed her." He looked down at the table as he continued. "It wasn't a romance, not for either of us. It was just a sideline for me and a business proposition for her. She never expected more than some presents and a nice time while it lasted."

"You sure about that, Tony? Women have a way of getting involved even when they know it doesn't make sense."

"Not Elisa. She was pretty, she was fun, she was good in bed, okay? She had a way of making you feel more important, more manly, than you knew you really were. But deep down, she was only out for herself. Like when she opened a present, you could almost hear the calculator working."

And you found this attractive enough to betray your family? My emotional danger bells started to ping. "Did she see other men, or just you?"

"Hell, I was paying for the apartment, all the expenses, gave her an allowance. She damn well better not have been seeing anyone else."

Did he really believe that he could buy loyalty? That his money guaranteed her faithfulness? Especially since the relationship was founded on his own adultery. *Denial reigns*, I thought. "Okay, let's start at the beginning. When and where did you meet?"

"It was last March. She was a receptionist at Dunwoodie's—they handle my real estate insurance. I went in to meet with John Dunwoodie, and there's this stunner sitting at the front desk. We flirted a little, you know, while I waited for John to get off a call. Then afterwards, I asked her out to lunch."

The little mental pings grew louder. I didn't say anything, but my disgust must have shown on my face.

"Look, the new baby was making Gracie sick every morning and tired every night. I just wanted someone to enjoy some time with. I'm not proud of it."

"You know, if you walk away from this, you better think twice about how you behave. A stay-at-home wife and mother of five could get a whole lot of your personal income, and I know how to find it for her."

He blanched at that and leaned back in his chair. "Hey, it won't happen again. I already promised Gracie."

"Did it ever happen before Elisa?"

"Once, just once, a lot of years ago." Tony squirmed in his seat, refusing to meet my eyes.

Probably a lie, I thought, but I decided to get back on track. "After your lunch with Elisa, then what?"

"We went out for a couple of dinners, dancing. She complained that Dunwoodie's wasn't a very nice place to work, that John's wife, Jane—you know she's a partner?—was always on Elisa's case and Elisa couldn't do anything right. So I offered her a job managing the Concord Building."

"Was she qualified?"

"All she had to do was collect the rent checks and make a call if something broke down. I advertise that there's an on-site manager, but it's not like the manager's a super or anything."

"When did Elisa move into the apartment?"

"First of May."

"And how often did you see her?"

"Twice, maybe three times a week. Mostly daytime, after she quit her job at Dunwoodie's."

Convenient, I thought. *You already have two singletons and a set of twins, your wife's in the third trimester of her fourth pregnancy and you're having a nooner two or three times a week.* I didn't look up, just kept writing notes on my legal pad. The pinging in my head was now an insistent chiming. "Tell me about Elisa's background. Family, where she grew up, education, that kind of thing."

"No clue. We didn't talk about that."

"What did you talk about?"

"Movies, sports, her investments."

"Investments?" I asked.

"Yeah, she was into some limited real estate partnerships, and she liked to play the stock market. She was pretty good, too."

Twenty-four years old, real estate and stock market investments, 70K in a mutual fund. Elisa was one financially savvy woman.

"Did you ever meet any of her friends?"

"Nah, we mostly stayed in."

I'll bet you did, I thought, *in more ways than one.* "I need to talk to others who knew her. Did she have an address book? Planner? PDA? Cell phone?"

"Funny you should ask that. She misplaced her PDA about a week ago, and it was making her crazy. She practically took the place apart trying to find it, and then she turned my car inside out, but it never showed up."

"How about email? Do you know her login and password?"

He gave me the email address.

"And her password?"

He grimaced. "She never told me, but one day, I watched her log in. It's not that hard to figure out a password that way, you know?" I nodded. "Well, I tried it later, and it worked. It's 'one for the money.'"

"Spell it, please."

"Number one, number four, t-h-e-m-o-n-e-y," he told me.

The corruption of words by numbers is one form of what geeks call "leet speak." This one was ambiguous. The initial number could indeed stand for the word 'one,' as Tony interpreted it. It could also stand for the word 'I.' Either way, the password gave evidence to Elisa's priorities. "Okay, Tony, now for the hard part. Where were you last night?"

"Gracie and I had a fight. She was acting crazy, waving the credit card statement and the cellular bill in my face, telling me she'd hired you to trace the charges and the calls. I lost it, took off and drove around for about an hour. Driving helps me calm down."

I nodded. "Yeah, me too."

His voice softened and he looked down at his hands. "Well, the longer I drove and the more I thought about it, the more I realized that I really love Gracie and the kids, and I was a jerk about Elisa. I decided to drive over to the apartment and talk to Elisa, tell her it was all over. It was about eight o'clock when I got there and parked. I called her from the car. She didn't like me to surprise her."

I'll just bet, I thought. *Can't have boyfriend number one accidentally walk in on number two or three.* "So you were at the building last night?"

"Yeah," he confirmed.

This would look great to the cops. Motive, means, opportunity—the triple play, all wrapped up in one neat package labeled "Anthony Belloni." I kept my expression as neutral as possible. "Not good. Did you go in?"

"Nah, she didn't answer the phone. I sat there until about eight-thirty, thinking maybe she'd gone out for groceries or take-out. When she didn't show, I left. I drove straight home and begged Gracie to forgive me. I never saw Elisa last night, I swear." Again, he placed his right hand on his chest.

"Did you see anyone in the lot? Talk to anyone?"

"No, nobody drove in or out."

"What about garbage?" I asked, remembering the time I'd spent in the dumpster at the back of the lot.

He sat up with a jerk. "That's right. Somebody did come out the super's door and toss a big box in the dumpster. I remember thinking they should have torn the box down so it wouldn't take up so much space. You pay by the load, you know."

"Did you recognize them?"

He shook his head.

"Man or woman?"

"Man."

"Black man? White man?"

"White."

"What was he wearing?"

"Something dark, but his shoes were light, like running shoes."

"Hair color?"

"Kind of light brown, I think. It was dark, I couldn't see that well."

"How tall?"

He shrugged. "Couldn't tell."

"Did the dumpster come up to his chest, shoulders, head?" I asked.

Tony screwed his eyes shut in concentration. "When he stood at the front, it was about up to his armpits."

"Good job, Tony. How did he move? Fast? Slow? Easy? Stiff?"

"He walked fine, but I heard him grunt when he lifted the dumpster cover and tossed the box in. Like my old man used to do when he had to reach or lift."

I smiled. "My pop, too. I used to kid him when I was younger, now I do it myself at the end of a hard day."

"Ain't it the truth," he commiserated.

"Did he use a key to get back in the building?"

"Nah, he propped the door open with something as he came out, then just shoved whatever it was aside as he went back in."

So he might not be a tenant. "How many tenants in the building?"

"Six floors, eight units on each floor, total of forty-eight units."

"Any idea how many are men?"

"Not really. But Jeannie at my office can tell you."

"Did he go back into the building before you started the car to leave?"

"Yeah. I waited. I didn't want to draw attention to myself."

I took a deep breath. Didn't he see how this would look to the DA? "It isn't good, you being there last night. Let's hope that no one saw you at all, or someone watched you the whole time and saw you leave without going in. Did the cops ask you where you were last night?"

"Yeah, but Bart told me not to answer until he and I talked. I just kept telling them that I needed my attorney present."

"So you got home about nine o'clock. Did you stay home the rest of the night?"

He nodded. "Gracie was pretty upset. We talked, then I made her a cup of tea and rubbed her feet. She likes that. We went to bed and cuddled for a while, and she fell asleep."

The bells began to ring, loud and strong, as I remembered the times that I'd heard Bozo's excuses and apologies and promises. "Okay, let's get back to Elisa. Did she ever talk about enemies, about someone who had it in for her?"

"No." He shook his head. "Never."

"How about her email? Did you read it after you figured out her password?"

"Well, yeah, I did. I wanted to know if there was someone else."

So he wasn't stupid enough to think that paying the bills guaranteed fidelity. "Was there anything in her email that indicated someone was threatening her? That she felt in danger?"

"No, all she ever got in email was stock and broker stuff, and online shopping offers. Nothing personal."

"Maybe she had a separate email account for personal stuff, and the account she gave you was her public account."

He looked hurt at that idea. "You mean, she didn't trust me?"

The full peal was sounding now, DONG-DONG, like bells tolling for a funeral. I massaged my forehead. "Let me put it this way, Tony. Would you trust someone who cheated on his wife? Wouldn't you think that a person who'd do that to his wife was less than totally trustworthy?"

He raised his arms and extended his hands toward me, palms facing me. "I've had it with the sniping, Ms. Bonaparte." Stress on the "miz." "I'm telling you I didn't do this. If you don't believe me, then maybe I need to ask Bart to find another investigator."

"You're free to do that, Mr. Belloni." I stressed the "mister." We glared at each other for maybe thirty seconds, while my mind replayed the interviews with Gracie, Bart and now Tony. Did I think he was guilty of murder? No. Did he deserve life in jail because of infidelity? No. Had I let my emotions run away with me, lost my professionalism because of my own marital history? Maybe. Time to silence the bells and attend to business.

I kept my voice low, leaned forward and opened my arms in a posture of acceptance. "Tony, there's one thing you need to understand about me and about our professional relationship, if it's going to continue. I'll do my level best for you, but I can't help you if you're not honest with me. And I'm not going to BS you. I'm a straight-up woman." He nodded, so I continued. "How about if we reach an agreement? We'll tell each other the truth without recrimination. Deal?" I held out my right hand.

"And you'll keep what I tell you private? Not tell Gracie everything?" I nodded. "Deal," he agreed as we shook.

"I'll start trying to trace Elisa's background. Bart will be in touch today. He's working on getting bail set. Anything you need?"

"Not if I get out today. Otherwise, a change of clothes."

"Let's hope it's today. If not, I'll bring some stuff over later."

I buzzed, and the deputy came to escort Tony back to his bunk. I took a few moments to put papers and pen in my briefcase and smooth my skirt and jacket, trying to reorder my thoughts by reordering my belongings. I hate it when I lose control.

As I walked down the corridor, Wukowski came striding toward me. I decided to "make nice," as they say on the Polish south side of the city. "Afternoon, Detective Wukowski." I held out my hand and he reluctantly shook it. "I was just interviewing Tony Belloni." He nodded. *Help me out here*, I thought, *even a grunt is better than total silence.* "Has the coroner's report been filed?"

"Check with the desk." He stared past me, down the long hallway, making it abundantly clear that he had no time to chat.

"Sure thing, Detective." I slapped his upper arm playfully, knowing it would aggravate him, and gave him my biggest, most insincere smile. "Thanks so much for your help."

As I exited the building, the hot steamy air of a Milwaukee August caused even my scalp to break a sweat. I removed my suit jacket and slung it over my shoulder, raising a wolf whistle and a couple of rude comments as I walked to my car. I was pretty sure that Tony hadn't done the deed, but he hadn't given me much to go on. All I knew was that Elisa seemed to be a gold-digger with the ability to pan for some pretty good-sized nuggets. If she wasn't killed for passion, maybe it was for money.

Chapter 5

Innocence is lovely in the child, because in harmony with its nature; but our path in life is not backward but onward, and virtue can never be the offspring of mere innocence if we are to progress in the knowledge of evil.

—Clara Jessup Moore

As I drove east on Kilbourn, I thought about Tony and his mob connections. The Family was not a topic of conversation in my father's house. Our sole discussion about it occurred when I was eight years old, when I repeated the question that Ricky Oleniszak posed on the playground—Your old man's in the mob, ain't he?

"What did you say to him, Angelina?" my papa asked in a quiet voice, as he tucked me into bed that night.

"Nothing. I just walked away." I felt vaguely ashamed, not even sure what the phrase "the mob" meant.

Papa picked me up and set me on his lap. His suit smelled of pipe tobacco and fruit, a smell I continue to associate with calm and security. "You're a good girl, so listen to me and do as I tell you." He paused and settled against the headboard of my bed. "Long ago, in Sicily where we come from, there were rich and powerful men who mistreated the poor and the lowly." I snuggled against his chest, ready to enjoy the story that was about to unfold. "These men were outsiders who came to the land from other places. There was no justice. The rich ones owned the judges and the courts, and they manipulated them to their advantage. The only way that the Sicilians could survive was to band together and fight against the outsiders. So they formed a kind of union, a guild. They called it La Cosa Nostra. In English, Our Thing."

Papa's voice was low and steady, his body was warm and comforting, and the story reminded me of Robin Hood. "Did they rob from the rich and give to the poor, Papa?" I asked.

"Mostly, they just tried to protect their families and each other," he replied.

"Then what happened?"

"Some of the people felt that America would be a good place to live. They sailed here on big boats, started businesses and raised their families. Your grandpa was one of them. He came to America in 1922, to New York City, where he drove a truck for a grocery. Then his boss sent him to Chicago to work for another Sicilian, and when the business expanded, he moved to Milwaukee. That's how our family ended up here."

By then, I was yawning broadly. "Did Grandpa stay in the union?"

"Sort of," Papa responded. "The people in America called it the Mafia. Some called it the mob. They said it had a lot to do with crime."

I perked up. "It did?"

"Just like in any organization, Angie, there are good and bad people. Some bad people did bad things. Some people just joined to be part of the group and to have protection from others."

"Did you join?"

"I'm not really supposed to answer that, Angel." I waited, knowing that whatever followed would be important. "But yes, I did. When I was about eighteen, your grandpa asked me to come to a meeting. I knew that at the meeting, I'd be asked to swear allegiance to the group, and to promise never to tell its secrets to anyone. I kept that promise."

"What about now? Are you still in the Mafia?"

"I guess you can say that. Once you're in, you're in for life. But now, well, things have changed."

"Papa, if someone asks me, what should I say?"

"You say that your papa is a business man, that he runs a fruit and vegetable store. You say that your papa is a good papa and a good man, who goes to church and who takes care of his family. Then you stand up straight, look them in the eye and say nothing else. Understand?"

I nodded.

"Good girl. My little angel. Now settle down and go to sleep." He kissed my forehead and tucked me back in. He stood in the doorway for a moment, outlined by the hallway light. "If Ricky teases you anymore, you just tell him to ask his father where they got the money for the car dealership."

That was my introduction to the mob, the Mafia, the Family, La Cosa Nostra. After that, if I asked Papa a question about it, he'd just smile and shake his head. I was twelve when I realized that Papa and his friends weren't the only source of information on this topic. I'd just finished writing a paper on animals of Australia, which opened my eyes to the wonders of the public library and its vast sources of information. This was pre-personal computer days, so I spent hours in the reference section of the library, and I even learned to use the index of periodicals and the microfiche reader. It was heady stuff for a young girl, having the means to find out things that her family didn't want her to know.

I started with sex. My mom died when I was a toddler, so it was up to my aunt Teresa to have "the talk" with me when I was ten. It was all about periods and products and hygiene, and provided no information on how babies are conceived or born. Like all my friends, I wanted to know how you "do it." I found out from a book at the library. It was so shocking that I didn't tell anyone for a week. I made copies of the relevant pages on the library copier, folded the papers tightly and hid them in the toes of my dress shoes, at the back of my closet. Every night for a week, I took them out and snuck into the bathroom to read them. *Unbelievable*, I thought. *People really do that? My papa did that? To my mama? Yuck.*

After sex, I researched violence. Specifically, the Mafia. I read historical accounts of the Sicilian origins. I read the history of the early twentieth century gangs in America. I moved on to the *Milwaukee Journal* and *Milwaukee Sentinel* stories of illegal activity. Again, I was shocked at how close this was to me. The children and grandchildren of these men were my schoolmates. *Thank God, Papa's name isn't in here.*

***

That was the start of my detective career. I smiled as I remembered the innocence of that little girl, her confidence that truth existed and could be found in books and libraries, her belief in all that her papa told her. As I pulled into the parking space in back of my office, a sense of melancholy swept over me. She was so far away from me now that she seemed like a stranger.

I waved to Susan as I slipped into my office chair. She was on the phone, headset in place, talking to a client as she typed into her computer. Since the conversation was in Japanese, I easily tuned it out, letting it form a kind of background noise to my work.

Bart would be looking for my interview notes with Tony. As I started to enter the report into my PC, I thought about the days when only doctors carried beepers. When a person who needed to make a call from a public place used a pay phone. When a computer with 256K of memory only existed in a sealed corporate computer room and not in one's briefcase. When all telephones had cords. When papers and whole books were produced on a typewriter, using carbon paper to make duplicate copies. Not for the first time, I longed for the days when people and information were not expected to be constantly, instantly available.

Finishing my report, I composed an email cover letter to Bart, asking for a report of calls made to and from Elisa's home and cell phones. As Tony's attorney, he could petition the court to obtain the information from the phone company. I pushed the "Send" key and the letter and report were on their way.

It was three o'clock and I hadn't eaten since my breakfast bagel and coffee. I felt faintly light-headed and knew I shouldn't drive, so I walked over to Oriental Drugs and took a seat at the counter. As I waited for my tuna melt, I called Dunwoodie's on my cell phone. I may rail against instant communication, but I use it.

"Dunwoodie Insurance." The voice was surprisingly deep. I had to guess whether the receptionist was a male tenor or a female alto.

"I'd like to speak with John, please. Angelina Bonaparte calling."

"I'm sorry, he's with a client. Can I make an appointment for you or take a message?"

"I really need to talk to him today. It's about Elisa Morano."

I heard a long intake of breath. "Oh, isn't it awful?"

If she/he wanted to dish, I was prepared to play along. "You have no idea. I'm working for Attorney Bart Matthews as part of the defense team, and I had to see the pictures and everything."

"Omigod. That must have been terrible."

"It was. Just terrible." I paused. Even to further the conversation, there wasn't much more I could say without jeopardizing the police case and possibly Tony's defense. "I'm sure you understand that we need to look into Elisa's life, to find out if there was anyone who might have a motive for the crime. After all, if Mr. Belloni isn't guilty, and we don't believe he is, then there's a murderer walking free. That's why I need to talk with John Dunwoodie today."

"I understand. But John's booked all afternoon with a new client. Maybe Mrs. Dunwoodie could help."

I recalled Tony's remarks on the friction between Elisa and Jane Dunwoodie. Perhaps I could use it to my advantage. "That would be great. Does she have time to see me this afternoon?"

"One moment." I waited on hold, listening to WOKY, a local AM radio station. A few stanzas later, the voice came back on the line. "Mrs. Dunwoodie can see you at three o'clock for thirty minutes. Please arrive promptly as her time is limited." The voice was strained. I felt pretty sure that Jane Dunwoodie was standing at the desk, listening.

"I'll be there at three. Thanks for your help. And your name is…?"

"Bobby."

Was that Bobby like Robert or Bobbie like Roberta? As I said goodbye and hung up, I was betting on Roberta, based on her emotional response to Elisa's murder. I hoped that the physical appearance would answer the question for me. Androgyny makes me very uncomfortable. There are few things as essential as gender to our understanding of another person. Even sexual preference can be fluid, but gender is an archetypal marker that determines, to a large extent, how we relate to each other.

Chapter 6

Men of all professions affect such an air and appearance as to seem to be what they wish to be believed to be—so that one might say the whole world is made up of nothing but appearances.

—François, Duc De La Rochefoucauld

At ten minutes to three, I walked into Dunwoodie's. The unattended reception desk featured a single gardenia in a cut-glass vase, a computer and multi-line telephone set, and a wooden plate engraved with the name "Bobbie Russell." *Woman*, I congratulated myself. I sat on one of their incredibly uncomfortable visitor chairs, all hard plastic and molded curves that bore no relationship to the curves of an actual human body. A door opened and closed, footsteps sounded in the hallway behind the desk, and around the corner walked an absolutely drop-dead gorgeous young man. He might have been a model for menswear in his charcoal gray Hugo Boss suit, light gray pinstriped Armani shirt and subtly embossed slate blue tie. Very tone-on-tone, very fashion-forward, and very expensive. To top it off, he had the chiseled good looks of a young Rock Hudson, all angular chin and cheeks.

"Hi," he greeted me. "I'm Bobbie."

Making a conscious effort to keep my surprise from showing, I rose and extended my hand. "I'm Angelina Bonaparte. Angie. We spoke earlier. I thought I'd arrive a little early, just in case Mrs. Dunwoodie was free."

His handshake was firm and he looked me square in the eyes. "Sorry, she's on the phone. Can I get you tea or coffee?"

"No, thanks." I decided to take a calculated risk. "Great suit. I always wanted my ex to wear Boss, but he's such a slob."

"Well, thanks. My friend is in the rag business. He gets it for me wholesale." He looked me over, subtly. "I like your suit, too, but the hair! Just love it! Is it Kenneth?"

Bingo. Gay, or maybe bi. We talked fashion and beauty for a couple more minutes, then I started to dig a little. "Did you know Elisa?"

"No, they hired me after she left. I met her once, when she came into the office to get her last paycheck."

"Tell me what you thought of her."

"Well," he began, then stopped at the sound of a door opening. "Dragon Lady," he whispered as he nodded toward the hall. He held up one finger and I stopped speaking as he turned and called, "Ms. Bonaparte is here, Mrs. Dunwoodie."

"Show her into my office, please. I'll be with her in a moment."

As Bobbie started to usher me down the short hallway, I placed a hand lightly on his sleeve to detain him for a moment and whispered, "Can you meet me after work? Say five-thirty, at Blu in the Pfister?"

He nodded. "Love to."

Jane Dunwoodie's office was a surprise. I expected the typical business impersonal, but it was all traditional cherry furniture and molding, and light sage green walls decorated with tasteful prints. On the credenza behind her desk were photos, in silver and bronze frames, of what I took to be her family—she, husband John and two children. Most of the pictures were obviously posed studio portraits, the only exception being a little girl and cocker spaniel puppy. The door opened and the "Dragon Lady" entered, with a cup of tea in hand. I expected her physical presence to match the impressions of formidability that Tony and Bobbie had given me, and was surprised at the five-foot nothing, small-boned woman in a boxy beige summer suit who moved toward me. It's not often that I tower over an adult.

Jane didn't give me the opportunity to enjoy it. She seated herself behind her desk, carefully placed her cup on a small woven coaster and motioned me to a chair on the opposite side. A rather comfortable-looking set of upholstered chairs graced the opposite corner of the room. *Okay*, I thought, *it's going to be all business.*

"You wanted information about Elisa Morano?" she asked me.

I explained my role as Bart Matthews' investigator. "Anything you can share that will help us with Elisa's personal life will be greatly appreciated."

She frowned. "This is a business. Elisa worked for us, we didn't socialize with her. I don't think we can help you." She folded her hands on her desk and sat, silent and stiff.

"Then let's talk about work. How would you characterize Elisa's job performance?"

"It was satisfactory. We didn't have any problems with it."

That didn't correspond with Elisa's comment to Tony. "Apparently, Elisa thought otherwise. She seemed to feel that you were not happy with her work."

The pupils of Jane's eyes contracted, and she leaned forward. "Who told you that?" The words were clipped, angry.

"It's based on statements that Elisa made. It came up in the course of other interviews," I hedged.

She pursed her lips into a thin line and wrinkled her nose. *Incoming lie.* "I can't imagine why. Her three- and six-month reviews didn't reflect any problems. Of course, there were times when I had to correct her, but that's only to be expected with a new employee."

I decided to cut to the chase. "Did you know that she and Anthony Belloni were seeing each other?"

"Seeing each other! That's a nice way of phrasing it. More like screwing each other, wasn't it?" She glanced at a picture on her desk, one with its back to me. The vulgarity was in sharp contrast to her ladylike prim appearance and the room's solid respectability.

"Did you know about it?" I repeated in a monotone.

"Not when it started, but then he began to meet her for lunch and pick her up after work. I told her that I didn't appreciate that kind of behavior from my staff, that Tony was married and had children, for God's sake." Her eyes drifted back to the frame on her desk.

"How did she react?"

"She told me to mind my own business, that what she did outside the office was her own affair." Jane snorted. "Affair was an apt description." Her hands tightly clenched and released, the knuckles turning alternately white and red.

Jane Dunwoodie, I decided, was a very angry woman. Was her anger due to Elisa's behavior? Or because Elisa dared to defy Jane? "I suppose Elisa was right, in that regard," I said. "Her carrying on outside the office didn't really affect her work. I don't admire her morals, but I don't think it would be her employer's business."

A flush rose above the Mandarin collar of Jane's white blouse. Her unappealing features, too strong for such a small face and body, were alarmingly highlighted. "Don't misunderstand me, Ms. Bonaparte. I don't make it a practice to inquire into my employees' private lives. But

I can't stand by and see a valued client degrade himself and rip his family apart." She took a deep breath. "Elisa Morano was a selfish witch." Her lips trembled and I knew she wanted badly to use the B-word. "She never gave more than she had to, to get what she wanted. I saw it on the job—she wouldn't stay five minutes past closing unless we paid her overtime. And I saw it with Tony. I don't know who killed her, but as far as I'm concerned, they did the world a favor."

"That's quite harsh, Mrs. Dunwoodie. Are you saying that Elisa deserved to die?"

"I'm saying that I don't regret her demise." She stood and gestured toward the door. "I'm afraid that's all the time I have to discuss this."

I walked around the corner of Jane's desk, deliberately invading her territory under the guise of shaking hands, so that I could see the picture on her desk. It was just another family photo, apparently from several years ago. Jane's dark helmet of hair was looser, lighter. She smiled sweetly as she gazed at the baby in her arms. Every mother has pictures of those moments when life is so perfect that your heart feels ready to burst.

I shook Jane's hand and turned to leave the office. Pausing in the doorway, I asked, "Can I get a listing of the dates that Elisa worked here, and her salary?"

"Why?" she asked.

"It's just routine," I responded. "We'll want to compare her pay to her bank account, to see whether she had any money coming in that can't be accounted for."

"Tell Bobbie to print out her records for you." She picked up her phone, dismissing me without another word. I gently closed her office door behind me.

Back in the outer office, I told Bobbie that Jane had authorized me

40

to get copies of Elisa's records. Bobbie was already printing them out. He'd apparently heard our exchange. He handed me a file folder with about ten pieces of paper inside. I raised an eyebrow.

"She said 'records,' didn't she?" he asked. "Well, that's the lot." We exchanged conspiratorial smiles, both of us knowing that Jane hadn't intended for me to see *all* of Elisa's records.

Chapter 7

While all deception requires secrecy, all secrecy is not meant to deceive.
—Sissela Myrdal Bok

Wearing pantyhose for six hours in the damp heat of a Milwaukee August is inhuman torture. I drove home to change into linen walking shorts and a cotton camisole, topped off with a raw silk jacket. A quick spritz of facial freshener as I slipped bare feet into Prada slides, and I was ready to meet Bobbie at the Blu cocktail lounge on the twenty-third floor of the Pfister hotel.

The Pfister is an old Milwaukee gem, an 1890s Victorian built of local stone and graced with bright red awnings on the sidewalk level. Inside, a permanent art display decorates the walls of the five-star hotel. The builder, Guido Pfister, was a German immigrant who envisioned a "palace for the people." Guido died before the building was completed, but his son Charles finished the father's dream. Even today, guests claim they can see the portly, well-dressed Charles patrolling the halls.

The after-work crowd filled the elegant Blu lounge. I stood just inside the doorway and scanned the room. No Bobbie. As my eyes made a second circuit, they passed over a woman at a table for two on the perimeter of the room. The back of her head looked remarkably like my Aunt Teresa's. Even her shoulders reminded me of Aunt Terry's, set comfortably square on a rather stocky body. I looked again. Good lord, it *was* Aunt Terry! And a man! In a bar!

You have to understand my family history to know why this was so extraordinary. My mother died from complications of the flu when I was barely one year old. Papa's sister Teresa, at the time a novice in the religious order of the Sisters of Charity of the Blessed Virgin Mary, left the convent and moved into our home to take care of us. This was in the fifties, before the feminist movement, and no one in the family seemed to think it strange that a woman destined for a life of "charity, freedom, education and justice," as the BVM's core values statement avers, would give up her vocation to keep house for her brother and raise her baby niece.

Aunt Terry never really cut ties with the order, however. She attended Mass at Gesu church every morning and worked with the BVMs who staffed the grade school until it was closed in the sixties. She wore her hair short, declined to use makeup and generally dressed in white, black or gray, with sensible shoes and hose. To my knowledge, she'd never been on a date or even alone with a man who wasn't part of the family. In short, she looked and acted as if she were still a nun.

Which made seeing her in the Blu lounge with a man akin to seeing the pope slow dancing with a woman in a honky-tonk. I sat at the bar, watching her table in the plate glass window with its spectacular view of the Lake Michigan shore. The guy seated across from her was no one's prize. I don't mind bald, but his remaining circle of hair looked greasy as it hung over the collar of his rumpled suit. *If you're going to kick over the traces, Aunt Terry, why not start with someone better looking?* On the other hand, maybe all the years of determined singlehood had left her unable to recognize his shortcomings. She obviously needed help.

He left a bill on the table as they rose and he guided her from the room with his hand on her elbow, rather than the small of her back. I angled my head away, still watching the mirror. I didn't want to embarrass her.

I sipped at my White Russian and waited for Bobbie. A fellow at the end of the bar was trying to catch my eye, but I concentrated on my drink and avoided his stares by watching couples in the mirror. I sometimes play a game while I'm on surveillance—who's involved, who's trying to cross the line to involvement, who's just friends? Of course, I never get to find out the accuracy of my guesses, but it passes the time.

As I scanned the couples in the room, the low-level hum of conversation dropped to silence. Bobbie stood in the entry, all eyes upon his gorgeous face, form and clothes. He spotted me and strode purposefully to the bar, placing a hand on my back as he kissed my cheek. "Nice entrance for a gay guy, huh?" he whispered into my ear.

I smiled. "Every woman in the room wants to be with you. Come to think of it, probably some of the men do, too."

"You better believe it, honey." Slipping onto the bar stool next to me, he angled his body toward me and motioned to the bartender. "Bitburger, please." As he waited for his pilsner, he noted, "There's a guy at the end of the bar looking very dejected. I can stop acting straight if you want me to."

"Please, don't do me any favors. I've been studiously avoiding eye contact with him for ten minutes."

"I didn't see him as your type."

"What's my type?" I was intensely interested in his assessment.

"Sure you want to know?"

"In for a penny, in for a pound, as they say in England. Yes, I want to know."

He allowed his gaze to travel from my toes to the crown of my head. It was curiously clinical. Then he leaned back and smiled. "You like the younger guys for the thrill, but it doesn't last. You need an equal, Angie, not someone you can lead or, worse, intimidate. But a woman like you doesn't find many single men who are your equal, right?"

The flush started at my face and moved to my ears, neck and chest. He was way too close to the mark. "Sorry I asked," I muttered. The barkeep looked over and I saw his startled glance. *Great*, I thought, *he probably thinks I'm blushing with the anticipation of a sexual fling with a young stud.* If he only knew.

"Let's talk about Dunwoodie's and Elisa," I said. I opened the file folder that Bobbie had provided. "Looks like she only worked there eight months. Decent salary." I glanced at Bobbie. "More than decent. Mind if I ask how much you make?"

"Not as much as Elisa did," he responded. "But she had more experience than I do, and a college degree. I barely made it through tech school."

"How about bennies? 401K, for instance."

"No, nothing like that. Dunwoodie's too small, just John, Jane and little ole me. John did offer to give me advice about setting up an IRA, but they don't contribute."

"Must have been her prior employer, then. She had a fairly hefty balance for such a young woman."

Bobbie smiled. "That doesn't surprise me. She had a certain charm. It appealed to straight men."

"What about women?" I asked.

"She was strictly a threat, Angie. Not a gal pal kind of woman at all. Why do you think Jane Dunwoodie conducted the interviews for her replacement and hired me?"

"Jane worried that Elisa was making a play for John?"

"I don't think so." He paused and sipped his Bitburger, licking the foam from his upper lip. I heard a collective sigh from the room. "Jane has the money in the family and therefore the power. John's as close to a eunuch as a guy who still has all the equipment can be. She runs the business and the house. It's gotta be hell. The only time he has to himself is on the golf course."

"But Jane was still threatened by Elisa?"

"Jane has a Harvard MBA. Family money. Good-looking husband. Nice kids. Success in every area except looks. Then along comes Elisa, who only has to smile pretty and vamp a little to get the attention that Jane craves. Sure, Jane was threatened by her. Elisa had the one thing that Jane can't get, no matter how much she spends or how hard she tries—femininity to the max."

"I wonder who else resented Elisa's femininity and charm."

"Can't help you there, Angie." Bobbie glanced at his watch, an Accutron with three dials inside the larger face. "I promised to meet a friend at six. Call me at home if you need more info. My card is in the folder."

"Thanks, Bobbie. You've been a big help." I left fifteen on the bar and we walked out together. I hoped I didn't look like his mother or maiden aunt. As we waited for the elevator, I asked, "Any way I can talk to John Dunwoodie without the Dragon Lady running interference?"

"Try the Starbucks down the street from the office at ten o'clock. It's his mid-morning routine."

As we exited the hotel door, a silver Porsche convertible pulled up.

Bobbie waved to the driver and kissed my cheek. "That's my ride," he said. "Call me and let me know the scoop, okay, girlfriend?"

I grinned. "Absolutely. And thanks again."

He folded himself into the seat and the Carrera pulled out into traffic. So much for my Miata and my designer clothes. I wanted to be the straight female version of Bobbie Russell. In a perverse way, I suddenly understood Jane Dunwoodie's envy of Elisa.

Chapter 8

Reality leaves a lot to the imagination.

—John Lennon

It was only six. Time to make good on my promise to Gracie that I would see her today.

As you travel north, from Milwaukee to Whitefish Bay, Fox Point and then River Hills, income levels and lot sizes increase dramatically. Whitefish Bay is a moderate-income area, with a fair Italian population. It was the logical step up for the immigrants who originally settled in the old Third Ward of Milwaukee, where my papa still lived. Although now even the Third Ward was undergoing gentrification, much to Papa's dismay. He likes things to stay the same.

The Belloni home was just west of Lake Michigan, in a quiet area of stone and brick homes set on one-acre lots. From a block away, I saw the TV vans and the reporters standing on the sidewalk, recording sound bites for the ten o'clock news. Bart's Lincoln Town Car was parked in front of the garage. The Miata top was down, and as I turned into the driveway, they all rushed over to thrust their mics into my face and shout questions at me. I rolled on by and parked next to Bart's Lincoln. It was likely that I'd be seen on the news, from the back, and

I hoped that my linen walking shorts and silk jacket weren't too wrinkled. At least I didn't have to worry about my hair.

Before I could ring the doorbell, the door opened slightly and a hand motioned me in. "Angie, great timing," Bart boomed as I slipped inside. "Tony was released on bail about an hour ago, and I picked him up and brought him home. I'm just meeting with Tony and Gracie to bring them up to date. You can give us your report, too." He walked toward the back of the house. "We're in the dining room. I'm keeping everyone away from the front of the house."

Tony and Gracie were seated at the dining room table. As I entered, he rose. "Welcome to my home, Angie."

"Tony, how you doing?" I asked, deliberately countering his formality. This was no time to act the gracious host. I turned to hug Gracie, hugely pregnant, seated back from the table with her feet propped up on a footstool.

"I'm glad you're here," she whispered in my ear. I gave her shoulders a little squeeze, then walked to the heavy brocade draperies, tightly drawn, and peeked outside. A tall wooden fence, with mature trees and bushes planted in front of it, ran the perimeter of the property. A fenced pool took up a large part of the area, and a play set, only slightly smaller than something you'd find in an amusement park, was established in another corner. The drapes covered French doors that opened onto a wooden deck, with flower planters dotting the railing. Comfy-looking padded lounge chairs occupied one side of the deck, while the other was dominated by a huge stainless steel gas grill. Looking out, I pictured the kids playing on the swings and mom relaxing on one of the chaises while dad grilled bratwurst or Italian sausage. A nice family moment.

I turned back to the room and the image melted away, replaced by the reality of a man accused of murdering his girlfriend while his pregnant wife waited anxiously at home. Life can really suck. "Looks okay, I can't see how anyone can get close enough to hear us without trespassing," I said as I sat down next to Gracie, opened my briefcase and removed pen and paper, prepared to take notes. "Where are the kids?" I asked Gracie.

"They're with Tony's mom. I didn't want them exposed to all this."

I nodded, and glanced at Tony, who had the grace to look ashamed. "Good idea," I responded. "This should all blow over when the reporters realize there's nothing happening here and they won't get any good footage. Just keep the curtains and shades drawn and stay in the house for a couple of days. Reporters have short attention spans." I looked at Bart and waited, silent. This was his show to run.

He reflexively reached into his suit coat pocket for a cigarette, then realized where he was and slowly withdrew his hand. This meeting should last one hour, tops. Bart couldn't make it any longer without a smoke. He cleared his throat, loosened his tie, and let his eyes scan a paper that lay on the table in front of him. "I was just going over your report, Angie." I nodded. "Umm, anything in particular you want to say?" he asked me, shifting in his seat and clearly uncomfortable.

I did a quick mental review. Bart must be wondering how much Gracie knew and didn't want to give away any of Tony's secrets that she wasn't aware of. Time to cut to the chase. Laying my pen down, I looked Tony square in the face and asked, "Tony, is Gracie aware of all that we discussed? Is there anything you've told me or Bart that you want to keep private from her?"

I heard an intake of breath from Gracie. After a short count of three, which seemed to stretch on for hours, Tony shook his head. "I told her everything. No more secrets. None." Gracie exhaled.

"Good. That's how it should be." I kept my voice level and

unemotional, like a second-grade teacher reinforcing a correct answer from the class. It was one of those lose-lose situations, where Tony could accuse me of being judgmental and Gracie could take a 'my husband, right or wrong' stand if I came down too hard. And I didn't want to cause Gracie any more stress than necessary. Still, I was damned if I would praise the guy for his minor attempt to do the right thing. I transferred my gaze to Bart.

"Okay, then let's get down to business." His long fingers, fat like sausages, drummed on the surface of the table, part of the typical Italian-American dining room 'suite'—dark wood, ornately carved, with matching high-back chairs, sideboard and hutch. It brought to mind the many family meals at my father's table. Would Tony's kids have only a single parent when they sat down at the table, like me? I couldn't let that happen, not if he was really innocent of the murder.

"Here's how the cops see it." Bart stared past Tony, his gaze fixed on the drapes. "Tony's been carrying on with Elisa Morano, but now he's ready to end the relationship. He goes to her apartment, in a building that he owns. As the owner, he has keys for all the units. Maybe he plans the murder, or maybe they fight. Either way, the gun goes off and Elisa is dead. Tony panics and leaves. The cops just need to put a bow on it and carry the package into the courtroom." Tony started to object, but Bart raised a pudgy hand, palm forward, kept his gaze on the drapes, and continued. "Here's what really happened. Tony wants to break off with Elisa. He drives to her apartment and calls her, but no answer. He waits in his car in the building parking lot. A guy comes out to toss some stuff in the dumpster. Tony sees no one else and no one sees him. After waiting for a half hour, he leaves and drives around for a while, trying to decide what to do next. Then he comes home and he and Gracie talk it out. In the middle of the night, the cops show up and arrest him." He stopped and looked at Tony for the first time since his monologue began. "That about it?" he asked.

"Yeah, that's about it."

"Tony," Bart continued, "I can't lie and tell you this will turn out right. There's just too much circumstantial evidence against you. We need a solid alternative, someone else with at least as good a motive, and the same means and opportunity you had. Without that, we're sunk. I can offer the DA a deal, but that means you'll have to plead guilty to a lesser charge, maybe involuntary manslaughter."

Gracie started to cry, quietly at first, then louder. Tony sat, frozen to his chair, staring at Bart as if the reality of the situation just struck home. Neither man moved.

"Gracie," I said, "it won't help to break down now." I put a hand under her elbow to help her rise from her chair. "You show me where everything is and I'll make us a nice pot of tea." The two of us went through the swinging door to the kitchen. I left it open so I could hear the men. Gracie levered herself onto an upholstered bar stool at the huge kitchen island and pointed to the cupboard that contained the tea. I put a kettle on to boil, and set out a tray with carafe, mugs, spoons, napkins, milk and sugar. The tea was in bags, not loose, but it would do. When the kettle blew its cheerful little whistle, I poured the water into the carafe, over the tea bags. Gracie wiped her eyes, blew her nose and preceded me into the dining room, her feet pointed out and her hips rolling from side to side in the pregnancy stroll. The men's conversation, carried on in undertones, ceased when we re-entered the room. Bart's mouth was set in a grim line and Tony looked like he'd been steamrollered.

I set the tray on the table and started to pour the tea, asking each if they wanted milk or sugar. Bart took four sugars—yech, syrup, not tea.

Tony took his cup, walked to a sideboard, and poured a healthy slug of brandy into it. Then he raised the bottle to us in an unspoken question. We declined.

Tony collapsed into his chair, took a long drink, and looked at Bart. "So you're saying it's hopeless? Even though I didn't do it?"

"It's not over 'til it's over, Tony. All I'm saying is that it looks bad."

"Well, I ain't making no deal with the DA. I didn't do this, Bart. And if they send me up, I got a lotta enemies in prison. I won't make it out."

Tony's street kid origins were busting through his sophisticated businessman persona. As he spoke, Gracie's mouth opened in a sickening imitation of Munch's *The Scream*. I frowned at Bart and rolled my eyes toward Gracie. He got the message. "What Bart hasn't said," I interjected, in the hope of raising Gracie's spirits, "is that I'm looking into other areas of Elisa's life. There must be a reason for the murder, and if the cops are only looking at Tony, they won't find it. So I will." I set my mug on the table.

Gracie leaned over and took my hand. "Oh, Angie, do you think you can?" Tony straightened up and waited for my answer.

"I'll do my very best. I've cleared my calendar of all my other cases. If it's out there, I can find it." Maybe, I added mentally. But what else could I say? Gracie was close to her due date, and I could see the strain in her face and hear it in her voice. It was bad enough when she thought her man was cheating on her, but now she was afraid that he'd spend the rest of his—and her—life in prison.

From the corner of my eye, I saw the two men exchange a look. They knew, and I knew, that evidence doesn't always exist to prove innocence or guilt, and that people do get wrongly convicted from time to time. But like me, they were willing to put up a front to reassure

Gracie, so we did the shoulder-punch attagirl go-get-'em routine and I promised to stay in touch.

As I drove away, I kicked myself mentally for being twenty kinds of a fool. What if I didn't find anything? What would Gracie do if Tony went to jail? When would I learn to keep my mouth shut?

Chapter 9

Family life itself, that safest, most traditional, most approved of female choices, is not a sanctuary: It is, perpetually, a dangerous place.
—Margaret Drabble

It was almost nine o'clock when I got home. I scanned the collection of junk mail from my 'public' box in the building lobby. My personal mail goes to a rented box at a private service center. It's more secure, and they can sign for packages, so it's also more convenient. I ran all the unopened envelopes through the shredder, poured myself a tot of Baileys, kicked off my sandals and sank down on the couch. The sun had set and the lake was dark. The streetlights along Lincoln Memorial Drive outlined the shore far below me, like twinkling fairy lights. I took a small sip of Baileys and opened the folder that Bobbie gave me. Was it only four hours ago? I was dead tired, but I knew that I wouldn't be able to sleep until I'd reviewed the material and decided on the next day's plans.

I scanned Elisa's employment records from Dunwoodie. There were some promising leads—her address when hired, her next of kin, two references. The print started to swim on the page, so I tossed the folder on my coffee table and leaned back against the soft leather of the couch.

I closed my eyes and tried to relax with some yoga breathing. My brain refused to cooperate, flashing images of Gracie and the kids on visiting day at the prison, then Elisa's bloody police photos.

The phone rang, releasing me from the grisly scenes. Caller ID showed "Schroeder, K." It was Kevin. Lovely, sexy, funny Kevin. I wasn't in the mood to be lovely, sexy or funny back. I picked up the receiver and said, "Hello."

"Hi, Angie. It's Kevin." His voice, a pleasant baritone, usually sent a little frisson of pleasure down my spine. Not tonight.

"Hi, Kevin. How are ya?" I knew my voice sounded flat and uninviting, but I just couldn't make the effort.

"Good." He paused. "You sound tired."

"I am. It's been a bad two days. The Belloni/Morano case. Did you see it on the news?"

"Yeah, I did. What's your involvement?"

"I'm working for Belloni's lawyer, Bart Matthews. Trying to prove Tony innocent. At least, innocent of the murder."

"I didn't know you did that kind of work, Angie."

"It's not my usual assignment. But I know Gracie Belloni, and Bart asked me to help."

"Is it dangerous?"

The question hung there while I pondered my answer. Was Kevin being protective, or just curious? I decided to play it down the middle. "Not likely, but I'm being careful."

"I see. I guess I never thought of you that way before."

Okay, best to get it out into the open. "Does it bother you?"

"Actually…no. I find it a little exciting. Who knew I'd be dating a beautiful, dangerous woman. I feel like Bogie, in *The Maltese Falcon*."

"Well, I'm no Mary Astor," I snapped, then immediately regretted it. "Sorry, Kevin, I'm dead tired and I've had nothing to eat for about nine hours. I'm not fit to talk to."

"I could bring over a pizza. Or some Chinese? I'm great at neck rubs."

There was more than a hint of sexual undertone in the offer. I felt a little tingle and I knew that we could end up in bed if I agreed, but I wanted some magic for our first sexual encounter, not this wiped out feeling. So I quoted Sam Spade's line to Brigid O'Shaughnessy at the end of the film. "I won't because all of me wants to, regardless of consequences."

He chuckled. "Hammett has a lot to answer for. But I'm glad you want to. Ah, well, see you tomorrow night, Dangerous." Click. He hung up.

Tomorrow night. The benefit for the Muscular Dystrophy Association at the Italian Community Center. The one that I'd agreed to attend in support of my neighbor, Joseph, and his family. Me and Kevin. And Papa. And Aunt Terry. And lots of Papa's friends and business associates. My heart started to pound in time with the headache that was tuning up inside my skull. I needed to eat something, before nausea set in.

I toasted two slices of Brownberry twelve-grain bread, and slathered one side with chunky peanut butter and the other with Smucker's apricot spread. Then I smacked them together, cut the sandwich in half, poured a glass of soy milk and sat at my dining table to eat my favorite comfort food. PB&J may sound juvenile, but it's good for the nerves.

As I munched, I remembered the night when I invited Kevin to the benefit. It was an I-don't-want-to-go-alone-and-be-poor-single-Angie moment, and Kevin had immediately accepted. He was obviously looking forward to the get-together, and he knew a lot of the families from his work as a physical therapist. It might not be so bad. I might be able to keep him away from Papa and Terry. Maybe. In some alternate universe, where Italian papas and surrogate mamas don't care who their child dates.

Screw it, I thought, as I headed for a warm shower and bed. I fell asleep and dreamt of Papa chasing Elisa with a knife, and Terry slow dancing with Kevin.

***

My digital clock read 6:13 when I woke. Saturday morning. I rolled over and hugged the pillow, remembering when my kids were little. On Saturdays, they would jump in bed with me and Bozo, watching cartoons and waiting for Mommy and Daddy to get up. Now Emma and David were grown, with spouses and children and homes of their own. Now they worried about me. Now they waited for me to "grow up" and "settle down." And they'd be at the benefit tonight. Damn! How could I forget? Papa bought tickets for all of us, after Joseph melted his heart one day in the elevator.

Groaning and muttering curses on myself, my family, and the fate that put me in this position in my fifties, I dressed, splashed water on my face and headed out the door for an early morning run. More from force of habit than from real precaution, I scanned each jogger, runner, walker, biker and blader in my vicinity. Milwaukee's lakefront is a beautiful, preserved area that many East-siders enjoy recreationally, but a woman can't be too careful.

At McKinley Marina, I bought a cup of coffee from the refreshment stand and sat on a bench looking out over the lake. *Get a grip*, I thought. *You're not a kid. You don't need anyone else's approval. It doesn't matter if Papa or Terry or Emma or David like Kevin.* But it did. Deep down, it did.

Why? I asked myself. I mentally ticked off the possibilities. One—

because you care deeply for Kevin and believe he might be the one you want to have a long-term relationship with. No, I answered. I like him and I enjoy his company, but that's as far as it's gotten, so far. Two—because you're afraid that he'll embarrass you in front of your family. Unlikely, I responded. He's gracefully survived a couple encounters with friends my age, who all liked him and told me what a great guy he was. Three—because you're afraid of the whispering, the innuendos about May-October relationships, the 'what does he see in her?' comments.

Yes, that's the one. For all my bravado, for all the self-confidence that I exhibit, inside there was that little seed of doubt. Doubt that Bozo planted when he started running around. Doubt that grew with every man like Tony. Doubt that bloomed with every woman who was younger, prettier, firmer, sexier. I didn't want to play the fool, or even look it.

Angry with myself, I slammed the coffee cup into the wastebasket and started my run back home. I showered, dressed in twill pants and a cotton top, and headed for the office. In order to concentrate solely on the Belloni case, I needed to clear my calendar. I called a colleague from the old Walterman days and asked him to handle a missing kid case—a seventeen year old who left home when her parents insisted that she stop seeing her boyfriend. Other than routine paperwork cases, it was the only active investigation on my plate, except for Belloni. I handled some bills, did a few credit and background checks on the Internet, wrote up my report for Bart and sent it off by courier to his office. It was only two o'clock. Kevin was picking me up at seven. I didn't need five hours to get ready. When you're slightly panicky about a guy meeting your family, having too much time is not a good thing.

I decided to take care of some routine chores, and headed for the grocery store. My cupboard and fridge had been bare long enough. I stocked up on pantry and frozen foods, and enough fruits and veggies to last the week. A package of FCBs (flattened chicken breasts, suitable for many a singleton's meal when garnished with different sauces), two sirloin beef patties, a nice Riesling. A tiny box containing four Godiva chocolates. I would eat one a night until they were gone. There's no point in wasting calories on cheap chocolate, always opt for the darkest and richest.

At my front door, I juggled the two bags of groceries and my purse as I tried to fit the keys into the lock. The door opened before I could complete the maneuver. Lela stood in the doorway, hands on hips. "Girl, it's about time you got some food in this house. If there was another empty pizza box in the garbage, I planned to call Nutrition 9-1-1." She took one of the bags and preceded me into the kitchen.

Lela (not Lila, and don't forget it!) is a six-foot, 30-something, beautiful black actress who works sporadically at her craft and weekly for me. Don't ever call her a cleaning lady, she'll eat you alive. 'Cleaner' or 'cleaning person' are fine with her, but 'cleaning lady' sets her off. She tidies up, vacuums, mops, wipes down, runs the dishwasher, changes the sheets, does the laundry and generally makes it possible for me to live without personal chaos. I just call her my angel.

"How's life treating you?" I asked as we put the groceries away.

"So-so. Had an audition for the Rep. Waiting to hear. Want any of this meat to stay out for tonight?"

"No. I'm going to the MDA benefit at the Italian Community Center. There's a meal."

"Who you going with?" She stopped packaging meat for the freezer and waited for my answer.

"Kevin." I didn't look at her, just kept shoving cans in the pantry.

"Young studly Kevin? You go, girl."

"Yeah, well, you know how my dad dotes on Joseph next door. Thinks he's the bravest little boy in the world?" She nodded. "Papa bought tickets for the benefit, for the whole family. A table. Him, Aunt Terry, my son David and his wife Elaine, my daughter Emma and her husband John, and me and Kevin." I grimaced.

"So, you're worrying about what? That Kevin won't know which fork to use? That he'll disgrace you in front of your family?"

"No. I'm not worried about Kevin. I'm worried that I'm going to look like a middle-aged woman with a much younger man. That people will wonder why we're together, what he sees in me."

Lela stepped back, put her right hand against her cheek and looked me up and down, slowly. "What does he see in you? Hmmm." She tapped her index finger against her cheek. "Maybe he sees a woman who's got it together. A looker. With a good heart. A woman who's always trying to help someone else. Who's funny and smart. A woman that any man over the age of thirty with an IQ of more than ninety would be proud to be seen with."

I hugged her, not caring that my face was at her bosom level. "Could you record that for me, so I can play it back at regular intervals?"

"So, let's put the rest of this food away and then you show me what you're wearing," she said.

My dress was a killer, if I do say so myself—a long, red, beaded, backless, halter number. The strappy red stilettos and small beaded red bag would blend into the background, focusing all attention on the dress. I planned to keep the jewelry simple—diamond studs in my earlobes and a beautiful platinum-and-diamond watch that Papa gave me when Emma was born.

"Mmm, mmm, mmm," Lela slowly shook her head. "You will

knock them dead. I mean stone cold dead, girl. You planning to bring ole Kevin back here for a nightcap?"

"We'll see."

"That man deserves a medal if he's with you in that dress, all night, and then he don't even get a little." Lela always slipped into jive when she lectured me, which she did at regular intervals. "My Sam call that a blue ball night."

I laughed and shook my head. "Maybe Sam's just giving you a sob story so you'll put out."

"Sam don't need no sob story for me to put out, honey." She laughed a wicked laugh and waved as she left the bedroom. "I already put clean sheets on the bed!"

The front door slammed and I was once again alone with my thoughts. It was four-thirty. The house was clean, the laundry was done, the bills were paid and the office duties were current. There was no way I was going to concentrate on the Grafton novel, so I watched one of those home decorating shows on HGTV for a little mindless entertainment. Am I the only one who thinks that Moroccan harem is not a good look for a dining room?

At five o'clock, I broke down and turned on the shower. While I waited for the steam to rise, I plucked my eyebrows and made sure that none of those nasty post-thirty chin hairs were poking out. Then I cleaned my face with oil and rinsed it off in the shower. Shampooed my hair and applied conditioner. Applied more conditioner to underarms and legs, and shaved. Exfoliated elbows and feet. Washed with my favorite ginger-and-green-tea body wash, then rinsed off from top to bottom and followed with a cold spray. Brrrr. Toweled off, swabbed ears. Slathered on face cream and body lotion. Rubbed paste into my hair and combed it into place. Slipped into a robe and slippers and padded into the kitchen for a cuppa. The microwave clock read 5:45.

At six, I sat down to watch the local news. Just as I suspected, they showed my back entering the Belloni residence the night before. Thank God they didn't film my butt from one of those odd angles that make you look like a pear. The newscaster pronounced in serious tones that 'alleged suspect Anthony Belloni confers with his attorney, Bartholomew Matthews, and local investigator, Angelina Bonaparte.' Of course, she mispronounced my surname. She also managed to imply that it was all a Mafia conspiracy, with 'mob ties' being pursued by the DA's office. *Bart will have her hide*, I thought. I clicked off the tube and started to dress.

When Kevin rang the buzzer at seven, I was gowned, made up, bejeweled and as ready as I'd ever be. I opened the door and, for a few seconds, he just stood there, looking gorgeous in his rental tux. Then he stepped back and said, "Whoa," placing his right hand over his heart.

I smiled. "I hope that's approval," I said as I motioned him in.

"Nothing but," he replied. Then he closed the door and kissed me. No tongue, no heavy breathing, just a sweet, soft, appreciative kiss. "Mmmm," he murmured as he held me for a moment.

"Mmmm?" I questioned.

"You smell good. Why is it that girls smell so good?"

"Must be the bathing. And maybe the lack of testosterone."

"Yeah, I bet you're right."

It was silly banter, the kind that women and men exchange when they're pleased with each other. I handed Kevin my silk stole and he carefully wrapped it around my shoulders and offered his arm.

"Kevin, I did tell you that my family will be there? That my dad bought the whole table?" Of course I told him, but I wanted reassurance.

"Duly noted and warned, Angie. I promise to be on my best behavior. Feel free to poke me with one of those extremely sexy shoes if I say or do anything inappropriate."

"Deal," I said as we headed for the elevator.

The air was balmy, one of those starry August nights where the humidity drops while the temperature hovers in the eighties, and the city wants to stay up late. We drove in Kevin's Camry and chatted of inconsequentials—the Brewers home stand, the weather, State Fair. At a red light, a block from the Italian Community Center, he took my hand and kissed my palm. My heart did a little back flip of enjoyment, then another of concern. Would he pull a stunt like that in front of Papa?

"Don't worry," he said in an ironic tone, apparently reading my mind, "I know—no PDA allowed when we get there." He grinned, the light changed, and we drove on.

I handed Kevin the tickets before we got out of the car. I had no wish to challenge the man-as-host tradition. The Pompeii ballroom was decorated in white—white napery on the large round tables, floating white water lily centerpieces, shimmery white draperies along the walls. There was no way to miss my red dress against that background. I lifted my chin, squared my shoulders and smiled, on the principle of 'act like you wish you feel.' Sometimes it works.

We stood near the door for a moment, looking for our table. Aunt Terry spotted us and waved. I waved back to let her know I'd seen her. People were milling around the room, talking and looking for their places, so I couldn't see who else was with her. "Looks like we're at the other side of the room, Kevin." I pointed to Terry, her hand still in the air. "That's my Aunt Teresa, my surrogate mom."

"Let's beard the lion in his den, shall we?" He took my arm and we crossed the room, our progress interrupted several times by couples or singles who knew Kevin. Each time, he introduced me simply as 'Angelina Bonaparte,' with no further explanation. I liked that. I also liked that he placed his hand lightly on the small of my back, making it clear that we were not just business acquaintances or, heaven forbid, relatives.

When we got to our table, Papa rose and came around to give me a hug. At five-ten, he towered above me, even in my heels. His vintage fifties tuxedo still fit, its satin-trimmed lapels soft against my cheek. "*Bella*, Angelina," he whispered in my ear. Then he turned to Kevin.

"Papa," I said, "I'd like to introduce Kevin Schroeder. Kevin, this is my papa, Pasquale Bonaparte."

"Sir," Kevin said formally.

Papa looked him up and down as they shook hands. He'd always told me that a man's handshake was an important indicator of character. Kevin must have passed the test, because as they shook, Papa slapped Kevin's right arm with his left hand and said, "Call me Pat."

Papa went back to his chair and Kevin and I sat. By the time I introduced Kevin to Terry, then Emma and her John, and finally David and his Elaine, I was starting to relax. Then I noticed the empty chair between Papa and Terry. Kidding, I asked her, "Where's your date?"

"Oh, he'll be here in a minute. He went to the men's room."

Clunk. My chin hit the floor. I just stared at Terry. I couldn't think of a word to say. The waitstaff broke the silence when they started to fill water glasses and ask folks to take their seats. Then the man I saw with Terry at Blu sat down next to her and she introduced him. "Fausto Pirelli, this is my niece Angelina and her friend, Kevin Schroeder."

Aunt Terry was only seventeen when she entered the convent, and eighteen when Mama died and she left it to care for me. That made her ten years older than me, a slightly frumpy 60-something. She'd made an effort tonight, dressed in a black (what else?) chiffon number that, unfortunately, did nothing to conceal her extra pounds. Her hair was plainly styled, as always, but she wore small clip-on gold earrings.

Fausto looked about seventy-five. His handshake was okay, not slimy or soft, but his hair hung over the collar of his ill-fitting dinner jacket. He needed some fashion direction. But then, so did Terry. I mumbled the polite phrases and reached for a glass of water.

At my elbow, a waiter asked, "Wine, ma'am?" I nodded and he filled my glass. My kids know how I hate being called 'ma'am.' David grinned at me from across the table, and I saw a tiny movement of the tablecloth that made me think Elaine poked him.

The meal was served, chicken marsala with rice and veggies. Not the best, but at least it was hot. Papa asked Kevin what he did for a living, and was suitably impressed to find out that his PT work involved a lot of the families in the room. Score points for our side. Emma and Elaine began a side conversation about school starting and how glad they'd be to have a moment's peace at home. I smiled, remembering Emma as a little girl, whining at me through the last weeks of summer—"I'm bored." Emma and John have little Angela, now eight and the apple of my eye. David and Elaine have ten-year-old twin boys, Patrick (the Anglicized form of Pasquale, for my dad) and Donald (for Elaine's dad). Those two are holy terrors. What one doesn't come up with, the other one does. It's only fair, though, since David ran me ragged all through high school. The parents' curse, that you should have a child just like yourself, certainly came back to haunt him.

As we chatted about the start of school and shopping for school clothes, shoes and supplies, I caught Kevin watching me. "My grandkids," I said, defiant.

"I figured," he replied. Then he leaned over to reach the basket of rolls, put his lips to my ear, and whispered, "Did you get married at fifteen?"

"Bless you," was all I could say. After all, at thirty-eight, he was closer to my kids' age than to mine.

As coffee and dessert were served, the lights dimmed and the speeches began. First, a nationally-produced film on the work of the Muscular Dystrophy Association, with stories guaranteed to evoke a tear. Then a speaker from the local chapter, who spoke of the higher prevalence of the disease as one moves away from the equator, and among women, and among those aged twenty to fifty. Of the difficulty in diagnosing. Of the limited treatment options. And lastly, the stories of families living with the disease and not only surviving, but thriving in love. I dabbed surreptitiously at my eyes, careful not to smear my mascara. I didn't want to look like a raccoon when the lights came up.

The band was well-known locally, a staple of the lakefront festivals and clubs. They started out with an old Sinatra tune, "I'll See You in My Dreams." Before Kevin had a chance to ask, Papa rose and held out his hand to me. Ever the gentleman, he extracted a clean white linen hanky from his breast pocket and draped it carefully across his right hand so that, as we danced, he wouldn't contact my bare back. We swung into a slow rhythm. I remembered him dancing with me as a toddler, my stockinged feet perched on the tops of his wing-tips as he moved across the living room floor. I think my mama was still alive then, for I can vaguely hear her laugh, soft and melodious, as she clapped her hands.

"So, Angelina, you like this man?" Papa's question interrupted my reverie.

"He's a nice guy, Papa. Yes, I like him."

"But he's not the one for you, Angel." Papa shook his head. "You need a man you can respect, who won't back down and let you have your way."

I leaned back slightly and looked Papa in the face. "Kevin and I have had no major disagreements yet. Maybe he won't back down. And anyway, what's wrong with a woman getting her way, sometimes?"

He just shook his head.

It's hard for a woman born in the fifties and raised pre-Friedan to navigate the post-feminist waters. I often feel like I have a foot in both camps and no real place to rest in either one. The Eisenhower-era family standards that I was raised with betrayed me, but I wasn't able to shake them entirely. Papa knew.

It turned into a pleasant evening, dancing with Kevin and Papa and Fausto, with David and John, with friends and acquaintances. I let myself enjoy and refused to contemplate what might happen later. When Terry headed for the ladies' room, I grabbed my bag and followed her. In the hallway, I stopped her and asked, "So, Aunt Terry, what's up with Fausto? Anything you want to tell me? Or ask?"

Emma rounded the corner and joined us."Yeah, Aunt Terry, you secretive little devil. How come you never told us you were dating?"

She blushed and stammered and finally came out with, "We've only been out once before. For a drink."

Blu, I thought.

"What do you think of him?" she asked.

Emma and I exchanged glances. "Well," I started, "he seems nice. Polite. Do you like him? That's what's important."

"I honestly don't know," she admitted. "I haven't been on a date for fifty years. I don't know how to do this." Her voice rose and she sounded like she was starting to panic.

I took her hand and patted it, and Emma put an arm around her shoulders. "Just take it slow, Terry. At your own pace. If you feel like seeing him, good. If you don't, tell him 'not today.' He needs to respect your wishes in this matter." I was sounding like Papa, lecturing me as a teenager. "Have you known him long?"

"His wife, Maria, and I went to school together. He's a little older. Maria died two years ago, and I think he's lonely. But honestly, Angie, Emma, I don't know if I want to change my life like this. I don't know if I'm up to it." She looked at me for reassurance.

"Any woman who can run Papa's house and manage a teenaged rebel like me, and walk with Father Groppi in civil rights marches, and teach literacy and raise money for the retired Sisters, is up to any challenge she wants to take on." My voice was firm, assured.

"That's right," Emma added. "If you want him, you can have him, Aunt Terry. But only if you want him. If you don't, then just toss him out." She snapped her fingers as she waved her free arm to the side.

We broke up, laughing. *But*, I thought, *it's a lot like me and Kevin. I can have him if I want him. But do I?*

As the evening wound down, we all kissed and hugged good-night, and David whispered in my ear, "Nice guy, Mom. Is he a keeper?"

"Not sure," I whispered back, and he gave me a little squeeze.

"Don't wait too long to decide," he advised. "I want to see you happy."

When we stopped in front of my building, Kevin put his arms around me and drew me into a long, long kiss. "Can a guy get a nightcap?" he asked.

I knew he wasn't just asking for a drink and I'd never been one to take sex lightly. I hesitated, unsure whether I really trusted him, whether this was really the right guy, the right time, the right circumstances. He noticed. He trailed a finger along my jawline. "Call me when you decide I'm not one of the bad guys, Angie." The words were soft, his eyes looked hurt.

A big lump in my throat prevented me from speaking. I just nodded, pressed a kiss on his cheek, and left the car. He waited until I was inside the lobby before driving away.

In the bedroom, I carefully hung up my dress and put my shoes and bag on the closet shelf. In the bathroom, I washed my face and brushed my teeth, and changed into cotton PJs. In bed, alone, I cursed my inability to trust.

Chapter 10

A daughter is a mother's gender partner, her closest ally in the family confederacy, an extension of her self. And mothers are their daughters' role model, their biological and emotional road map, the arbiter of all their relationships.

—Victoria Secunda

I slept fitfully, wrestling with the sheets and my damnable scruples. Hugging a pillow was no substitute for wrapping my arms around a warm, sexy body. At six o'clock, I gave up the struggle to escape into sleep and went for my morning run.

The streets were quiet—no bladers, few joggers or runners. The cars that passed me all seemed to consist of well-dressed families on their way to church, evoking memories of little Angie, scrubbed, neatly dressed and wearing her best shoes, clutching her aunt's hand as they went to Mass. Old St. Mary's, a church built by Italian immigrants, smelled of incense, votive candles and the furniture polish that the nuns used to clean the wooden pews. The flickering banks of candles cast shadows on the statues of the Virgin Mary and St. Joseph. The faces of the figures seemed to watch the child and it both frightened and thrilled her to think that all the saints of heaven were there to call upon in time of need.

As I pounded the pavement along the lake front, I pondered my lost faith. Certainly, I still believed in God and in the presence of spirit. What I'd lost was belief in religion, in an organized body that could interpret the Truth and dictate my conscience. I'd "fallen away," as Aunt Terry put it. In reality, I'd run away, as soon as I realized that the old men in Rome who fronted for God had no concept of the lives of ordinary men and women, especially women. I was still waiting to see if there was something to run to, rather than just from. The morning fog that shrouded the lake seemed a fitting metaphor for the gray cloud that seemed to hover over my heart and mind.

Kevin. Cute, funny, sexy Kevin. What was I going to do about Kevin? The rhythm of my feet faltered slightly as I stepped aside to avoid a pothole in the running path. My life was going along rather smoothly just now—great home, a job I enjoyed, family and friends whom I could depend on for love and support. Did I need the complication that a lover would bring to my well-ordered existence? I'd already done the background work (credit, employment, criminal and civil court checks, even a limited health history that bordered on the illegal) on Kevin and found no reasons to reject him. Now I needed to decide. He wouldn't hang around forever, waiting for Angelina Bonaparte to make up her mind. Inaction was one way of letting him go, but I told myself that I preferred to make an outright choice. So what's it going to be, Angie?

My head was running the Billy Joel song *Honesty*. Do you really think everyone is untrue? I challenged myself. Or are you just finding what you're looking for? Are you setting yourself up for betrayal? Are you just flat-out scared? The little Angie chided me—scaredy cat, scaredy cat.

Basta! Enough! I walked the last block home, took a shower, and dressed in black silk slacks and a white cotton tank top. Small gold earrings lent a slightly formal look to the outfit. I carried the matching black silk jacket, suitable for professional interviews. It might be Sunday, but the investigation needed to move forward.

The counter man at the Starbucks on Farwell looked me up and down. "Whoa, Angie, looking good."

"Thanks, Mo." I smiled. He was a senior citizen who worked part-time to supplement his Social Security income. Mo generally only saw me on Sundays, dressed in sweats. "I have some interviews today, hence the clothes," I explained.

"Hence. I like that. No one says 'hence' anymore. It's like 'hark.' A forgotten word."

"Must be the librarian in me, peeking out from behind the private eye."

"Nice image. How many more of you are there?"

"Way too many."

"I hear ya. So, what'll it be? Latte and a scone?"

"Exactly right, Mo. I must be getting predictable." I waited as he heated and frothed the milk. Mo was an artist. I like to watch people who do things right.

"Nah, you're still a woman of mystery," he tossed over his shoulder. "It's just that most folks eat the same thing for breakfast. I wonder why that is."

"No idea. But thanks, Mo. You made my day." At the little table, I took a bite from the scone and munched contentedly as I extracted my rolled-up *Journal Sentinel* from its plastic sleeve. Sunday papers feel so substantial, until you take out the employment section, the automotive section and all the ads and coupons. Then you're down to about twenty pages of news. I glanced up and noticed that Mo was leaning on the counter, watching me intently. Geez, I sure hoped he wasn't getting a real crush on me. I liked the old guy and didn't want to change coffee shops.

Snapping the paper open, I was greeted by individual head shots of Elisa, Tony, Bart and myself. The headline read "Mob Murder?" Crap. Papa would have a fit, in his restrained way. Bart would go ballistic, and there was nothing restrained about that. Over the top of the paper, I saw Mo, grinning broadly and shaking his head.

They'd pulled together the current story of Tony and Elisa, and some old Mafia history. It labeled Papa "Don Pasquale Bonaparte" and me a P.I with "connections," implying that I worked for the Family. It called Bart a "mouthpiece." I was pretty sure that the reporter would get a piece of Bart's mouth today, and maybe some other parts, too. I read the entire story, looking for inconsistencies and new bits of information. A good crime reporter will usually have a friend in the police department. It's not only the Washington administration that leaks. But the story told me nothing I didn't already know.

I shoved the parts of the paper that I wanted to read later back into the sleeve, then tossed the rest into a recycle bin as I waved to Mo and left the shop. Time to get to work.

The first person I wanted to interview today was Elisa's mother, Janet Morano. She was listed on Elisa's Dunwoodie application as next of kin. I decided to show up at her home without calling first—a blatant violation of social rules, but this wasn't a social occasion. My small stature, white hair and non-threatening sympathy might get me entrance that a phone call wouldn't.

Mrs. Morano lived on Oklahoma Avenue, in a four-family building on the Polish south side. There was no security, so I just walked in and knocked on her door. She had enough sense to open it with the chain still on. "Yes?" she asked me.

"Mrs. Morano, I'd like to extend my sympathy and talk to you for a few minutes. I'm working on the investigation of your daughter's death." I deliberately didn't tell her that I was a private investigator. Let her think I was with the police department, until I was inside the apartment.

She slid the chain off the door and motioned me inside. I stepped into a typical two-bedroom, one bath, living room and kitchen apartment. The "front room" was dark, its roller shade pulled down and the drapes pulled almost-but-not-quite closed. I extended my hand to Mrs. Morano. "Angelina Bonaparte," I said.

Her eyes widened. "You're the one in the paper. You're not the police."

"That's right, Mrs. Morano. I'm a private investigator. I'm trying to find out who really killed Elisa. I'm sure that's what you want, too. Please hear me out."

She hesitated for a moment, then indicated a chair. I sat, my legs primly crossed at the ankles, radiating respectability. The room was cooled by a standing rotating fan. I was pretty sure that she'd bought the furniture as a "suite," consisting of couch, chair, coffee table, end table and lamps. The scratchy upholstery of the chair rasped against the silk of my slacks. Although I tried to sit completely still, I expected to be in static electricity hell when I left.

"Coffee?" Mrs. Morano asked.

"Only if it's prepared. Don't go to any bother."

"I have a pot on the burner. Sugar or cream?"

"Cream, please." I usually drank it black, but the "burner" phrase warned me. She returned with a cup of sludge, which I dutifully sipped as she settled herself on the couch.

In her youth, Janet Morano must have been beautiful. I guessed her to be around my age now, in her fifties, but life had not been kind to her. Her dyed-auburn hair, dull and thin, hung limp to her shoulders. Her eyes were red, the eyelids droopy, giving her a tired look. *Smoker*, I thought, noticing the faint odor of cigarettes and the fine network of wrinkles that radiated from her lips. Her small frame carried no extra weight, but she didn't seem healthy-thin. More like dieting-to-excess thin. With make-up and the right clothes, she would probably still turn some older guy's head. But today, she was just a tired, sad woman.

"You don't think Tony did it?"

She was direct, at least. "No, I don't. I wouldn't work on this case if I thought he was guilty, I promise you." I put my hand on my heart. "I'm a mother, too, Mrs. Morano." I hesitated. "Are you aware of anyone who might hold a grudge against Elisa? Or be angry enough to...?" I let it hang there. You don't use the phrase "murder your child" to a mother.

She looked me in the eyes, her gaze flinty. This was no shrinking violet, even if she had been crying. "Elisa was beautiful," she said. I nodded. "Other women, they were jealous. They resented that she could get the things they wanted."

"Things?" I waited.

"You know, jewelry, furs, the apartment. I told her, get it while you're young. It won't last forever."

Aha. The light dawned. My distaste must have shown on my face, because Janet started to justify herself.

"After all, a woman's only pretty for a little while. And men only want pretty women. They use you up and then they go looking for a younger model. You better have something put aside when that happens. Look at me." She stopped and made a Vanna White gesture, arm flowing gracefully to the apartment and finally resting on her chest.

"Married for fifteen years, Elisa only nine, when the bastard walked out and sold the house right out from under us. He claimed he had no money and had to sell it in order to pay our debts."

"Did you hire an attorney, try to track his assets?"

"Honey, I never worked until the divorce, then I had to get a minimum wage receptionist job. Those snotty little girls right outta high school lookin' down their noses at me 'cause I don't know stuff like Excel and Word. I didn't need computer skills to get married and keep house and raise a baby, right? But after my husband left, I had nothin.' Nothin' to fight him with."

I shook my head sadly. It was a story I'd heard many times.

"So," she continued, "I made sure Elisa knew to take the money and put it away where only she could get it. Used to be, marriage meant security for a woman. If he wanted to play, he had to pay. Now, with community property, he just walks away scot free."

God, I thought, *am I as bitter as she is?* I didn't want to be Janet Morano, not in reality and especially not in spirit. I needed to get the interview back on track. "When was the last time you heard from Elisa, Mrs. Morano?"

"Oh, maybe last May. Yeah, that's right, she called to give me her new address and phone number when she moved into the apartment."

I looked down and wrote in my notebook, trying to conceal my surprise and pity. Her daughter hadn't called or even met her for lunch in three months? I don't live in my children's pockets and they don't live in mine, but that level of disassociation amazed me.

"Did you know about her relationship with Anthony Belloni?" I asked.

"Yeah, she told me. I figure, if he wants to support her, why not?"

"Maybe because he's married?" I responded.

"Listen, honey, he woulda been humpin' somebody. Elisa might as well get something for it. He treated her nice, at least. Bought her nice stuff."

"Did they ever fight? Did he ever touch her in anger?"

"Nah, she knew how to keep him happy." I raised an eyebrow. "Not just the sex stuff. She would make him a nice meal, let him talk about his business, build him up a little, you know? Men like to be treated like little kings, right? He had no complaints."

"Did she ever mention a fight with anyone else? Someone who might have a grudge, who might want to do her harm?"

"Nah. I mean, she and that Jane Dimwitty—" she sniggered— "Elisa called her that as a joke. Well, they didn't see eye to eye, 'cause that Jane thought she was so much better than Elisa. But she didn't have any contact with Jane after she left the job. She got her last check from John, not Jane."

"Any old boyfriends who might be carrying a torch? Someone she broke up with, who maybe still hoped to get back with her?"

"Not that I know about. Well, there was this guy she dated in design school, Richard Llewellyn. They went out for about six months. But he moved to Dallas after graduation. I remember Elisa thinking he might ask her to go with him, but he didn't. So I guess he wasn't too broke up about leavin' her."

"Would you have his address or phone number?"

"No. But it must be in her book. Or in that little electronic thing she always carried."

"The police couldn't locate her address book or PDA, Mrs. Morano. They're assuming that the killer took them."

"No kidding? Well, sorry I can't help you there, but Elisa didn't share that with me. We weren't real buddy-buddy, ya know? Sometimes I thought she mighta been embarrassed by me, once she started to move up in the world."

"I'm sure you're wrong about that, Mrs. Morano. What daughter wouldn't admire a mother who could go out into the world, work to support herself, make a nice house with nice things, and keep her looks? I'll bet you were her role model." It was lies, all lies, but I couldn't leave her thinking that her selfish grasping daughter was ashamed of her, even if she'd been the one to teach the child to be selfish and grasping. She shouldn't have to live with that.

A tear rolled down her cheek and she reached into a pocket for a tissue and dabbed at it. "You think so?" she asked.

"I'm sure of it." I handed her a card. "Please call me if you think of anything else, or if you come across Mr. Llewellyn's contact information." As I stood, I noted that the silk of my slacks was clinging to my legs and I had that high-water effect working. I stood in the building hallway after the door closed, shaking my legs one at-a-time and trying to get the static electricity to discharge. A little girl and her mother came through the outside door and the child started to giggle and point, "Look at the lady dancing, Mommy." Some days, life is determined to make a fool of you.

Chapter 11

The central struggle of parenthood is to let our hopes for our children outweigh our fears.

—Ellen Goodman

Sunday afternoon. Lunch at Papa's, with Aunt Terry, my kids, their kids, any friends that anyone cares to bring along. Your basic Italian family get-together. As I stepped into the back door of the Bay View Foursquare home of my girlhood, my upbringing slammed into me, full force. Papa stood at the kitchen counter, chopping onions and garlic for his masterful spaghetti Bolognese. Aunt Terry rinsed salad greens at the sink. Emma was setting the dining room table, and David stood in the doorway between the kitchen and the dining room, glass of wine in hand, kibitzing. I slung my jacket and purse over a stool, kissed Papa on the cheek, and addressed the room in general. "Hi, everyone. Anything I can help with?"

Terry cast a sidelong look in my direction, and Papa snorted.

"What?" I asked.

"Ma," said David, "*Nonno* isn't too happy about the headlines." David knows that I hate to be called "Ma." He raised one eyebrow, lifted his glass of wine in a toast, and walked out of the room, leaving me to face the music.

Papa stopped chopping and turned to me, wiping his hands on his white chef's apron. "Angelina, I'm a grown man and the newspapers can say what they like about me. I've dealt with it before. But no man wants to see his daughter's name and picture spread across the front page like that."

I knew I was in trouble when my full first name surfaced. If I heard 'Angelina Sofia,' then I was in deep disgrace. "Papa, I'm sorry that it happened, but it was out of my control."

He shook his head. "Why do you want to do this work? You have a good degree, be a librarian, for God's sake. That's a proper job for a woman." He turned his back to me and resumed chopping, with increased vigor. "Ever since you broke up with that *faccia di stronzo*, you've been acting like a crazy woman. You don't go to Mass, you date men as young as your son, you...you...investigate!" He spat the word out. "What kind of work is that for a good woman? What kind of life? Is that how I raised you, Angelina?" He slammed the knife down on the cutting board and turned back to me.

Terry started to speak, to intervene, but I stopped her with a raised hand. I took a deep breath, angry at the personal attack and unwilling to debate about woman's work with Papa. I decided to respond to the spirit of his words, rather than the words themselves. "Papa, I know you're worried about me and you want the best for me. But you raised me to be a woman who would follow her own path. To think for myself. To question and judge. You raised me to care about people. That's what I do, Papa. That's why I can't be a librarian, there's no heart in that work for me anymore." I walked over to him and put my hands on his shoulders. Looking up into his eyes, I continued. "I spent the first half of my life pleasing others, Papa. Most of the time, it made me happy, too. I'm glad I got the chance to raise a family and be a wife.

I don't regret it. But now, I need to find out who I am without those others to define me." I squeezed his shoulders lightly. "Maybe that will include Kevin, maybe not. I just don't know yet. Give me time, Papa."

Behind his back, Terry gave me the thumbs-up. Papa scowled and turned to the stove, muttering under his breath. Then he turned back to me and gave me a grudging embrace. I knew I'd smell like onions and garlic all day, but I didn't mind. "Angel," he whispered, "it's more important to be happy than to be strong or independent or right. I found that out just in time, when I married your mama. Don't wait too long to be happy. I want to see you happy."

"I know, Papa."

As I stepped back, Aunt Terry piped up. "It's been quite a while since you've been to Mass yourself, Pasquale. I wouldn't mind a little company from either of you."

Papa and I looked at each other, co-conspirators in the effort to avoid the dreaded nun's pew where Terry invariably sat during Mass. I poured myself a glass of wine, escaped into the living room and sank onto the couch. Little Angela curled up by my side. "*Nonna*, is *Bisnonno* mad at you?" Her dark curly hair and big brown eyes dominated her heart-shaped face. *Someday*, I thought, *she'll be a boy magnet.* I sighed, wishing that day would never come, and suddenly understood Papa's feelings a little better.

Setting my glass of wine on the coffee table, I put an arm around Angela and smiled down at her. "Not exactly mad, sweetie. He's just a little worried because your *nonna* is working on something that concerns him."

"Is it grown-up stuff, or can you tell me about it?"

Her serious face brought me down to earth. What were the odds that someone at her school would know about the headlines and tease her? I hoped small, but I decided I'd better explain to all the grandkids, just in case. First, though, I sought permission from my kids and their spouses. They all agreed, with reservations, so we trooped back into the living room together.

"Angela," I said, "please go ask your cousins to stop their video game for a minute, and come out here. I need to talk to all of you." She walked purposefully into the den, where the boys were engaged in a competitive game of Mario Brothers. David and Elaine don't allow them to play the violent games. I heard their protest, and Angela's "Now, boys!" in a very motherly tone. I smiled as they all assembled in the living room and sat on the big leather couch, a row of expectant small faces waiting for *Nonna* to speak. The Sunday paper was lying on the coffee table in a heap. I picked through it until I found the front page and turned it to the three children's faces before me. "Angela, Patrick, Donald," I said, to get their attention. "Take a look at the pictures in the paper today." It felt almost like storytime at the library.

"*Nonna*, that's you," Donny exclaimed.

"Right, that's me." I pointed to Papa's picture. "And that's *Bisnonno*, great-grandpa, when he was a little younger."

"Wow," said Patrick. "Are you famous?"

"Well, not exactly. See, *Nonna*'s working on an investigation that involves a murder, and that's why my picture's in the papers."

"Why is *Bisnonno*'s picture there, too?" asked Angela.

"It's kind of hard to explain," I responded. "You see, when he was a young man, *Bisnonno* had some friends who were part of a gang, and one of the new gang members is suspected of murdering a woman. *Bisnonno* had nothing to do with this, but they decided that his picture might make the story more interesting."

Although I was careful to avoid any mention of it, Donny broke in with his usual precocious understanding. "You mean the Mafia, right? Like in *The Sopranos*?"

"Have you seen that show, Donny?"

"No, Mom and Dad say it's too violent."

"Well, they're right about that. But you're right that some people think that *Bisnonno* was part of the Mafia. That's why they dug out his picture and put it in the paper, even though he had nothing to do with the story they wrote about. It's called sensationalism—they just want to create a sensation so people will buy the paper." The three serious faces of my grandchildren looked at me, waiting. "So I wanted you to know why *Nonna* and *Bisnonno* were in the papers today. Just in case someone at your school says anything to you about it. Okay?"

They nodded in unison.

"Any questions?"

They shook their heads.

"Okay, then. Who wants to play kickball in the back yard?"

"Me."

"I do."

Emma waggled her finger at me. "Mom, you're incorrigible. And wonderful. Don't wreck your clothes."

"Yes, ma'am," I responded, as we both laughed at our role reversal. I gathered David and his Elaine, and Emma's John, and we all headed outside with the children to play. Emma, ever the lady, waved us on. I played on the children's side. We beat the adults soundly and ate a hearty meal afterwards in Papa's formal dining room.

Then, while the men snoozed in the living room and the kids watched *Shrek* in the den, we women cleaned up the kitchen and dining room and gossiped. Of course, our talk turned to men. To Terry's Fausto. To my Kevin. We both played it cagey, deflecting Emma's and Elaine's questions and comments and keeping our thoughts to ourselves.

Chapter 12

Anyone who has obeyed nature by transmitting a piece of gossip experiences the explosive relief that accompanies the satisfying of a primary need.

—Primo T. Levi

It was only four when the family party broke up at Papa's. I decided to make a few calls in Elisa's old neighborhood, but first I had to change clothes. The smell of onions and garlic from Papa's embrace was apparent, even to me. I drove home, showered and dressed in a plain linen shift and sandals, and then set out to the address Elisa gave when she was hired at Dunwoodie's. It was in the village of West Milwaukee, a one-mile square area squeezed between Milwaukee and West Allis, in a lower middle class neighborhood that was one step up from the barrio of Milwaukee's south side. Maybe some of Elisa's old neighbors would furnish me with an alternate murder suspect.

Milwaukee bungalows lined both sides of the street, most with side drives and detached one-car garages, some well-maintained, but many showing signs of neglect. The owner versus renter mentality was obvious. In the fifties, these houses would have been shaded by towering elms whose canopies met in the sky above the street pavement. Dutch Elm Disease hit hard in the late fifties and early sixties, decimating the elm population in most of southeast Wisconsin. I missed the stately old trees.

I parked on the street in front of Elisa's former house, one of the rentals. Tobacco-spit brown paint peeled from the clapboards, the roof was patched with mismatched shingles, and the steps up to the front porch looked none too sturdy. I pressed the doorbell, not confident that it would work, but heard the ding-dong of an old-style ringer sound within the house, followed by footsteps. I took a couple of steps back, not wanting to seem threatening to whomever would answer. The door creaked open and a middle-aged man, wearing a sleeveless tee shirt and khaki pants, stood behind the screen door. "Yeah?" His expression was sullen.

"Good afternoon," I greeted him. "I'm hoping you can help me. I'm trying to locate someone who knew Elisa Morano when she lived at this address."

He studied me in silence for a few seconds. "Why?" The question was direct but his voice was non-confrontational.

"I'm a private investigator." As I spoke, I extracted a business card from my purse and offered it to him. "Did you move in here after Elisa left?"

He eased the screen door open, took my card and studied it for a moment. "You the one in the papers this morning?"

"That's right." I waited, wondering if the newspaper article would be a help or a hindrance.

"Well, I didn't know her. I moved in here after her old roommate left. Marsha."

"Can you tell me Marsha's last name and new address?" I had my Cross pen poised over an open steno book.

"Her last name is Cantwell. I accidentally opened a bill addressed to her here, after she moved out. Don't know where she moved to. I sent the bill to the landlord."

"And how might I get in touch with him?"

"You might call him." He was mocking me now, but I kept my temper under wraps, held the pen over the paper and waited. "Ben Sobczak, 555-8703," he said.

"Thanks. If you think of any other information that might help, please give me a call."

He flicked my card against his thumbnail and responded, "Yeah, right," as he closed and latched the door.

Back in the car, I got a voice recording and left my cell phone number and a request that Ben call me at his earliest convenience. I added that it had to do with locating a former tenant. Landlords get all kinds of repair calls and tend to avoid answering the phone directly. I was hoping he would call me back right away, but after five minutes of waiting, I decided to ring a few more doorbells.

The house across the street was the "after" image of the one I'd just visited—nicely sided and roofed, neat little front yard with flowers along the walkway, porch with table and wicker chairs, one occupied by an older lady rocking away as she sipped from a tall blue glass. That glass looked awfully good in the early evening heat. I walked over and stood at the bottom of the steps to the porch.

Before I could speak, she greeted me. "Nice night, init?" The South Side dialect was in full force.

"A little warm," I responded.

"Only if you run around. You need to find a place and set."

"You're right." I smiled as I looked her over. About seventy, wispy gray hair, no makeup, forty pounds overweight, wearing slippers and a clean snap-up-the-front print dress, what Terry would call a "housecoat." I suspected that the lady sat here on her front porch in good weather, or in the bay window of her front room in bad weather, and watched her neighbors, day after day. An investigator's dream, if she would talk.

"Ma'am, I'm trying to locate one of the young women who used to live in the house across the street." I gestured at the rundown monstrosity. "The gentleman who lives there now couldn't help me. I wonder if you can."

"He ain't no gentleman and I ain't surprised he cou'nt help you. Don't do nothin' but go to work, come home, and drink. Recycle bin full of beer cans and bottles, every week. Not part of the neighborhood at all." She shook her head at this lack of spirit and I echoed the gesture. "Come on up," she invited. "Have a seat."

Hallelujah! I thought, as I ascended the four broad wooden steps and sat in the unoccupied rocker.

"Care for an iced tea?"

"I would love one."

She heaved herself up and flip-flopped into the house. In a moment, she was back, carrying the twin to her glass, filled to the brim with ice cubes and tea, and a lemon slice floating on the top. She set the glass on the table, along with a long-handled spoon and a small sugar dish, filled with little paper packets of sugar and sweetener. "I'm Mabel Lembke," she introduced herself.

"Angelina Bonaparte." I pondered giving her a business card, but decided to wait. I didn't want to spook her. If she was the neighborhood tabby, as I suspected, she'd probably talk to me with no provocation.

"You can't be lookin' for Elisa. She got herself killed last week. So it must be Marsha you want, right?"

I noticed the phrasing. Elisa "got herself killed." As if Elisa was responsible. "That's right, I'm trying to find Marsha Cantwell. But it's in regard to Elisa Morano, so if there's anything you can tell me about Elisa…"

"Honey, I can tell you a lot about that one. She'd talk nice to your face, but behind your back it was another story. They lived there about a year, her and Marsha. Both students at that art school, MIAD. Don' know what it stands for. Anyhow, I been here more than fifty years, since I married Mr. Lembke, so I know most everyone on the block. Them girls moved in about a year ago May. An' I think to myself, uh-oh, party time. But they was quiet and gave us no trouble. Truth to tell, I think they was too ashamed of the place to bring people home."

"Did they socialize much with the neighbors?"

"Nah, but they was friendly when you run into them on the street or at the store. An' last winter, when I slipped on the ice and broke my wrist, Elisa called the ambulance and rode with me to St. Luke's." She laughed. "She called it St. Lucrative's."

"Your husband wasn't home?"

"Joseph's been gone these twelve years, now. An' our kids don' live by me, so it was a blessing Elisa was there. But, you know, after that, I started to get charges on my credit card that I didn't make. An' I always wondered if she memorized the number while she sat with me in the hospital intake. D'you think that's possible, to memorize one of them long numbers?"

"I couldn't, but I bet there are people who can."

"That's what I thought. O' course, it coulda been somebody who worked there. I guess I'll never know, for sure. But I watched her after that, an' I din't like what I saw."

I cocked an eyebrow and waited.

"I mean," Mabel continued, "she shoun'ta treated Marsha that way, talking about her behind her back, about how plain she was and how she'd never get a man. And then Marsha does herself up a little, ya know, new hairdo and some makeup and nice clothes, and this fella in their class shows a little interest." She leaned over to me. "Then one night when Marsha's outta town, visiting her family over the holidays, her boyfriend Al comes over. Stays all night. I'm out clearin' the dusting of snow off the front walk next morning when he strolls outta the house, bold as you please, gets in his car and leaves. I'm leanin' on my broom and watchin,' and there's Elisa, the *kurwa*—that's Polish for whore, honey—grinnin' in the doorway. So I waves to her, and she comes out and tells me this story about how the furnace went out and Ben the landlord wou'nt answer the phone, so she calls Al and he comes over to help and ends up sleepin' on the couch 'cause his car wou'nt start. Funny, I says, it started fine just now.'

"Did Marsha find out?"

"Yeah." She sat back and took a sip from her glass. "Yeah. I tol' her. In this day and age, you can't be too careful. I tol' her to go down to the clinic an' get tested. Was I wrong?"

"I don't know, Mrs. Lembke. Who can say? How did she take it?"

"At first, she stuck up for Al and believed the story Elisa gave her. Then, about Easter, she musta found out the truth. It was like the light went right outta her. She moped around the whole month of April, and in May, Elisa moved out. Marsha cou'nt handle the rent all on her own, so she moved, too."

"Do you know where?"

"Yeah, I wrote down her address while I was getting' the tea. I heard you talking to the *dupa* across the street." She reached into the big square pocket of the cotton housedress and removed a slip of paper. "My number's on there, too. When you see her, tell her to call me. I worry about that girl. She's missin' a layer a skin, ya know? Like everything is just a little too much for her, like she's got no defenses. Maybe I shun'ta told her."

"Mabel, I appreciate your help." I handed her a card. "If you think of anything else, especially anyone who might have a grudge against Elisa, will you call me?"

"Sure. Yeah." She smiled. "Come on back and visit sometime. Let me know the details, okay?"

"I will." I gave her a conspiratorial grin and waved as I drove away.

Chapter 13

A threat is basically a means for establishing a bargaining position by inducing fear in the subject. When a threat is used, it should always be implied that the subject himself is to blame by using words such as "You leave me no other choice but to..."

—CIA Manual

Monday mornings are my organization time. I hate the feeling that I might be overlooking something important, so I always start the week with a clean slate by taking care of paperwork. I arrived at the office, latte in hand, at seven forty-five. Centered on my desk blotter was a legal-size envelope with "Bonaparte" block lettered in black marker.

I get my share of threats as a result of doing divorce investigation. Most arrive via phone. A few are via U.S. mail. I make it a point to trace them and have Bart or my client's attorney send legal notice that the police will be notified should anything untoward happen to me. I can't afford to take these things with a grain of salt, even though I know they're usually just the release of pent-up frustration.

As I donned latex gloves, I mentally reviewed what I knew of letter bombs. Most of them don't make it to their destination, due to postal handling. This one had been hand-delivered, sometime over the weekend. I sniffed it—no odor. I dusted the envelope for prints—none present. I gently lifted it by the corners and held it to a strong light. Inside, I could see what looked like a sheet of paper with cut out letters. Should I call the bomb squad and risk looking like a fool? This didn't feel like a bomb to me. I slit the envelope and eased out the contents.

It was only a piece of paper. Sighing with relief, I unfolded it and read "*Elisa Morano got what she deserved. Drop the case or the same could happen to you.*" It looked like the writer had run a glue stick across the page and then stuck magazine and newspaper cut-outs down to form the message. "*Elisa Morano*" was one piece, apparently cut from a local headline. Again, I tested the contents for fingerprints, but no luck. I reinserted the page into the original envelope, put it all into a plastic evidence baggie, and peeled the gloves from my hands.

The letdown that comes after an adrenaline rush suddenly overwhelmed me. I sat down, uncapped my latte and poured it into my office mug. Sipping, I considered my options. My run-of-the-mill threats are of the vulgar name-calling variety, unpleasant but not logical or specific. This letter seemed less emotional and more serious to me. It didn't attack me personally, it didn't vent about Elisa, it simply stated what the writer considered to be the facts—Elisa Morano was guilty (of something), she was tried, sentenced and executed, and the same would happen to me if I didn't back off. I have to admit I was a little shook up. I rose and locked the office door.

At eight thirty, I heard the rattling of the doorknob. "Angie, you in there?" It was Susan, my office mate. "Angie, I can't find my key. You there?"

"Coming," I called as I rose to open the door.

"What's up?" she asked. "You don't usually lock yourself in. I thought I'd have to track down the super." She settled her briefcase and purse on her desk and hung up her suit jacket. Her blue-black hair, cut in a plain pageboy style, lay in a heavy curtain across her cheeks as she peered at me.

"Susan, somebody left a threatening letter on my desk. I'm trying to figure out how they got in. Would you check your bag for your office key?"

Like most people, she had several rings clipped together onto one bigger bundle. "The office key must've gotten detached somehow. Let's see," she said, as she started to remove the contents of her purse and place them on her desk, one item at a time. From one compartment, she withdrew wallet, checkbook, credit card case, business card case, black ink pen, blue ink pen. From another, lipstick, comb, small mirror, purse-size package of tissues. From the outside zippered pocket, cell phone. Susan was nothing if not organized. She turned her purse upside down and shook it. A single wrapped mint fell out. "That's really odd," she said, "I was sure it would be at the bottom."

"Susan, when I got here this morning, the envelope was on my desk, just my name on it, no postage or other address. It contained a letter warning me off the Belloni case."

Her eyes opened wider and her mouth formed an "O."

"Were you in over the weekend?"

She shook her head.

"Then unless the super let someone in, I think we can assume that the person used your key."

"But, Angie, how could someone get my key? The key ring is never out of my purse."

"I wasn't in the office on Friday. Were there times when you were here alone?"

"Well, sure. I had one new client and a couple of audits, but I didn't have someone here every minute of the day."

"Is it possible that you went down the hall to the bathroom and left your purse in your desk and the door unlocked?"

She flushed slightly and her voice took on a defensive tone. "It's possible. I can't remember. And I'm not a hostile witness, Angie."

Uh-oh, I thought. My investigator mode kicked in too soon, probably the result of my earlier scare. I needed to back off a little. "Sorry, Susan, don't take this personally. I just need to understand what might have happened so that I know how to proceed. It's one thing if someone used your momentary absence to filch the keys, it's another if they were professional enough to pick the lock. I already checked the door and I didn't see any evidence of tampering, but it isn't always obvious. That's all I'm trying to determine."

"I see," she said, unbending slightly. "Well, unless the key is on the floor of my car, someone took it. I can't figure any other way that it would be missing. The ring is either in my hand, in my purse or in the car ignition. Let me go check the car."

As the sound of her heels clacked down the hallway, I examined her filing cabinets and mine with a magnifying lens. There were no scratches on hers, but I found slight traces on the lock of the cabinet that contained my A-B-C-D files. I decided to leave it for the police. I felt I'd have to call them, since theft and illegal entry were involved.

Susan returned, glum. "No luck, there's no key in the car and I'm positive I didn't leave it anywhere else. I'm really sorry about this, Angie. You're always drilling security into me. I should have known better."

"Listen, kiddo," I said as I put an arm around her shoulders, "it's not the end of the world. As far as I can tell, the only other thing that's disturbed is one of my filing cabinet locks. Why don't you take a look through your things, then we'll know what to tell the police."

"Police," she squeaked. "Mr. Fong will be here at ten o'clock. He's so old-style conservative! He'll drop me if he thinks I'm involved with the police. Please, Angie, can we wait to report the break-in until after he leaves?"

"Probably. I'll need to talk to Bart Matthews first, anyway. I'm going to call a locksmith and get new locks installed this afternoon. Will you be here to let them in?"

"Sure. And I want to pay for it."

"Don't worry, Bart will bill the client. After all, it's a direct result of the Morano-Belloni investigation."

As Susan tidied her purse and prepared for Mr. Fong, I retreated to the conference room and called Bart's office. His seventy-something secretary, assistant and all-around aide, Bertha Conti, answered the phone in her no-nonsense tone, "Law offices of Bartholomew Matthews."

"Bertha, it's Angie Bonaparte. How are you?"

"Fine. What can I do for you, Ms. Bonaparte?"

Great, I thought, *Bertha's in her usual poker-up-the-butt mood*. Papa told me her story, how she'd been hired as the young widow of a Family soldier who'd been shot and killed in an inter-Family feud while they were still newlyweds. Bertha herself was German, but you'd never know she hadn't been raised with the code of *omerta*—silence about anything related to the Family. She applied merciless control and order to Bart's otherwise chaotic life.

"I hate to bother Bart, but there was a nasty surprise waiting for me when I got to work this morning. A threatening letter, regarding the Belloni case. I need to talk to him before I go to the police, get his take on it."

"Hold on." Her voice was low and raspy. You can't work for Bart and not smoke. "I'll get him on the line right away."

In a few seconds, I heard clicking and Bart picked up the line.

"Angie, what the hell's going on? You're getting threats?"

"Typical letter, Bart. Cut-outs glued on stock paper." I read it to him. "But here's what's bothering me about it—the letter isn't emotional, it's logical; there were no prints on the envelope or the paper; the perp used keys to get into my office over the weekend and leave it on my desk; he also tried to pick the lock on my filing cabinet."

"Did he succeed?"

"Doesn't matter. He went for the *B*s, so, worst case, he got my notes on Gracie's original case. I filed everything else under M, for Matthews-Belloni. After all, you're the real client now. Bottom line, if he got into the A-B-C-D files, he didn't find anything related to the murder investigation."

"Well, your filing may be unorthodox, but I'm glad of it."

"Bart, I should notify the police about this."

I heard him light up and take a drag. I waited.

"I'm not sure that's a good idea, Angie. This is Family business. We need to do some damage control. Why don't you bring it over here so I can look at it?"

"Once it leaves my office, Bart, I can't call the police. They won't take it seriously, you know that as well as I do."

"Is there anything their lab can do that you didn't already do?"

"Maybe check the envelope flap for saliva, run a DNA test on it. Hang on." I retrieved the baggie from my desk, donned the gloves again, and lifted one corner of the envelope. "Damn, it's one of those self-stick types that you don't have to lick."

"Not likely that they'd spend the time and money on it, anyway, Ange. How about the building security? Any cameras?"

"No, that's one reason I rent here. Some of my clients don't want to be taped by surveillance cameras. And I already checked with the security company. No unusual activity this weekend."

"So how do you figure it happened?"

"Sometime Friday, my office mate went down the hall to the ladies' room and left her purse in the unlocked office. It wouldn't be that hard to slip in, grab the office key from her ring, and use it to access the office after hours."

"Not good."

Bart and his network of attorney friends send a lot of business my way. I needed to reassure him of my security measures. "I talked to Susan about it, Bart. She's properly sorry and I know it won't happen again. I'm getting new locks installed and I'll be looking into motion detectors, too. Believe me, the security of my clients' information is my number one priority."

"You know, Ange, there's an office available next door to me."

"My lungs could never stand the strain, Bart." He started to laugh, but it degenerated into a hacking cough. "You okay?" I asked.

"Yeah, just my normal routine."

"Bart…"

"Don't start with me, Angie. I'm fine. Now listen, I prefer to sit on this until we know more. I don't see what the cops can do that you haven't done already, and I don't want them in the middle of this until we know the source. If the perp is someone in the Family who had it in for Elisa because of Tony, I don't want the cops digging into it. I'd rather handle it internally. Are you okay with that?"

"Under one condition. I want your assurance that Marco will be made aware of this and that he'll take steps to keep it from going any further if it is an inside threat." Marco Alberici was the titular head of the Milwaukee branch of the Family. My skin prickled at the thought of getting involved in a possible feud, but I didn't think I had a choice.

"You have my word on it. Messenger the evidence over, would you? I want to keep it in my safe." He took a drag and exhaled. "Another thing. One of us will have to call your dad. Once I go to Marco about this, Pasquale will find out anyway. I'd rather it came from you or me."

Crap. I hadn't thought about Papa. This would just reinforce the lecture he gave me yesterday. There was no way to keep it a secret, but I wasn't in the mood for a replay of his Sunday talk. "You call him, Bart. And try to convince him that it's probably harmless. He's already on my case about this not being a woman's job."

"Hah. I bet that went over big. Listen, I want you to call Bertha's number and let her know where you are and who you're with, day and night, until we close this case. Got it?"

"Damn it, Bart, I don't need a babysitter, especially not Bertha. She hates me."

"She hates everyone. Probably me, included. So don't take it personally. Besides, I hired you and I'm responsible for your safety. The least you can do is let me know where to start looking for your body if you fail to show up. It's so much easier that way." His sarcastic tone couldn't completely hide the tension behind his words.

"Okay, Bart. But you tell Bertha what to expect. I don't have time to listen to her carefully ordered and numbered set of rules."

It was nine forty-five. My voice mail had a message from Ben Sobczak, Elisa's former landlord. "Marsha didn't answer her phone, but I left her a message to call you. Marsha ain't been doing so good. Go easy on her." Mrs. Lembke had already provided the address and phone, so I planned to interview Marsha today. I just hoped that Sobczak's forewarning wouldn't put her on her guard too much.

I donned gloves to place the threatening note in a courier bag, threw the gloves in for good measure in case Bart didn't have any at his office, called the company and arranged a pickup. Susan promised to check the courier's ID before handing over the bag. She was relieved that I didn't plan to call the police. She didn't seem to realize it meant that there was no real evidence as to the perpetrator. Grabbing my purse and briefcase, I headed out to talk to Marsha.

The temperature this morning was in the eighties, with humidity over ninety percent. I folded the jacket of my peacock blue suit and laid it carefully on the passenger seat of the Miata. My tan camisole, decorated at the neckline with small blue crystal beads, let the sun warm my arms and chest, but the airflow kept me cool as I motored west along National Avenue with the top down, back toward the village of West Milwaukee.

Marsha was living only a few blocks from the flat that she'd shared with Elisa. This didn't surprise me. Most people are creatures of habit who find it hard to break out of their familiar ruts, even when change would do them good. I didn't know if Marsha would be home, but I decided not to call first. Both Mrs. Lembke and Ben Sobczak mentioned her fragility. A phone call might be enough to send her running, if she had anything to hide.

I pulled up in front of the address, a four-family cinderblock with lawn chairs, kids' bikes, tricycles and big wheels scattered in front. A buzzer system was located at the entry door. The small card next to Marsha's address read "*Alan McGuire/Marsha Cantwell.*" Was it possible that she'd moved in with Al, the creep who'd slept with her roommate? I pulled out the slip of paper that Mabel Lembke had given me, walked to the side of the building and called her on my cell phone.

"Mrs. Lembke," I asked, after she answered and I identified myself, "do you remember Marsha's boyfriend Al's last name?"

"Sure. Irish kid. McGuire. Don't get a lot of them on the sout' side. Why you askin'?"

"Well, I think I located Marsha and it looks like they might be living together. I just wanted to be sure that Alan McGuire was the same Al you mentioned."

"No kiddin'? Guess she forgave the bum, huh?"

"Guess so. Thanks for the help. I'll give her your number. If she calls, it might be better to let her tell you."

"I hear ya. Go easy on her, Angie. And call me when you know what's what."

Quid pro quo, I thought. She was almost a professional source. "I will," I promised.

I approached the front door and pressed the buzzer. No answer. I pressed again, this time laying on it for a few seconds. Again, no answer. They were probably at work.

As I turned to leave, the door burst open and a small child raced out, uprighted the red bicycle that lay on the grass, jumped on it and pedaled furiously down the sidewalk. She was the embodiment of Einstein's energy-matter equation in what appeared to be a little four-year-old body. The bike wobbled back and forth on its training wheels that hovered inches above the pavement, providing stability but allowing her to learn how to balance on two wheels. Sweet freedom, that first sense of speed and mobility.

Her mother exited behind her, a baby strapped to her chest in one of those sling contraptions that today's young parents use. "Oh, I'm sorry, did Missy bang into you?"

"No, don't worry about it." I shook my head as I saw little Missy reach the end of the block and turn back. "Don't you wish God gave parents the same energy that he gave children?"

"You have no idea," she said, as she settled into a lawn chair and adjusted the baby. "I never knew I could be so tired."

"I remember," I said. "It does get better, but not right away."

She smiled at me and glanced tenderly at the baby.

"How old is the little one?" I asked.

"Seven weeks." She looked up at me, shading her eyes from the sun.

"Maybe you can help me," I said. "I'm trying to get in touch with Marsha Cantwell. One of her old neighbors, Mrs. Lembke, gave me this address."

"Well, she lives upstairs from us. But I'm pretty sure they're both at work."

"That's what I thought. Maybe I'll try tonight. Any idea when she usually gets home?"

"Around four. She leaves for work real early, like my John, but she gets home a lot earlier than he does."

"Do you know what kind of work she does?"

She shook her head. "I'm not sure, they keep to themselves. Didn't even come outside for the block party in July." She paused. "If I see her, should I give her a message?"

"No, but thanks. I'll probably be back later."

As I settled into the driver's seat of the Miata, Missy pedaled up and screeched to a halt. Her big eyes, startlingly blue, raked the car. "Nice wheels," she commented in a surprisingly adult manner.

"Well, thanks. I like yours, too."

She waved, looked over her shoulder at her mother, and cycled away. Such innocent joy in a fine summer day and a nice set of wheels. *If only we could all remember to feel that joy.* I decided to take an hour to smell the roses.

The Domes were just down the street and I had a season ticket. Formally titled the Mitchell Park Horticultural Conservatory, the Domes are a set of giant glass greenhouses shaped like beehives. Each dome spotlights a unique theme—arid, tropical, floral. The floral dome changes with the seasons and holidays. Today, I strolled among brilliant summer flowers and tropical plants. There were few people and I savored the peace and beauty around me, refreshing myself and feeling a slight lifting of the heaviness that seemed ready to descend on me. Too many pressures, both personal and professional, and not enough spiritual refreshment, I diagnosed. I promised myself that I would call my best friend, Judy, tonight. It was too long since we'd had a girly chat or a movie. She'd set me straight on Kevin and probably a few other things. I smiled as I exited into the sunlight.

When I stressed that it was an emergency, the locksmith and the security company had promised to be at the office this afternoon. I had time before I needed to be back at Marsha's and I wanted to understand how the security company's motion detectors worked before I let them install anything. I drove back to the office.

Susan was out. The door was locked tight. The locksmith stood there, talking on his cell phone, leaving me an angry message. I hastened down the hall with my hand outstretched. It doesn't do to get on the bad side of a tradesman, especially if it's a trade you may have need of in the future. "Sorry I'm late, I hope you weren't waiting long. I'm Angelina Bonaparte."

"Smitty. Smith Locks and Keys." He waved his hand at me, but didn't shake. Considering the graphite that had settled into his skin, I appreciated the nicety. After examining the door, Smitty recommended a multiple-deadbolt high security lock and suggested that the pebbly glass in the upper half of the door be replaced with laminated glass that would withstand a bullet or bomb. "No sense putting in a good lock when any fool can crack the glass, reach in and disengage it. Right?"

I nodded. "Right. Do you do the work?"

"No, but I have contacts. You'll get a good price, I promise. Your old man, he got me out of a jam a while back."

"I see." I didn't want to know what kind of jam Smitty had been in and how Papa had managed to extricate him. "I appreciate it, Smitty, and I'll be sure to let Papa know how helpful you've been. Can you get it done today?"

"Sure, I'll make the call now."

The message light was blinking on my phone. It was Susan, telling me that she'd had an emergency call from a client and couldn't be back until two o'clock. An emergency call? For an accountant? Did someone lose a decimal point? I was a little hacked off, but reasoned that if I hadn't taken an hour to wander around in the Domes, there would have been no issue. So in a way, it was partly my fault for goofing off. *C'est la vie.* It all worked out anyway.

Just as the glazier and Smitty finished their work and left, the security consultant arrived. He looked about eighteen years old to me, all hair and teeth and new blue suit. But my confidence level rose as he demonstrated the motion detectors and how they could be connected to the building's alarm system. He seemed to know his stuff.

"What are the odds of a false alarm?" I asked.

"Low, in a business. It's mostly pets and kids that trigger the falsies. We'll set the sensitivity so that mice or insects won't set it off. And since we also protect the building, the monitoring charges are a lot less than if you went to another company." He showed me a rate chart.

"Do it," I said. I'd clear it with Susan when she got back. We set up a day for the wiring and other physical work, and he left.

Susan still wasn't back. She wouldn't be able to enter the office without the new keys. I called her cell phone, got voicemail, and left a message telling her that it was now two o'clock and I would be in the office until three, waiting to hand over her new door keys.

While I waited, I made notes on my interview with Elisa's mother, Mrs. Lembke and the woman outside Marsha's building, and reviewed the Morano folder from Dunwoodie's, trying to decide who to tackle next. By then, my watch read two forty-five. I wanted to be in place outside Marsha's building by three-thirty, just in case she got home early. I couldn't wait for Susan any longer.

Just as I grasped the doorknob to the stairway, the elevator doors swung open and Susan rushed out. "Angie, I'm so sorry." She was breathing rapidly and looked flustered.

"Don't worry about it, Susan. I have to go, we can talk later. Here are the new keys." I handed her a ring with two new keys, one to carry and one for a spare, and told her to keep the spare at home, in a safe place. She nodded, and I pounded down the stairs to my car.

Chapter 14

A fraudulent intent, however carefully concealed at the outset, will generally, in the end, betray itself.
—Titus Livius (Livy)

As I neared Marsha's building, I pondered the best approach to take. Everyone I spoke to mentioned her fragile state. I've found through experience that those who are unsure of themselves like others to project calm authority, but not overwhelm. So I'd be a little bit Mom and a little bit buddy. I waited in the alley behind the building, where the tenant parking spaces were.

At four-fifteen, a Honda Civic, several years old and sporting rusty fenders, pulled into the spot assigned to the McGuire/Cantwell apartment. A young woman, dressed in a black business suit, exited the car and bent into the back seat. As she retrieved her briefcase and turned to lock the car, I pulled on my suit jacket and approached her. "Ms. Cantwell?" I asked. She jumped, as startled as a newborn hearing a loud noise. *Whoa*, I thought, *go easy*.

"Yes?" As she responded, she backed up several steps.

I slowly walked over and stopped ten feet away. "I'm Angelina Bonaparte. I'm an investigator working for the lawyer who represents

106

Anthony Belloni. I'd like to talk with you briefly about Elisa Morano." I extracted a business card from my briefcase and held it out to her, silently willing her to approach me.

She did. After glancing at the card and putting it in her jacket pocket, she looked me over. I returned the compliment, noting a twenty-something woman in a chic suit (Ann Taylor?) and pumps, whose mousy brown hair was expertly enhanced by auburn highlights and whose makeup, while subtle, did a lot to glamorize rather plain features. In short, her appearance took me by surprise. It just didn't match Mrs. Lembke's appraisal or Mr. Sobczak's concern.

"I suppose I'd better talk to you." Her voice was a monotone. "Come on up."

I followed her into the hallway of the building and upstairs to her apartment. It was neatly but plainly furnished, with no decoration on the walls and not much flair to the furniture. I wondered at her background as a design student, given the blandness of the living room.

After setting her briefcase in the coat closet, Marsha sank onto the couch, folded her hands, crossed her legs at the ankles and looked at me. No gesture or offer of a seat, no words of welcome, no smile. She was an empty container, with no animation or interest in me.

Unbidden, I took a seat in a leather recliner, set my purse and briefcase on the floor, and leaned forward. "I understand that you and Elisa went to design school together and were roommates for a time." She nodded. "You met in design school?" Again, she nodded. It was like interviewing someone spaced out on tranqs. Could that be the problem? Drugs? I decided to step lightly. "Would you say you were friends?"

Friends. That simple word broke her shell of listlessness. Her lip curled up in a snarl, her eyes flashed, and her hands clenched together tightly as she leaned toward me. "I used to think we were friends. I used to call her my best friend." Those final two words snapped, enunciated precisely and with venom.

"Something happened to change the relationship?" I kept my voice neutral.

"Did she suffer when she died?"

The question and the longing behind it pushed me back in my chair. This lady was a ticking bomb. I didn't want to be the one she exploded on, but I needed information and she certainly seemed a likely candidate to replace Tony on the Elisa hit list. I decided to stay factual and low-key. "There was a lot of blood. The coroner's report indicates that she died quickly."

"Too bad." Marsha stood and began to pace the room, then stopped with her back to me, looking out a window. "No...no, I didn't mean that." She covered her face with her hands and her body shook. I couldn't tell if she was crying or if they were tremors of rage.

Moving into Mom mode, I told her, "It's best to acknowledge the dark feelings that we all have. Expose them to the light. That way, we can work through them instead of hiding them. Secrets take on a life of their own. They fester and grow."

"That's what my therapist says." Her voice was a low murmur. She gave herself a little shake and turned, looking me in the face with an expectation of interaction.

"I'd say your therapist is right." I waited, but she just watched me with what seemed like hungry anticipation, so I plunged ahead, keeping my voice natural and my face unexpressive. "Why did you hate Elisa?"

Marsha's face crumpled into a mask of grief. The transformation shocked me. It was as if the pieces of a jigsaw puzzle, all complete and ready to admire, were suddenly jumbled and their linkage destroyed, so that nothing matched. She began to cry, and I sat quietly, waiting, as her sobs rose and fell. Gradually, slowly, the crying jag eased and she curled up on the couch, her back against the cushions, her knees tucked up despite the skirted suit, her arms wrapped around them. She was a picture of misery.

She spoke, at first low and haltingly, but then more forcefully and fluidly, as if reciting a soliloquy that she'd rehearsed. "She ruined my life. She took everything away from me, everything that mattered. But not at first." She paused and looked at me. "Did you ever know someone who was so special, they made you feel special, too?" I nodded, as Marsha's eyes sparkled and she smiled. "Elisa would light up a room. She made me feel pretty and smart, better than anyone ever said I could be. She helped me shop and get my hair styled, took me to parties, introduced me to her friends. We worked together on school projects. She made me think I could be somebody, not just the plain little bookworm that I'd always been, but somebody pretty and smart and fun and sexy. It was all so wonderful."

Then her mouth turned down, and her eyes took on the dead look I'd first seen at the car. "But it was all a lie. All fake. She never liked me, never cared about me. She just wanted someone to do her schoolwork, someone plain who wouldn't be a threat to her. I heard her on the phone, laughing at me, calling me her butt-ugly roomie, telling her boyfriend that she needed me to pay the rent and do the grunt work at school that she didn't want to do." Tears pooled and overflowed down Marsha's cheeks. "Then she cheated on me with Alan."

I noted that it was Elisa who cheated on her, not Alan. It was Elisa whose emotional fidelity was most important to Marsha. I took a tissue from my purse and handed it to her. She wiped her eyes and blew her nose.

"At first, when Elisa left me, moved into Tony's apartment, I couldn't sleep. I couldn't eat. I knew I had to move. I couldn't afford the rent by myself, but I couldn't make myself look for a place or for another roommate." Her voice dropped and she looked down at her drawn-up knees. "Ben, my old landlord, he found me when he came over to get the rent. I tried to OD, but I couldn't even do that right. He took me to the hospital and he and Mrs. Lembke from across the street decided to call Alan." She looked up and gave a shudder of breath, reminding me of my daughter Emma as a little girl and how she would always end a crying episode with that same stuttering intake. "I'm going to make some tea," Marsha said. "Would you like a cup?"

I nodded and followed her into the small kitchen, where she put a kettle on to boil.

"Lemon? Sugar? Cream?" she asked me. I declined them all and sat at the two-person drop leaf table. She busied herself setting out cups, spoons, tea bags and sugar bowl. When the kettle howled, she poured water into our cups and sat across from me, adding sugar to her tea and stirring.

She looked up at me and tucked her hair behind her ears. As she continued to stir, she spoke. "Alan was great. He talked to the doctors and got me released into his care. He brought me here and moved my stuff into storage. Don't get me wrong." She raised her hands, palms up, and looked at me from lowered lids. "We're just roommates, we sleep in separate bedrooms. That's all Dr. Nichols thinks it should be, for now. Alan found Dr. Nichols and got me into treatment. But even now, sometimes all I want is to get back to the golden days, the days when Elisa was my friend. Now it will never happen. I'll never see her again."

It was gut-wrenching, listening as she mourned. Again, I thought of my Emma, crying her eyes out as she told me that her best friend Gina had a new best friend and didn't want to play with her anymore. Marsha evoked a lot of girlhood images. But she was a grown woman, and I was here to do a job. "Marsha, were you with anyone the night Elisa was killed?"

"Sure, Alan and I were home that night. We watched TV, I did some work and went to bed early. Why?" Suddenly she understood, her eyes popped and her head snapped back. "You can't think that I…"

"Did anyone else see you? Did you get any phone calls that night?"

"I honestly don't know. Alan will be home around seven, he might remember." Her voice rose, a little panicked.

I patted her hand. "Don't be too concerned. Most people don't have alibis for every minute of the day and night. But I wouldn't be surprised if the police want to talk with you."

"They were here yesterday. But all they asked was what I knew about that night and whether Elisa ever mentioned threats. Should I tell the police what I told you?"

Aha, I thought, *I'm one step ahead of Wukowski and Iggy*. Her simple-minded question aroused my motherly instincts. "Maybe you want to talk to a lawyer. Know anyone?" She shook her head, so I grabbed my purse, took out a card for the Legal Aid Society and set it on the table. Private investigators see a lot of wreckage, I'd learned to carry the tow truck numbers with me. "Call them," I told her. "They can help. Marsha, is there anyone else you can think of whom Elisa hurt, someone who might hold a grudge against her or want to get even?"

"I don't think so." She slowly shook her head. "No, there's no one else. Everyone loved Elisa."

Yeah, right, I thought. "What about her boyfriend? Did she break up with him, or did he break up with her?"

"He moved to Dallas after graduation. They kept in touch for a while, but Elisa didn't want a long-distance relationship."

I asked for his name and contact information, and she left the room and returned with an address book. It was the same name that Elisa's mother had provided—Richard Llewellyn, a good Welsh name.

"What are your plans?" I asked, concerned about her welfare.

"Well, after graduation, which I made by the skin of my teeth and my good work record from before Elisa moved and I fell apart, I got a job with MacNeil and Associates."

I was impressed. "Excellent firm. You should be proud of that. They did some design work for the attorney I'm currently working for."

She nodded. "It's been great. I'm working with good people, learning a lot. And I'll probably get my own place in a month or so. Dr. Nichols thinks it would be best."

"So you and Alan are over?"

"I'm not sure. He wants to get back together; he swears that night with Elisa was a one-time thing, that he'd never cheated on me before and it will never happen again. But I think I need to be on my own for a little while, to decide for myself what I want. I guess I've always let others make the decisions for me. At least, that's what Dr. Nichols thinks, and I agree. I'm trying to keep up my image." She giggled a little. "You know, the clothes and hair and makeup, the stuff Elisa taught me. And a lot of the friends I made from knowing Elisa are still my friends." She smiled shyly. "They like me, not just Elisa's tag-along friend. They like me!"

"Of course they do," I said. "Sounds to me like you're doing pretty well for yourself. You have a great job with a future, you know how to dress and present yourself, you have friends who stand beside you even through the tough times. You're pretty lucky, Marsha. Pretty blessed."

Her eyes widened as she nodded. "I know. I don't get it, but my pastor tells me that it's all grace, a gift, and I should just be thankful. And Dr. Nichols tells me that we can learn from even the worst events in life and use them to grow."

"I'm not sure I understand about the grace part, but I remember a passage from the Bible that says that God can make all things work for good. So maybe they're both right."

"Yeah. I never thought of it that way."

As I gathered my purse and briefcase and we walked to the door, I asked her to call me if any thoughts surfaced concerning Elisa. Driving away in the Miata, I pondered the effects that we all have on each other, the ripples that we set into motion, the tidal waves that can overtake us. Elisa Morano had a lot to answer for. I didn't like her. I didn't like the mess she left behind. I was afraid of what the next interview would uncover, but Gracie and Tony and Bart were depending on me. And it was my job.

Chapter 15

Sexual attraction keeps throwing self-interest off course.

—Mason Cooley

Not for the first time, I questioned why living in this world was so damned hard. Why don't we act decently toward each other? Why do we lie and cheat? Why do we hurt even those we love? Why do we get sick, or injured in accidents, and suffer, and die? Years ago, I walked away from the Catholic response—original sin, inherited from Adam and Eve. A God who would punish every person on the planet for the disobedience of two was not a God I believed in or wanted to deal with. I couldn't get into New Age philosophy, either. It made no sense to me that I was God, or that the world was a mirage. I even toyed with atheism, but the order of the universe and the wonder I felt in nature kept pulling me back. I believe in God, in a creator. I'm just not sure what meaning God has in the here and now, in the everyday lives of people, in my life. Longing for the truth, not entirely sure if it exists, willing to keep searching, but afraid I'll never find it. Not a comfortable way to live.

It was seven-thirty on a warm August night. The sun wouldn't set until nine o'clock. I was too disgusted with Elisa in particular and the world in general to go back to my condo, so I turned south and headed for the gym. Sometimes a good workout can set my mind straight. I sure hoped so.

Rick's isn't one those glamour-girls-in-thongs places, where women and men spend more time posing for each other than they do exercising. It's an honest-to-God gym, with mats on the floor and a boxing ring and weights. It smells dank and sweaty, despite Rick's best efforts to clean and spray. There aren't a lot of women at Rick's, but those of us who do frequent the joint are serious.

I changed into sweats and a tee shirt, and walked out into the gym. A kickboxing class, newly added to the roster to attract more women, was underway on the mats. Ignoring them, I warmed up on the treadmill and then took out some of my hostility toward life on the bag. Left, right. Uppercut. Cross. Bob and weave, dance and jab. I kept at it for about twenty minutes, until I was exhausted and soaking wet.

The kickboxing class was just ending and the participants were milling around, talking and kidding with each other. I sure hoped they knew that none of that fancy crap would save their butts in a real encounter with a bad guy. A woman's upper body strength is about sixty percent of a man's, so in a fight, there's only one way a woman can win—disable him quickly and run.

As I looked around for Rick to help me off with the gloves, I saw Iggy talking to another man, whose back was to me. I waved my gloved hand in a greeting, and he smiled and walked over to me. "Hey, Angie. How's things?"

"They've been better, Iggy. But then, they've been worse, too." I raised my hands and he pulled off the gloves. "Thanks," I said.

"No prob." He turned and called to the man he'd been talking with. "Wukowski, look who's here."

Shocked, I stared as Wukowski turned and walked over. He was dressed like me, in sweats and a tee shirt, but in his case, he wasn't dripping with sweat. I felt at a definite disadvantage as he approached, my five-foot-three dwarfed by his six-foot-something. "Ms. Bonaparte," he greeted me formally.

"Detective Wukowski," I just as formally responded. I could stand on my dignity, too, even if I didn't feel especially dignified at the moment.

Iggy just shook his head and rolled his eyes. "When are you two gonna get over it and act like human beings to each other?" he asked. But he pronounced it 'human beans.' I had to smile. Either Wukowski heard what I did, or he took my smile as a sign of agreement with Iggy's pronouncement, because he smiled, too.

It transformed the man. An absolute metamorphosis. From rod-up-the-rear, Joe Friday, 'just the facts' ice-man to crinkly-eyed, genuine human being, good-looking in a Dana Andrews tough-guy way. I stared. I looked him up and down. I appreciated his face and body for the first time. I started to blush, and hoped they would put it down to post-exercise blood flow.

Wukowski spoke first. "Yeah, well, maybe you're right, Iggy." He looked at me. "You a member?"

I nodded, unsure if my voice would squeak and betray me. The silence was like a fourth person in the conversation. Iggy, bless him, seemed to sense our discomfort. "How about we shower and get a cuppa coffee? Maybe kick the Morano case around a little?" Wukowski tensed and started to speak, but Iggy grabbed his arm and pulled him toward the men's locker room. "Fifteen minutes, okay, Angie? At least you don't need to mess with your hair. My wife, she takes an hour, just on her hair." He shook his head in wonderment at women in general and his wife in particular, and continued talking as they moved away.

Rick ambled by me and tapped the gloves that I still held in my hands. "All done, Angie?"

I nodded, assessing Wukowski from the rear until he and Iggy disappeared into the locker room. Bulky, but not fat. Substantial. The way I like men to look. "Cherce," as Spencer Tracy once remarked of Katherine Hepburn. Damn it, this was not a complication I needed.

"Angie? You okay?" Rick stood before me, his face searching mine carefully for signs of distress.

"Sorry, Rick. Yeah, I'm okay. Just trying to figure out how to approach Wukowski. We're working a case from different sides."

He nodded, and motioned me over to a quiet corner of the room. "You know about Wukowski? About him and his partner, Liz White?"

Liz White. The name suddenly exploded in my head. "The policewoman who was ambushed and killed?" Two years ago, the story had captured headlines for weeks. She and her partner were investigating a homicide involving a drug dealer, when she suddenly disappeared. The police chief shut the city down, searching for her. Finally, seven days after her disappearance, someone dumped her body under a freeway overpass. In a plastic trash bag. Tortured. Mutilated. With a note purported to taunt her partner and the squad, a note which was never made public. I remember the newspaper photo of her partner, in dress uniform, ramrod straight, stone-faced, hand to forehead as the rifle salute pierced the air at her funeral. So that was Wukowski.

Rick continued. "I never saw a guy so shook. It changed him completely. For weeks, he'd show up here and hit the heavy bag until I thought he'd drop. The other cops, they talked about how he'd spend all night watching the houses where the deals went down, trying to find out who killed her. How he refused to take on another woman partner.

How he and his wife split up. Then, about four months ago, he started looking normal again. Put some weight back on. Started to smile and kid around a little."

"Any idea what caused the turnaround?" I asked.

"No clue. All I'm saying is, the Liz White killing hit him hard, where it hurts. He's doing better, but I don't think he's really over it." He paused. "The thing is, I like him, Angie. And I like you. I don't want to see you take the brunt of his hurt."

"Thanks, Rick. You're a good guy." I gave him a big hug and hit the showers, where I cooled off and contemplated my approach to Iggy and Wukowski. They didn't want to have coffee with me because they loved my company. Iggy'd already paved the way by mentioning the case. There had to be a reason why they were willing to engage in an exchange of information. Maybe the DA thought the case against Tony wasn't strong enough, or maybe the police investigation uncovered some evidence that pointed in another direction. Whatever their reasons, I was willing to cooperate if it would help Bart's defense. I'd have to be cautious, though, and not reveal anything that might jeopardize Bart's case. Even the truth can be damaging, if it's revealed too soon or too late or to the wrong parties.

How to approach Wukowski? As I toweled off and applied lotion to my arms and legs, I thought about my reaction to his physical presence. I enjoy men, don't misunderstand, but I don't usually react that way to a guy who disrespects me, no matter how good looking or manly he is. When he and Iggy showed up at my home on the morning of the murder, Wukowski went out of his way to try to intimidate me physically. Then he tried to tell me how to conduct my business. And at the jail, he simply dismissed me as being beneath his notice. It might be the old good cop/bad cop ploy, it might be his issues with women after his partner was killed, but I didn't think that was the entire explanation. Something about the way he acted made it personal, as if he disliked me and not just the idea of a woman investigator infringing on police affairs.

Other than separate locker rooms, Rick's only concession to his female clientele was a small vanity area for doing one's hair and makeup. I worked styling paste through my wet hair and combed it into spikes, then left it to dry as I applied moisturizer, mascara, lipstick and blush. I didn't want to look like a slob who just finished working out, but neither did I want it to appear that I was trying too hard to look good. I didn't understand why I cared, but I decided that I'd analyze it later. Somehow it was important that I strike the right balance. This man/woman stuff is tricky.

Iggy and Wukowski stood at the exit door as I came out of the locker room. We walked into the parking lot together, and Iggy suggested that we take one car. I dumped my workout bag into the Miata and turned to get into the back seat of Iggy's Impala, but stopped short when I saw that Wukowski was already seated there. *Odd*, I thought, *that he'd cede the front seat to me*, but I climbed in and buckled up. "Where we going?"

"You eat supper yet?" Iggy asked. I shook my head. "How about Paul's?" he suggested.

Paul's is a little greasy spoon diner that sits on a triangular lot where Kinnickinnic meets Lincoln. They serve the greatest chili dogs you'll ever eat—Chicago red hots, roasted, not boiled, plumped in a chewy bun and smothered in homemade chili, chopped onions, mustard and relish. I started to salivate before Iggy turned the key in the ignition.

As we pulled out of the parking lot, Wukowski leaned forward. Casually placing a forearm along each seat back, he rested his chin in the middle of his clasped hands and started to talk. I didn't hear a word he said. All I could think of was his spicy aftershave and his breath on my ear. I felt the heat start to rise and my chest start to tighten, and I cursed myself for a fool. *Damn it, Angie, get a grip. This is business.* I slid as far right as I could, pushing myself into the car door, and turned toward Wukowski. As I hoped, he backed up. *Thank God, breathing space.*

When Iggy parked on the street in front of the diner, I bolted out of the car. The men exited at a normal pace. They both stared at me, confused looks on their faces. *Time for a little misdirection*, I told myself. "C'mon," I said, "I'm starving." I led the way and slipped into a booth, staying on the outside of the bench so that they'd have to sit together on the other side. The place was empty, not unusual for eight-thirty at night. We all perused the menu, although I knew exactly what I wanted.

Paul, the owner, cook and all-round maintenance guy, leaned across the nearby counter and yelled at us. "I'm on my own today, Lottie called in sick. What'll it be?"

Iggy and Wukowksi deferred to me, so I shouted back at Paul, "Two chili dogs, the works, an order of cheese fries and a diet cola."

Wukowski started to laugh. "A diet cola?" Emphasis on diet.

I grinned at him. "A woman's got to save a few calories wherever she can. Besides, I just worked out. I'm entitled."

He shook his head and called out an order for coffee and the breakfast skillet—fried eggs on top of fried potatoes with diced ham, cheese, green peppers and onions. "Not exactly a cardiologist's delight yourself," I teased him. Iggy yelled over for a coffee, cheeseburger with raw onions, and fries. Paul slammed the drinks on the counter and turned back to the grill. Wukowski stood up and stacked the two cups of coffee in their saucers, then carried the beverages over to the booth.

We settled back to wait for our food.

"So, Angie, what's happening on your side of the Belloni case?" Iggy asked.

"Not a lot. I've been interviewing her former coworkers and friends."

Wukowski leaned forward, suddenly grim. "You licensed to carry?"

I looked at him for a moment. He was asking if I had a legally-licensed gun. "Why do you ask?"

"This is a murder investigation. Somebody killed somebody. That makes it dangerous."

The threatening letter flashed into my mind. I could see the pasted cut-outs on the paper. I felt the fear that the logical, cold threats evoked when I first read them. I also felt like a three-year-old being reprimanded for bad table manners. Iggy opened his mouth to intervene, but I spoke first. "I'm well aware of the meaning of murder, Wukowski. I'm not an idiot. I take sensible precautions."

"Sensible precautions," he repeated. "Like what?"

"Are you honestly asking me if I know how to conduct my business?" I stared at him, anger boiling up at his tone and his words. I've faced prejudice against woman investigators before, usually in the form of 'what's a nice little thing like you doing in such a bad business?' Wukowski was more blunt and confrontational than most. I wasn't about to swallow it.

"I'm trying to tell you that whoever offed Elisa was a very angry person. I want you to understand that they won't take kindly to any investigator, male or female, police or private, trying to unmask them." He stopped for a moment, took a sip of coffee and swallowed. "I've asked around and you're not exactly known for criminal work. So I'm just trying to find out if you can handle yourself." He stared straight at me, the green of his eyes almost obliterated by the dark black circles of his pupils.

The intensity of his words and his look slammed into me and pushed me into the back of the booth seat. I paused. To his credit, he didn't base his observations about the killer's intentions on females or private investigators. I also had to concede that his observations about me were accurate. Most of my work involves divorce or corporate background checks, with an occasional missing person case thrown in. Those kinds of cases have the potential for violence, but they don't start out that way. I cooled down.

"You're right, Wukowski, I don't do a lot of criminal work. I only took this case because Gracie Belloni begged me to, and Bart Matthews has thrown a lot of other work my way." I took a sip of cola and continued. "I guess nobody knows how they'll react to an attack until it happens. All I can say is that I'm licensed and I can handle a gun. I know enough self-defense to get me out of a jam, but I'm not stupid enough to think I can take a man in a real fight. I have a lot of common sense. I keep good records and I let someone know where I'm going and when I can be expected back." He didn't need to know that I'd only started to check in with Bertha this morning. I paused, unwilling to play the final card, but needing to acknowledge the truth. "Anybody who knows my old man knows it would be unhealthy to hurt me." It was my turn to stare at him and I did. He blinked first.

"All that's on one side," he said softly. "On the other is someone who would kill a young woman in her own home and repeatedly, viciously stab her, even after death."

I nodded, wishing that Bart hadn't instructed me to keep quiet about the letter. "You're right. I'll be extra careful."

"Food's up," Paul called. We all breathed a sigh of relief. Wukowski and I were seated on the outside of the booth, so we rose and brought the plates to the table. Before I sat, I took off my silk jacket and hung it on the hook at one end of the booth. Chili dogs are too darned messy to eat while wearing anything that has to be dry-cleaned. I then grabbed a handful of paper napkins and tucked them into my sleeveless camisole and across my lap. It didn't escape me that, with the jacket off, Wukowski was surreptitiously eyeing the small amount of cleavage that the cami displayed. *Good*, I thought, *let* his *hormones ra*ge. I attacked my food with gusto.

We didn't even try to maintain a conversation, we just ate like three people who haven't had a meal in a while. By the time we finished, there was a small mountain of chili-smeared napkins on the table next to me, but not a spot on my clothing. I balled up the napkins, stacked our empty plates and carried them to the counter. Then I reseated myself, propped my elbows on the table, leaned forward and asked, "Okay, what is it you want to know? And what can you give me in exchange?"

"We're not here to trade information with you, Ms. Bonaparte." Wukowski stressed every syllable of my surname. "If you have information that can lead to the successful apprehension of the perpetrator, it's your duty as a citizen to tell us. It's also your legal responsibility as a licensed investigator."

Iggy rolled his eyes. "Wukowski, I swear you're the biggest A-hole I ever had for a partner." I suspected he was too polite to say the entire word in the presence of a woman. "If Angie's willing to work with us, what's the harm?"

They glared at each other for a moment, then Wukowski said, "It's police business, Iggy. And it's murder. She sticks her pretty little nose into this, it might just end up getting chopped off. Or worse."

My brain flashed the picture of Wukowski saluting at Liz White's funeral. I felt a tiny twinge of compassion, but not enough to stop me from doing my job. "Hey, you two," I interjected, "I'm sitting right here. How about you stop talking about me like I'm in another room and we start talking to each other?"

Wukowski gave the smallest of nods, and Iggy spoke. "Whatcha got?"

"Not enough to hang a dog," I responded. "But more than enough to cast doubt on Tony being the killer. Elisa Morano left a trail of pain everywhere she went. She was a user, plain and simple. One of those beautiful women who thinks she's entitled, and doesn't care how she gets what she wants, as long as she gets it."

They waited. Then Wukowski spoke, quietly, incredulously. "That's it? That's all you've got? Some pop psychology that wouldn't convince my granny?"

"No, Wukowski, that's not all I've got. But, like you, I have a professional responsibility to uphold." I wanted to make it clear that the police were not the lone guardians of justice. "You'd be the first ones I'd tell, if I knew who committed the crime. But I don't. And unless it's in my client's interests, I can't say a lot more. So maybe you want to make it in my client's interests?"

Ignowski leaned forward and shouldered Wukowski slightly, pushing him into the back of the banquette. "Angie, I'm gonna be square with you. We ain't got shit. Not for proof, anyway. Obviously, Tony's prints and hair and DNA are all over the apartment, but any good lawyer can talk his way out of that. After all, they were...cohabiting, right?"

I nodded, amused that Iggy thought he needed to clean up his language for me.

"But," he continued, "we got nothing to place him at the scene that night. And you're saying that there are plenty others who would want to see her dead?" I nodded. "So seems to me, we got a problem—one very dead woman, multiple suspects, no evidence strong enough to convict. How 'bout you help us out? Tell us about the others. The ones who maybe hated her enough to kill her."

Sipping my diet soda, I thought about what Iggy just said. They didn't know about Tony sitting outside her apartment that night. They didn't seem aware of the undercurrents surrounding Marsha or Alan or Richard Llewellyn. Obviously, they hadn't interviewed Mrs. Lembke or Bobbie Russell. They didn't know about the letter. I couldn't hold them accountable for that, but Wukowski's 'just the facts' approach to interrogation wasn't working too well. I wanted to shove my female, non-professional, pop psychology methods in his face. But I just smiled sweetly and responded with a shake of the head.

We paid the check and they drove me back to the gym. No one spoke. When we got there, Wukowski dove into a red Jeep Wrangler, slammed the door and peeled away. Iggy waited while I started the Miata. I waggled my fingers in acknowledgement and drove home.

Chapter 16

What's of significance is sweet, however mistaken; one could make up one's mind to what's insignificant even. But pettiness, pettiness, that's what's insufferable.

—Ivan Turgenev

My satisfaction was short-lived. I mentally chastised myself for being mean-spirited and wondered if I'd forfeited all chance to exchange information with Iggy and Wukowski. *Damn it*, I thought, *I let Wukowski get the better of me.* I hate that feeling.

I parked the Miata in its underground space, grabbed my gym bag, purse and briefcase and took the stairs to the lobby, reminding myself as I climbed to call Bertha and let her know I was safely home. The last thing I wanted tonight was a couple of goons pounding down my door.

At least, I thought it was the last thing I wanted. Until I opened the stairway door and saw Kevin sitting on a lobby couch, reading a magazine. He tossed it down and came toward me, hands outstretched. "Angie, I owe you an apology."

My right eyebrow rose, involuntarily. My kids always referred to it as the Mean Mommy look. "Really? What for?" *Showing up at my home unannounced?* I thought. *Invading my privacy? Catching me unprepared?*

Kevin didn't know me well enough to be alarmed. "I was concerned that maybe I came on a little strong on Saturday." The elevator doors opened and a couple whom I didn't know exited. "Can I come up?" he asked. "Just for a moment. I'd like to talk."

The couple stood at the mailboxes, listening. "Okay. Sure." As the elevator doors closed on us, I turned to Kevin. "Look, it's been a long day and I'm not sure I'm really up to it. Maybe this isn't a good idea right now."

"Ten minutes, Angie. I'll even throw in a foot rub."

Confident bastard, aren't you? I thought. Then I stopped myself. *Where was this hostility coming from? Kevin isn't Wukowski. Give him a chance.*

He took the gym bag so that I could unlock the door. There, on the threshold, lay a white envelope, lettered in black magic marker— Angelina Bonaparte. Kevin bent down to retrieve it.

I body-blocked him with my shoulder and said, "No. Leave it. Don't touch it. Just come inside." As I put my purse and briefcase in the coat closet, I explained about the threatening letter at the office and gave him orders to go before I called Bart and the police.

"No way, Angie. I'm staying until the police get here. Maybe I should search the place?"

"That's sweet, Kevin. But if the letter-writer could get inside, I don't think he'd be stupid enough to leave the letter as a warning."

"Oh, yeah, guess you're right." He looked a little deflated and I realized that I'd just called him stupid and taken away his opportunity to act the macho man for me. He recovered, though. "I'll put some water on for tea while you make those calls."

The phone was ringing as I headed for the bedroom. "Angie, it's Bertha. Why didn't you call me? I was just about ready to notify Bart."

"Calm down, Bertha. I just got home. And you'll need to call Bart anyway. There was another note under my door when I got here. The envelope looks just like the one from my office. This time, I think I have to let the police know."

"I agree. I'll talk some sense into Bart. This can't go on."

Three minutes later, Bart called. "Angie, I talked to Marco this afternoon. As far as he knows, there's no Family involvement. Bertha tells me that you want to talk to the police?"

"I think I have to, Bart. They might be able to swallow my silence on the first note, but if they find out there was a second and I didn't tell them, they could bring me up on charges for impeding an official investigation."

"Okay. Go ahead." He took a drag on his cigarette. "I'll drive over to the office and wait for them to pick up the first letter." We both knew that the police would lose no opportunity to cause inconvenience to Bart. This way, he retained some sense of control. And he didn't have to open his safe in front of them.

As I hung up and dialed Iggy's home number, Kevin appeared in the doorway. I held up a finger and mouthed, "Five minutes." He nodded and walked away.

It wasn't the most comfortable call I've ever made. Iggy was uncharacteristically angry, and rightly so. I could do nothing but apologize and assure him that the current letter was still lying, untouched, on the floor of my foyer. "Be sure it stays that way," he growled. "I'll be there in thirty minutes."

I, not we. Did that mean that he would be alone?

No such luck. Kevin and I were sipping tea when the doorbell rang, twenty-five minutes later. I eased it open, careful not to tap the letter with the door or my foot. Two bulky men blocked the light from the building hallway. I stepped back, but held the door in place. "Come in," I said, "but watch out for the letter, it's right behind the door."

"Nice of you to be so careful to preserve evidence, Ms. Bonaparte." Iggy was still mad.

Some fence-mending was in order. "Iggy, Wukowski, I'm really sorry that I didn't call you this morning. I felt that I had to honor Bart's wishes. He's the one paying me, after all." Wukowski moved inside, brushing against me as he eased past.

"That's the difference between us, Ms. Bonaparte," Wukowski answered. "We work for the law."

It was a low blow, but accurate. I couldn't fault him. "I'll be in the living room," I said. "Call me if you need anything." As I walked away, I felt their eyes on my back. They waited until I was out of range to start talking. I could hear the point-counterpoint of their conversation, but not the actual words. I sat next to Kevin on the couch and tried to explain that I was *persona non grata*, and that if the police seemed angry, he should ignore it.

Minutes later, Wukowski appeared. "We bagged it and dusted the door for prints." He stopped and looked at Kevin, hostility evident in the tightness of his shoulders and his clenched hands. "We can compare them to the ones on file from your P.I. application, Ms. Bonaparte. But I'll need your…friend's."

"Kevin Schroeder, Detective Wukowski." I made the introductions and they shook hands. From the way Kevin's eyes widened, I suspected that Wukowski's grip was just a little tighter than necessary.

"I didn't touch the doorknob, Detective," Kevin said.

"Nevertheless." In grim silence, Wukowski extracted a fingerprinting kit from his bag and looked at Kevin. "Unless you'd rather do this downtown?"

"No need. I'm glad to cooperate with the police."

"Unlike your girlfriend," Wukowski muttered, just loud enough for us to hear.

Kevin smiled slightly and slipped an arm around my shoulders. *Okay*, I thought, *let's play games.* I put my arm around Kevin's waist and we walked together to the dining room table, Wukowski clumping along behind us. After he took Kevin's prints, he asked for his contact information.

Then he turned to me. "What time did you leave the premises this morning, Ms. Bonaparte?"

"About seven. I stopped for a latte and got to the office at quarter to eight."

"Latte." He snorted slightly. "And you didn't get home until...?"

"Until fifteen minutes before I called Iggy. I didn't check the clock."

He let that slide and looked at Kevin. "Mr. Schroeder." He pronounced it with a long O, Shro-der, although I'd given it the proper German pronunciation, Shra-der, when I introduced them. "Can you account for your whereabouts today?"

"Now just a minute, Wukowski," I protested. "Kevin has no part in this case."

His voice was a monotone. "Forensics will open the envelope downtown. We're only assuming this has something to do with the case." His head swiveled from me to Kevin and back again. "What if it's a love thing gone bad?"

It was my turn to snort. "Love thing?"

He reddened and repeated his question to Kevin. Iggy entered the room as Kevin gave a rundown of the day, stopping when he got to my building and followed a couple into the lobby so that he could wait for me. "So, you two didn't plan to meet tonight?" Wukowski asked.

Kevin shook his head and looked slightly embarrassed. I was determined that Wukowski not move on to the next logical question, so I put my hand on Kevin's shoulder and squeezed. "Kevin doesn't need a reason to see me." Liar, liar, pants on fire. The girlhood taunt rang in my head.

"I see," Wukowski said, his voice disinterested.

He and Iggy exchanged glances, then Iggy spoke. "We'll be in touch. And Angie, any more of these, we want to know right away."

So I was back to "Angie," at least in Iggy's books. I nodded. "I promise, Iggy."

As I saw them out and locked the door, Kevin disappeared into the bathroom. "Any rubbing alcohol in here?" he called. "I need to get this ink off my fingers."

"Look in the top right-hand drawer, where the Band-Aids are," I called back.

I poured two small snifters of B&B and waited. Several minutes passed, then I heard water running and Kevin emerged. "I think we deserve a drink, don't you?" I asked from the couch.

"You read my mind." He sat down next to me and pulled me into the crook of his arm.

It should have been a perfect night—a woman willing to surrender her foolish fears to a man she liked and found very attractive, flavored with a hint of danger and rescue. It should have been perfect. But it wasn't.

The man could not make love! He was tentative, he was apologetic, he was inept! *No wonder he's still single,* I thought as he fumbled around. Pity, and a desire to put myself out of my misery, led to the inevitable— I faked it.

Afterwards, he wanted to snuggle and seemed ready to settle in for the night. He had a goofy grin on his face, like he'd done something spectacularly wonderful. *You dolt*, I thought. My body was humming like an electrical circuit about to overload.

I told him how embarrassed I'd be if the police came back to talk further and found him with me. I said I had a very early appointment. I confessed that I snored. In fifteen minutes, he was out the door. I sat in the steam shower for an hour, guzzling a snifter full of B&B and mourning my lost illusions. Then I changed the sheets and fell asleep.

Chapter 17

When I am an old woman I shall wear purple
With a red hat which doesn't go,
and doesn't suit me,
And I shall spend my pension on brandy
and summer gloves
And satin sandals, and say
we've no money for butter.

—Jenny Joseph

Tuesday morning. Only six days since Elisa's murder, assuming that it happened before midnight on Thursday. As I ran that morning, I pondered the fact that I was no closer to a solution to the puzzle of who had killed Elisa Morano. I certainly knew much more about her and about her interactions with others, which would help Bart in his defense, but I had no more clue now about who'd done the deed than I did when Iggy and Wukowski first woke me out of a sound sleep in the early morning hours of Friday.

I planned to meet John Dunwoodie for coffee at his favorite Starbucks, the one that Bobbie Russell told me Dunwoodie frequented every day at ten o'clock. If his wife, Jane, really did resent Elisa Morano because of her sex appeal, I wanted to appear as unsexy as possible while still looking professional, so I showered and dressed in a plain white pantsuit and light blue blouse.

First, though, I called Bertha and let her know where I was headed. She mentioned that Bart had finally gotten the requested records for Elisa's home and cell phones and would have copies ready for me to pick up. Since it was eight-thirty, I figured that I'd have time to swing by Bart's office before intercepting John Dunwoodie.

Milwaukee's Third Ward is the Little Italy of the city, populated in the 1880s by Italian immigrants when the Irish moved up and out. Today, it's a haven for art galleries and cafes, as well as upscale restaurants and clubs. But scattered throughout, one can still see the old ironwork buildings, most no more than three stories high due to the lack of elevators. Bart's offices are in one of those buildings, on Plankinton Avenue. I parked and entered the building.

The security system was supplemented by round-the-clock guards, consisting of college students who needed additional income. A Family consortium owned the building and paid top dollar to assure they got the best from the local engineering school, MSOE. The daytime guards were mostly female, the nighttime guards were all male. It might be sexist, but Bart told me that it worked better that way, since the women tended to deal better with clients, who were there during business hours, and the neighborhood at night demanded more physical presence than most women could provide. Except for Mighty Mary, a former bouncer, who could take just about any average-sized man. I always wondered if Mary was a guy on hormones or a woman on steroids. But I never had the nerve to ask.

Was the lobby desk unstaffed today? No, as I approached, I could barely make out the head of a very diminutive young woman, dwarfed by the bank of security monitors which showed her the access points to the building and displayed any activity in the newly retrofitted one-person elevator and each hallway and stairwell.

"Angelina Bonaparte to see Bertha Conti," I told her.

She stood and looked me up and down. "ID, please," she said in a surprisingly authoritative voice. I handed it over and she examined it thoroughly. "Is Mrs. Conti expecting you, Ms. Bonaparte?" She scored points for using the proper address for Bertha, who was always "Mrs. Conti," never "Ms."

"No, I'm working on one of Bart's defense cases. Bertha called me this morning to tell me that some records we subpoenaed were in. I decided to pick them up on my way to another appointment."

"One moment, please." She punched a button on her console, spoke quietly into the phone, and then nodded at me. "Go on up." As I climbed the old marble stairs to Bart's second-floor office, I couldn't help feeling that she was watching my butt. I tugged the short jacket of my pantsuit down slightly.

When I opened the public door to Bart's office, Bertha looked up. "Ms. Bonaparte," she intoned throatily. She might be close to eighty, but Bertha's a tall woman still, one of those older Germans who maintains height and bone density. She wore a short-sleeved white blouse and navy skirt, and her glasses hung from a chain around her neck. "No nonsense," her clothes proclaimed.

"Good morning, Mrs. Conti. You have the phone records for me?"

She handed a sheaf of papers to me. A quick scan told me that, like most of us, Elisa called the same numbers repeatedly. Bertha had already anticipated my next question. "I started reverse lookups on the most frequently-called numbers." She handed me a typed list. Not surprisingly, Tony Belloni's cell phone was at the top. More surprisingly,

John Dunwoodie's cell phone and residence were also on the list.

"How far back did we request the records?" I asked her.

"Just the last three months."

"Odd. Elisa hadn't worked for Dunwoodie since May, but she called him or his home repeatedly since she left their employment."

"That is odd," Bertha responded.

***

I got to Starbucks at about nine forty-five, ordered a latte, and settled with my morning paper at a table close to the counter. At ten, the door opened and a stunningly good-looking man walked in. About forty, with thick wavy hair, graying at the temples. Six-one, one-ninety. Wearing a gray Armani suit, light yellow shirt, blue tie. Very put-together.

As he stepped to the counter, the barista called, "The usual, Mr. Dunwoodie?" He nodded and headed my way.

I smiled as he passed my table, and he smiled back. It was not the casual smile of a stranger who wants to acknowledge another, nor was it the smile of a man appreciating a woman. He had full lips, like a young Victor Mature, that curved in a cupid's bow. Womanly lips. Predatory lips. For the first time since the investigation started, I felt the threat that the letters stated. *Watch yourself, Angie*, I told myself. *There's a killer on the loose.*

Dunwoodie placed his briefcase and newspaper on a table behind me and walked up to the counter to pick up his order. I waited until he settled in to approach him. "John Dunwoodie?" I asked. One eyebrow rose slightly as he looked me up and down. A player, definitely a player.

"Yes, Ms. ..."

"Bonaparte, Angelina Bonaparte. I believe you know my father, Pasquale."

It was like a scene change in a play. One act, you see a bedroom, then the curtain descends and when it rises, you see an office. Suddenly, he was all business. "Pat? Sure, I know Pat well. Done a lot of business with him over the years. How is he?"

"He's very well, thanks for asking. May I join you for a moment?"

"Please do," he said, as he placed his briefcase and newspaper on an empty chair.

I took a few moments to sit and arrange my own briefcase, paper, and purse on the floor and to place my latte on the table. His business persona was firmly in place when I spoke. "I'm here professionally, Mr. Dunwoodie."

"Call me John," he said, but there was no hint of flirtatiousness in the statement. "If you're in need of insurance or investment help, Ms. Bonaparte, I'd be happy to make an appointment to meet you at my office. This isn't the most confidential place to talk."

"It's my profession, not yours, that brings me here, John. I'm a private investigator, working for Bart Matthews on the Belloni defense. I tried to see you at your office, but your wife was most insistent that you couldn't take the time to talk with me." I smiled a sheepish smile. "I hope you don't mind this little subterfuge."

He responded with a just-one-of-the-guys grin. "No, of course not. Jane does tend to guard my time. But I'll be glad to help you if I can."

"I need to gather some facts concerning Elisa Morano's employment with you. She worked for your agency for five months?"

"That's about right."

"Would you say she was competent?"

"Yes. I mean, I had no problems with her."

"But Jane did?"

"Well, Jane has very high standards. She tends to be a perfectionist."

"So she and Elisa didn't get along?"

"Oh, I wouldn't say that. There might have been some friction, but after all, when you work together for hours a day, that's bound to happen. It wasn't anything out of the ordinary."

"How would you characterize your relationship with Elisa?"

"Relationship? She was an employee."

He took a sip of his coffee and a bite of scone. I didn't care if he talked with his mouth full, though. This wasn't an etiquette class. I kept at him, sensing that his was the kind of personality that could be pushed. "Would you say you were friends?"

"No. We never saw each other outside the office."

"Did she ever ask your advice about men? About Tony?"

"No. I told you, it was a boss-employee relationship, strictly business."

"Then how do you explain the calls she made to your cell phone and home? Even after she left your employ. Some days, there were four or five calls." I pulled Bertha's sheaf of papers from my briefcase and brandished them at him. "That doesn't seem like a boss-employee relationship, does it? I wonder what we'd find out if we subpoenaed your phone records. Were you calling Elisa as much as she was calling you, John?"

His eyes opened wide and he started to choke. He coughed and sputtered and wiped tears from his eyes, sipping at his coffee and trying to regain his composure. The barista brought a cup of water to the table and stood by, asking, "You all right, Mr. Dunwoodie?" He coughed some more and nodded as he sipped the water.

"Sorry," he said, "I inhaled a piece of scone."

Very convenient, I thought. *Gave you plenty of time to think up a reason for those calls.* I wondered—can a person force themselves to swallow down the wrong tube, as Terry would say.

"You okay, now?" I asked. He nodded. "Then let's get back to the phone calls, shall we?"

"Look, it's not what you're thinking. Elisa had investments that we managed for her. She was calling me about her accounts." He clasped his hands and leaned toward me, a picture of sincerity. I was sure I was about to hear lies. "My wife, Jane, she's…kind of jealous. Not that I ever gave her reason, but she just couldn't handle having such a pretty woman in the office. So when Elisa left, we agreed that it would be best for her to contact me on the cell phone, so Jane wouldn't know."

"And the calls at home?"

"Well, I'm not in the office a lot. Jane really runs the business. I do a lot of the PR work—golf, lunches, you know." I nodded. "So if Elisa wanted to make a change to her account, she'd call me at home sometimes. If Jane answered, she'd either hang up or pretend it was a wrong number."

"I've seen some of her fund statements. She had quite a balance for such a young woman. How much did she start out with?"

"I don't recall."

It was the Ronald Reagan defense tactic. I wasn't having any. "Estimate."

"I'd say about 50K."

"And you never asked her how she came by that much?"

"Look, Angie, if I asked those kinds of questions, I wouldn't have any clients. I never asked your old man where he got his money, either."

"My papa isn't the one under discussion here." He blinked and sat back in his chair. "So in five months, you grew her initial investment of fifty thousand by another twenty thousand? You're good, John."

"No, she put more into the fund. It wasn't just growth."

"And again, you didn't ask the source?"

"I knew she was seeing Tony. I figured…"

"So there was nothing personal between the two of you?"

"Nothing. I swear."

"And the threatening letters?" I waited.

"What letters?"

"The ones I got at my office and my home, yesterday."

"I had nothing to do with that. Nothing. Not only do I have no reason to threaten you, I'd be a damned fool to mess with Pasquale Bonaparte's daughter."

"That's right, John, you would." I set my business card on the table. "Call me if you come across anything else related to the case. Elisa's address book, PDA and cell phone are still missing. Of course, they should go to the police if located, but I wouldn't mind having a quick look at them first."

He picked up the card and tucked it into the inner breast pocket of his suit. "Does Jane need to know about any of this?"

"No reason that I can see right now. But if I think for even a minute that you're not straight with me, or that you're hiding anything, I won't hesitate to use whatever means I have at my disposal to get at the truth. I hope we understand each other."

He nodded.

Chapter 18

"I hate discussions of feminism that end up with who does the dishes," she said. So do I. But at the end, there are always the damned dishes.
—Marilyn French

I felt restless when I got to the office. Itchy. Closed-in. Unhappy. What did I have to be unhappy about? I asked myself. I had a good job that I liked, a nice home, good health, responsible children, wonderful grandkids. What more could a woman ask for? A man, the answer came back to me. A life partner. Someone to tell your troubles to. Someone to laugh with. Someone to hold hands with. And, yes, I sighed, someone to have good sex with—'good' being the operative word.

Susan wasn't in, so I decided to make a personal call to my best friend, Judy. She would set me straight, if anyone could. Judy and I met at the park, back when our kids were toddlers. She'd been the sixties mom, always joining some group to make the world better and trying to drag me along, trying to raise my consciousness, as we used to say. I would just smile and go home to my husband and kids, secure in the rightness of my ways. Judy and her husband, Hank, were what my Aunt Terry called the "Battling Bickersons." They fought over things both little and big—whose turn it was to clean the bathroom, whether women would govern more peacefully than men, if shaving one's legs and underarms was a sign of oppression. Several times, Judy spent the night on my couch while I snuggled next to Bozo and thanked my lucky stars that I was happily married. Ironically, her marriage had lasted and prospered. And mine? Well, irony didn't quite cover it.

She answered on the third ring, with her familiar "Yes?" Never "hello."

"Judy, it's Angie."

"Hey, girl, long time no talk. How are ya? How was Saturday?"

"Saturday was great. A romantic fantasy. Then reality set in."

"Tell me all. Is it a man?"

"More like a lack of."

"Kevin's history?"

I started to snivel. I hate that, a lot.

"Angie, are you okay?"

"Yes, I'm just feeling sorry for myself. You know, poor middle-aged single woman blues. Kevin and I had a nice time on Saturday, but I sent him home alone. Then last night, he came over with flowers and one thing led to another."

"And…?"

"Studly turned into dudly."

"Omigod, noooo!"

"Yep, a night of fumbling frustration."

"Maybe he was just nervous. Maybe you can show him what to do."

"Honest, Judy, I did everything but paint a bull's eye on it and he still couldn't…" I started to giggle. "At one point, he whispered in my ear, 'Some women call me Kevin from heaven.' I don't think there's any hope that he even realizes how bad he is."

Judy snorted into the phone. She always snorts when she laughs.

"'Kevin from heaven?' No, no. That's just WRONG! Drop him like a dirty diaper, Ange."

We both broke up laughing, Judy snorting loudly through the phone wires, as we remembered the early years, pre-disposables, when our kids wore cloth diapers. While playing in the park one afternoon, my David filled his with a particularly nasty load. I decided it was too toxic to lug home, and planned to deposit it, nicely bagged, in a park trash can. Unfortunately, the park sanitation service was emptying the can and refused to take it. So I tied the bag into a knot and swung it in front of the garbage collector's face, yelling "You call yourself a man? I deal with shit worse than this every day." Judy stood behind me, diaper bag raised, shouting, "Right on, sister." The garbage collector just sighed and took the bag, muttering "damned feminists" under his breath. From that female bonding moment developed our almost thirty-year friendship.

When we finally got our snickering and snorting back under control, Judy invited me to dinner. "With Hank?" I asked.

"Sure. You know he loves you."

"Anyone else?" Judy was famous for her attempts to fix up all her single friends, male and female.

"Well, there's a new guy at Hank's office I thought I might ask."

"Not this week, Jude. I need a break from men. Besides, the Morano/Belloni case is taking all my time."

"Yeah, I read about it in the papers. I bet your Papa was plenty mad at them dredging up all that old Mafia stuff."

"Not as mad as he was at me for being in the middle of it. You know Papa, he wants me to be a proper wife, stay home and cook and let my husband take care of me."

"You'd think he would've learned his lesson, after Bozo."

We made promises to get together for a movie or a meal, and I hung up, feeling better about myself and life in general.

I had one more interview to complete. Janet Morano had given me a number for Llewellyn. I thought it was his home number, but my call was answered with "Dallas Design Center."

"May I speak with Richard Llewellyn, please?" I asked after a moment's hesitation.

"I'm sorry, Mr. Llewellyn is not in the office. Is there someone else who can help you?"

"No, I don't think so. I really need to talk to Richard. It's an urgent family matter." Not exactly family, but I couldn't tell an office receptionist that his ex-girlfriend was a murder victim and I needed to find out if Richard was implicated.

"I see." She pondered that for a moment. "If it's really an emergency, I can give you his boss's cell phone number. They're on a buying trip in Mexico, and I don't have Mr. Llewellyn's cell. But I should warn you that Mr. Harper won't be happy if Mr. Llewellyn is called back. Mrs. Arthur was supposed to accompany Mr. Harper but her son broke his arm and she begged off, so Mr. Harper is pretty anti-family at the moment."

"I just need to talk with him. I don't think it will require him to cut the business trip short. Have they been gone long?"

"They left last Wednesday. I expect them back tomorrow."

I took Mr. Harper's number and ended the call. The trip began the day before Elisa's murder. It didn't seem likely that Richard could make a round trip from Mexico to Milwaukee in one night without his boss's knowledge, but I had to confirm.

I called the number and spent ten minutes with Harper, who refused to let me talk to Llewellyn until I'd promised that "the boy" would not need to leave.

A little judicious questioning revealed that Harper was the kind of domineering older man who felt sure that his subordinate could do nothing right and who was determined to "teach him the business." By the time I got to talk to Llewellyn, I felt confident that he'd not been out of Harper's sight except to sleep, and that only for six hours. Then I had to break the news to him.

"Richard, when was the last time you talked to Elisa?" I asked him.

"Gosh, I'm not sure. About a month after I moved. I called and invited her down for a week, but she was just starting a new job and she couldn't get time off. Is there a problem with Elisa?"

"There's no good way to say this. I'm afraid that Elisa is dead. She was murdered." There was no sound on the other end of the line. "Richard? Are you okay?"

"Yeah. Yes, I'm okay. I just can't believe it. Elisa dead. My God. How did it happen? Who did it?"

"We're not sure. She had a boyfriend, he's the police's number one suspect. But at this point, it's all circumstantial."

"I just can't take it in." In the background, I heard Harper calling. "I'm sorry, I have to go. Would you call me and tell me what the findings are? And when the funeral is?"

We exchanged cell phone numbers, and I hung up, sorry for Llewellyn's distress at Elisa's death, as well as his work circumstances. I expected that he would recover from Elisa, since they hadn't kept in contact. I hoped he would get design experience and move on from that awful Mr. Harper.

Bart's report was next on my to-do list. I had a lot of data but it wasn't organized yet. When in disarray, I make lists, tables and spreadsheets. It may not give me any answers, but it shows me what I've got to work with. Two hours later, I had compiled the following list of suspects, with their relationship to Elisa, their means, motive, and opportunity.

- Anthony Belloni—boyfriend, access to guns through Family connections/conceal adultery; jealousy-other men?; threat to marriage/present at Elisa's apartment on night of murder.
- Grace Belloni—wife of boyfriend, access to guns through Tony/ jealousy; anger at "other woman"; threat to marriage/ no known opportunity unless Tony is covering for her absence from home.
- Jane Dunwoodie—ex-boss; unknown access to guns/ jealous of Elisa's sex appeal; disapproved of Elisa's work ethic; unknown opportunity.
- John Dunwoodie—ex-boss, unknown access to guns/ sexual interest in Elisa?; money manager; misuse of funds?; unknown opportunity.
- Bobbie Russell—replacement, unknown access to guns; homosexual; no known relationship with Elisa; unknown opportunity.
- Janet Morano—mother, unknown access to guns; anger at daughter's lack of contact or support?; unknown opportunity.
- Marsha Cantwell—friend; unknown access to guns; jealousy; sexual betrayal with boyfriend Alan; personal betrayal by role model; mental instability; unknown opportunity.
- Mabel Lembke—neighbor; unknown access to guns; gossip; disapproval; possible theft of credit card info; unknown opportunity.
- Alan McGuire—one-night stand; unknown access to guns; regret; conceal infidelity; angry at being led astray?; unknown opportunity
- Richard Llewellyn—boyfriend; unknown access to guns; jealousy? did he stay in contact?; unknown opportunity

I scanned the list, trying to pick the most likely killer. Logically, the cops had it nailed. Tony Belloni was the guy. But logic be damned, my gut just wouldn't go with it. There had to be something else. Something I was overlooking. There just had to be. Oh, well, at least Bart had some options. That was more than he started with. I typed my report on my laptop, printed and proofed it, and called for a messenger.

Ten minutes later, the knock on the office door broke my reverie and made me jump. I'm not usually the nervous type, but recent events were taking a toll. "Come in," I called, my tone reflecting the irritation I felt at being caught off guard. The door opened slowly and a very short Asian woman peeked around the frame, looking apprehensive.

"I'm sorry," I told her, "I was expecting a messenger service. I didn't mean to bark at you. Please, come in."

She peered at me, hesitant. Did she understand English? A lot of Susan's clients were first-generation Americans.

I stood up slowly and came around my desk. "Are you here to see Ms. Neh?" I asked, deliberately making my voice soft and gentle. I eased the door open wider and repeated myself. "Please, come in. Susan will be here in a few minutes, I'm sure." I smiled reassuringly. She was one of the few adults whom I towered over. She probably stood only four foot six and weighed about eighty pounds. I guessed her age at seventy, but with Asians, it's hard to be sure. *She must be someone's great-grandmother*, I thought. "I'm Susan's office mate, Angelina Bonaparte. And you are...?"

She stepped into the office and closed the door behind her. Then she looked me up and down, nodded once, and spoke in the purest upper-crust British accent. "Mrs. Marjorie Ellingsworth."

I managed to stop myself from opening the door and looking for

Queen Elizabeth doing a ventriloquist act from the hallway. "Would you care for a cup of tea, Mrs. Ellingsworth? Or coffee?"

"No, thank you, my dear. If I might sit down and wait for Ms. Neh?" She settled herself in one of Susan's office chairs and placed a canvas carryall, the kind that older women use for groceries, on her lap. From it, she extracted a black quilted satchel purse, which she set on Susan's desk.

My eyes wanted to pop out on springs, like a cartoon character's. It had to be a Bally Miss Satchel, priced conservatively at nine hundred dollars. I looked Mrs. Ellingsworth over more carefully, noting her black scoopneck St John knit dress with small cap sleeves and cute pleated detail at the knees, easily worth four hundred. Only her shoes spoiled the picture—they were simple black ballet flats, available at any Famous Footwear for thirty dollars. I should know, I wear them often enough with jeans. The incongruity was explained by the large bulges on the inside of each shoe—bunions, the bane of many a heel-wearing woman's older life. In all, her clothes and accessories alone were worth almost one-and-a-half thou, and none of it was dowdy. I quickly revised my take on Mrs. Ellingsworth. Wealthy, fashionable widow? *Au courant* granny? Sex toy for a centenarian?

Just as my goofy fantasies started to explode into giggles, another knock came at the door. Without waiting for my response, the messenger entered the office and handed me an ID. I filled out the paperwork for my delivery to Bart and he left, never saying a word. Mrs. Ellingsworth sat ramrod straight in her chair, with her back to the door, her toes barely touching the floor as her ankles crossed daintily, the picture of ladylike posture. But her head swiveled as far around as possible without moving her torso. Apparently even ladies are curious. I just smiled mysteriously and sat back down at my desk. If the old dame wasn't going to open up to me, I sure wasn't going to open up to her. Let her wonder.

At ten-thirty, Susan bustled in, all a-twitter. "Oh, Mrs. Ellingsworth, I'm so sorry to keep you waiting. I had an early appointment and the construction on I-94 is just awful."

"So my chauffer told me, dear. No need to fuss, I've only been here a few minutes. Ms. Bonaparte was very gracious."

It was time to give Susan and her client some privacy. Mentally, I pronounced it like Mrs. Ellingsworth would—prih-vacy. "If you'll excuse me, Susan, Mrs. Ellingsworth." I started to shut down my laptop and gather my purse and briefcase. This was one of the drawbacks of sharing space, but my work took me out of the office so much that it was seldom a problem. "I'll be back around noon, Susan, if you want to get a bite?"

"Sounds good," she told me.

As I left the office, I saw Mrs. Ellingsworth extract a flash drive and several inches of paper from her canvas bag. I wanted to be that kind of old lady, some day.

***

I returned to the office at noon, used the facilities down the hall and freshened my make-up. After knocking discreetly on the office door, I looked in to see only Susan. Plopping my stuff on my desk, I remarked, "That Mrs. Ellingsworth is quite the woman!"

"You don't know the half of it," Susan said. "I'm supposed to revise her estate plan to leave a bequest to her lover, who's younger than the oldest grandchild."

"Way to go, Marjorie."

"Jane Dunwoodie will have a fit," Susan noted, her mouth a tight line.

"What's Dunwoodie got to do with it?"

"They handle her insurance and some of her investments. I'll have to file her change of beneficiary with them and make sure her lawyer gets them a copy of her latest revised will."

"Latest?"

"Let's put it this way, Angie. If Mrs. Ellingsworth owned a football team, the second string would be on the field by now."

"Holy…. What do her kids say about it?"

"She has three grown sons. I'm not sure they know everything. They see Mom out and about on the arms of various much-younger men, but I think they prefer to look the other way and pretend they're just 'escorts.' It's less embarrassing to the family that way. If they knew that these guys move in and out of the will, they'd have a fit and probably try to have her declared incompetent." She stopped. "The thing is, I'm pretty sure Mrs. Ellingsworth has all her marbles, but I'm not sure I'm doing the right thing by helping her direct her money that way. I mean, she's spent a small fortune on some of these guys, even after they parted. She set one of them up in his own sporting goods shop."

"Hmmm. Well, it's not much different from Tony putting Elisa up in an apartment and paying her expenses. At least Mrs. Ellingsworth isn't married." I paused. "Is she?"

"No, her husband died decades ago. She took over an essentially marginal import business and made it into a multi-billion dollar enterprise. All the kids work for her and some of the grandkids do, too."

"The family members will get a fair share when she dies?" Susan nodded and I started to tick off points on my fingers. "One, she's single and available. Two, she built up the family business herself. Three, she employs those in the family who want to work for her. Four, she hasn't disinherited any of the family. Five, she enjoys the good things in life, like nice clothes and young men." I leaned towards Susan, all five digits on my counting hand upraised. "What's wrong with that picture?"

She started to shake her head. "You don't understand the Asian philosophy, Angie. An older woman, a widow, should remain quietly at home and allow the men of the family to run things and take care of her. She should never draw attention to herself."

I sighed. "Is that the kind of older woman you want to be some day, Susan?"

"Of course not."

"Then let's cut Mrs. Ellingsworth some slack. She isn't hurting anyone, unless you count a dent in her sons' dignity."

"True. But Jane Dunwoodie is a right little witch about stuff like this. She always makes me feel like I'm a pimp and Mrs. Ellingsworth is a low-class hooker. She'd probably tell the oldest son herself, if losing the Ellingsworth account wouldn't hurt her pocketbook so badly."

Interesting, I thought. "Why do you suppose that is?"

"Don't you know the Dunwoodie story?" I shook my head. "Let's get a glass of wine and some pasta, and I'll tell you all about it."

Albanese's wasn't crowded. We got a booth in the back, where we could talk with some privacy. After ordering, we sipped our Lambrusco and dipped the world's best crusty Italian bread, from Sciortino's bakery, into herbed olive oil. I leaned forward. "Okay, give. I'm dying to hear."

"It started when Jane had their third baby. They already had a four-year-old son and a two-year-old daughter. I guess Jane believed in spacing them out every two years. Anyway, the last baby, a girl, Lily, was born with cerebral palsy. Jane went into supermom meltdown. She couldn't accept that there was nothing anyone could do to make the child better. It wasn't so bad when she was just a baby, they're all pretty helpless then. It's not such a big deal if your kid doesn't sit up and crawl right on schedule. She's still your baby. But when Lily was about four, the seizures started. John told me they went to every top-level clinic in the U.S. and a few in Europe. The prognosis was always the same—increasingly frequent and severe seizures, leading to brain death."

For a moment, the room seemed to fade away, the sounds of cutlery and dishes silenced, and I remembered rocking my sweet babies and wondering what they'd be when they grew up. What if I'd been told they'd never grow up, never go to school, never have babies of their own?

Susan continued. "They tried everything—surgery, medications, behavior modification. For a while, it seemed like the house itself was a clinic. Then one morning, they found her in her crib, dead. She was only five years old."

I swallowed hard. "Was Lily the girl in the photo with the cocker spaniel? The one on Jane's desk?"

Susan nodded. "They called the dog Coco, because that's all Lily could say when they told her it was a cocker. I guess Lily loved that dog like some kids love their stuffed animals or blankies. And Coco was just as devoted to Lily. If a seizure started when Lily was in her room, John said Coco would bark like crazy and run in circles until someone came to check on her." She sniffled. "It's so sad. And I guess it explains Jane's attitude, but it doesn't make her any easier to get along with."

"Attitude?" I asked.

"That woman is so anti-everything that she puts the Pope to shame. I mean, radical. Anti-abortion, of course. But also anti-gay, anti-same sex marriage, anti-birth control, anti-morning after pill. She's even anti-organ donation, because they sometimes pull the plug to 'harvest' the organs. You name it, if it doesn't involve chastity until marriage, a man and a woman and all the kids they can have, and making every attempt to extend life no matter the quality, it's just wrong in her eyes."

"The hard part is, she's been through it herself," I observed. "You can't fault her for not understanding the issues, that's for sure. But heaven save us from those who think they personally know God's will and have to enforce it for the rest of us."

"That's for sure," Susan agreed. Nevertheless, we lifted our glasses in a salute to Jane's commitment to her dead child.

When the pasta came, we both tucked in with gusto. Appetite seems to improve after sadness for a tragedy that's a few steps removed. Susan wrapped her pasta around her fork like a real Italian. Of course, the Chinese invented noodles, and the Japanese co-opted them, but their etiquette allows one to put the bowl near the chin and scoop with the chopsticks. Even that's an improvement over those who cut their pasta into pieces like clods. I'd taught Susan the right way to eat pasta when we both worked for Waterman, with a big spoon and a fork, and she was a pro.

Replete with carbs and wine, we sipped our espressos. "You know, Angie, Jane Dunwoodie's been acting even stranger than usual lately."

"How so?" I asked.

"It's almost like she doesn't trust me anymore, like she's checking up on me. She came to the office last week and demanded detailed copies of one of my audits, even though I'd already provided her with the usual accounting statements. And remember the day the locksmith came? I was late because Jane called me out on an emergency, claiming I'd misstated a client's fund allocation and demanding that I meet her at her office. Of course, when we sat down and went over everything, it was okay, no problems. She apologized and laughed it off. But I can't help wondering why she's double-checking my work. I must handle half a dozen of her clients and we've worked together for at least ten years. Why this sudden lack of confidence?"

"That does seem odd, Susan. Maybe it's time for me to get back together with Bobbie and find out if there's anything shaking in the Dunwoodie office."

"Bobbie, the gorgeous gay guy?"

"The very one."

"Why are all the really great-looking guys gay and all the really nice guys married?" she asked. It was the single woman's lament, and it led into a deep discussion of her father's latest attempt to set her up with a nice Japanese fellow, and my Kevin fiasco. I even told her about my run-ins with Wukowksi and the attraction I'd felt at the gym. Hormones are scary.

It was one-thirty when we got back to the office. I checked my email and voice mail. One message—from Wukowski. I put it on speaker so Susan could hear.

"Ms. Bonaparte," he rumbled, "Elisa Morano's body has been released to the funeral home. Mrs. Morano informs me that she'll be cremated. The memorial service is set for tomorrow." We heard a hesitation, then, "I'd like to talk with you about attending, maybe get your take on some of the...people involved." I knew he wanted to say 'suspects.' "Give me a call this afternoon. Please." The 'please' hadn't come easy.

Susan raised one delicate eyebrow. "Are you going to call him?"

"Guess I'll have to. He *is* the police, after all."

"'Me thinks the lady dost protest too much,'" she quoted with a smile.

"Stuff Shakespeare," I said, as I headed for our small conference/interview room and closed the door behind me.

Chapter 19

Each man's private conscience ought to be a nice little self-registering thermometer: he ought to carry his moral code incorruptibly and explicitly within himself, and not care what the world thinks.

—Katherine Fullerton Gerould

"Detective Wukowski." He answered on the second ring, in his brusque baritone.

"Angelina Bonaparte, returning your call."

"Uh, yeah. Thanks for getting back to me."

Holy crap, was Wukowski being polite to me? Or was he maneuvering for a favor? I was betting on the latter. "What can I do for you, Detective?"

"I thought you'd want to know that there were no prints on the envelope or letter that we picked up at your apartment last night."

"Doesn't surprise me," I answered.

"Me, either. You have to live in the Amazon basin to not know about wearing gloves." We chuckled a little, slightly uncomfortable, as usual.

"Hope I didn't disturb your friend, Mr. Schroeder." This time, he gave it the long-A pronunciation. Making nice, my Polish friends would call it. "We checked out his story and didn't find any holes."

"Again, it doesn't surprise me. He's not involved with my professional life."

"And your personal life?"

"Why do you ask, Detective?" I made my voice silky. I wanted him to squirm.

"No reason." He cleared his throat. "The contents of both letters were identical, so it's not likely to be a personal vendetta. I mean, I don't think Schroeder's a likely suspect. I mean…"

"I get it, Wukowski. You no longer think it's a 'love thing.'" His silence was deafening. Had I gone too far?

Suddenly, sound exploded from the phone. Laughter—from Wukowski! "I deserved that. Sorry, Angie."

Hmm. First he was polite to me, then he laughed when I busted him, now he was apologizing and calling me by my first name. Was this really Wukowski, or an imposter? Or were they spiking the water at police headquarters with happy juice? I decided to push it a little further. "What's your first name?"

"Ted," he mumbled.

"Your badge says 'W.T. Wukowski.'"

"Yeah. Well, I go by my middle name."

"Oh." His first name must be pretty awful. Walter? Wilson? Wotan? I made a mental note to do some research.

The silence hung there for a minute, then he continued. "Any chance we can meet for a coffee or maybe a drink after work? Iggy and I have some ideas to run by you."

"Sure. Okay. Six o'clock?" I named a little corner bar not far from my condo. Milwaukee has more bars and more churches per capita than almost any other city in North America. I'm not sure if there's a relationship in that. Does too much prayer cause you to drink? Or *vice versa*?

I told Susan what had happened, and she immediately started to wag her finger at me. "Be careful, Angie. This isn't some boy. He won't be easy to manipulate."

"Are any of them?"

Simultaneously, we sighed.

***

I put in a little time on the Marcy Wagner case that afternoon. There had to be a way to locate Hank Wagner through his love of all things Trekkie. A web search for "Star Trek" produced almost seventy million hits. Refining the search to "Star Trek rare collectibles" produced a manageable listing, from which I selected one item—the Mego Star Trek Phaser Battle Game. It was listed on many web pages, but no one seemed to have it for sale. One of the references cited it as being worth a cool thousand dollars—for a table-top electronic game!

Serious fanatics don't change their habits just because they change their name and residence. It was possible that I could draw Hank out of hiding with bait like this. But I needed a strategy that would force him to make human contact, not just bid on a web site. I scanned the Yellow Pages for auctions and called the first one in the book—AAAA Auctioneers.

"Quad-A. This is Larry." His voice was brusque and he sounded busy. But a multiple A business name usually indicates someone who's hungry and wants to be the first listing in the Pages.

What the heck, I thought, *I'll try the truth. The worst he can do is tell me to get lost. If he does that I'll just go to the next auctioneer in line.* "My name is Angelina Bonaparte. I'm a private investigator. I have a client who's trying to track down her missing husband and recover her portion of their joint assets. I'm hoping you can help me with some pointers on the auction business." I waited.

A few seconds passed, then he spoke. "I don't get the connection between auctions and finding her old man. Is he an auctioneer?"

"No, he's a guy with a collectible fetish. It's a little hard to explain on the phone. Would you be willing to meet me and talk about it?"

"Is there any cash in this deal for me?"

"Probably not. My client is pretty strapped since he cleaned out their accounts. But I could buy you a lunch while we talked."

"Lady, I'm running this place pretty much single-handed right now. I don't have time to 'do lunch.'" The sarcasm was heavy. I waited out his silence. "Okay," he said in a resigned tone of voice, "I'll give you twenty minutes before I open tomorrow morning, if you bring the coffee. Six-thirty, sharp."

"Starbucks?"

"What else?"

"You got it. And thanks, Larry."

He hung up and I printed two copies of the material on the Mego game. I filed one copy in the Wagner folder and put another in my briefcase for the morning.

***

At five-fifteen, I shut down my laptop, tidied my desk and locked my files. After setting the motion detectors and the new door locks, I went down the hall to the women's bathroom, a remnant from times gone by, with an old-fashioned anteroom that boasted a vanity area. I plopped my purse and briefcase down and surveyed myself in the mirror. Of course, my hair didn't need any attention, but the subdued makeup I'd applied that morning to meet John Dunwoodie would look pretty washed out in bar light. I added a line of coppery eye shadow next to my eyelashes, smudged it with a Q-tip, and freshened my blush and lipstick. Then I stood to give myself a final once-over. *Professional woman*, I thought. *Successful. Not bad looking, either.* It would have to do.

Ed's Tap is a neighborhood bar that serves homemade soup, sandwiches and pizza. Marlene, a.k.a. Mrs. Ed, was behind the bar when I entered. All three-hundred-plus pounds of her. Ed weighs about one-fifty. I'm sure they've heard every Jack Spratt joke going, but they just smile and carry on running the bar. Ed cooks and Marlene bartends and serves the food. It seems to work for them.

I spotted Wukowski at a table in the back corner, but I stopped at the bar first. "Hey, Marlene, how's it going? I'll take a glass of wine back to the table with me. Save you a trip."

She extracted a bottle from the bar refrigerator. "Grab a geezer?"

I nodded. It was our personal nickname for Gewurztraminer, a mellow, fruity white wine. Marlene had busted my chops the first time I asked for it—"Ya think this is some fancy joint, lady? I got white and red, take your pick."—but the next time I stopped in, she flourished a bottle and served it as if she wore a wine steward's chain on her ample chest.

"He says he's waiting for you." She pointed at Wukowski with her chin and whispered as she poured. "Friend of yours?"

"Business associate."

"He's a cop, right?"

"Right. Just out of curiosity, Marlene, how did you know that?"

"I can spot a cop a mile away." She shook her head. "Don't ask. Just don't make it a habit to bring him in here, okay? It scares away my clientele."

I looked around the room as I walked to the back, wine glass in hand. A middle-aged couple occupied a table, drinking beers and ignoring each other. Another couple sat on stools at the middle of the bar, the man angled toward the woman, who looked straight ahead in an attempt to ignore him. *Pick-up or argument?* I wondered. At the far end of the bar, a fellow in work pants and steel-toed boots tucked into one of Ed's greasy burgers. The Tap didn't seem like a place where anyone would fear the police.

"Evening, Angie," Wukowski greeted me. "Iggy couldn't make it. He forgot about his daughter's piano recital. Marianne said she'd kill him if he missed another one."

"That would not be good." I sat across from Wukowski with my back to the room, which always makes me edgy. I noted that his back was to the wall.

Wukowski leaned across the table and asked, "Why'd she tell you to grab a geezer? I hope she didn't mean me."

"You've got ears like a bat, Wukowski." Somehow, I couldn't bring myself to use his "first" name. I explained the joke, but he didn't seem to get it. Then, just to tease him a little, I asked, "Were you more worried about her labeling you a geezer or about me grabbing you?"

"I'll take the fifth on that," he answered, but he smiled.

Damn, the man was stunning when he smiled. Just like at Rick's, I felt myself start to blush. Thank God the bar was dark. Time to change the subject. "Okay, let's move on. You said on the phone that you had some ideas to run by me. Shoot."

He cleared his throat and I thought, *disconcerting question or statement about to be made.* "Angie, we talked to Elisa's mother about an hour after you were there." He stared at me. I stared back, glad I'd taken the time to redo my make-up.

Wukowski's voice took on an accusatory note. "She didn't want to talk to us. Said that she'd already told you the story and that it was too painful to go over again. Of course, when we told her that we needed a statement and that we could do it downtown, she relented. It seems Mrs. Morano liked you."

"How nice." I smiled and sipped my wine.

"This is serious, Angie." He was back to the Joe Friday persona. "We're trying to catch a murderer."

"I know full well that it's serious. I'm trying to keep an innocent man from going to prison."

"Innocent?" Wukowski asked.

"Well, innocent of killing Elisa, at least. None of us is entirely innocent."

His eyelids lowered and his lips thinned. "No argument there. But that isn't getting us any closer to closing this case, is it?"

"You're right. You called this meeting. So why are we here?"

With a deep intake of breath, Wukowski started to speak. "It seems that some of the people who knew Elisa were more open with you than with us. Would you agree?"

I nodded.

"Tomorrow's the funeral," he continued. "Are you planning to attend?"

"I haven't decided," I answered. "It might be inappropriate, given that I'm working to defend the one who's accused of killing her. I wouldn't want to upset Mrs. Morano at her daughter's funeral."

"No worries there," Wukowski said. "She specifically asked for you when we told her that we'd be there."

"Well, as long as it's not upsetting to her mother, I'll be there. I'd like to see who turns up."

"That's the thing, Angie. You could help us out and still do your job. Just show up and keep your eyes open. Let us know if you spot anything unusual or suspicious. We'll do the same for you. How about it?"

I emptied my wine glass, then gestured to his beer bottle. "Another?" I asked. He shook his head, so I went to the bar and whispered to Marlene to pour slowly, while I thought about how I should respond.

Returning to the table, I started to explain my position. "The situation is somewhat difficult, Wukowski. My client is Bart Matthews and, indirectly, Anthony Belloni. I can't agree to do anything that would put Bart's defense in jeopardy. My first responsibility is to Bart."

"What about the law?" Wukowski growled. "You willing to break the law to protect Bart's client? You willing to let a murderer walk free?"

"I think of it like being a doctor or a priest in a confessional," I said in a low voice, attempting to defuse his anger. "I'm sure there are times a priest hears things that he wishes he could report. But he can't." I locked eyes with Wukowski. "I won't break the law to protect a guilty client, Wukowski, but I also won't betray anything that's told to me in confidence, unless it's to prevent the future commission of a crime. Not only is it my code, it's also the law that you're so fond of throwing in my face. In this state, a P.I. who's working for an attorney is protected under the attorney-client privilege. It's unethical for an attorney to reveal what's been told to him or her in confidence. It's unethical for me to reveal what my investigation uncovers, too, unless Bart authorizes it. Plain and simple."

"Some code. Lets a guy like Belloni off the hook."

"Are you so sure that Tony did it? Is that why you're here, asking me to cooperate with you? Because you're positive he's the one?"

He glanced down at the scarred wooden table, then around the room. Finally, he spoke. "You're right, Angie, we're not positive. We don't want to put the wrong person away and let the murderer go free. So will you help? Just keep your eyes and ears open tomorrow. Okay?" He was practically pleading with me.

"I'll do whatever I can, without violating my professional standards." I mentally ran down the table of "suspects" that I'd delivered to Bart earlier. "Who's number one on your hit parade, besides Tony?"

"Can't say." He stared at his hands. If he wore a wedding ring at one time, the tan line had faded away.

"Can't, or won't?"

"Can't. Not because I'm prevented, you understand. Because this case is a jumbled-up mess. Too many possibilities and not enough evidence." He peered into my eyes. "Who's number one on your list?"

I was flattered that he asked. It felt like an acknowledgement of my professional skill. Was there any reason not to talk with him? I had no evidence to bring to the table, but I did have a few good guesses that might direct the police away from Tony. I mentally tipped my hat to Bart and decided to plunge ahead. "Did you interview Elisa's old roommate, Marsha Cantwell?" I asked him.

"Yeah, we talked to her. Didn't get much, though. Just that they'd met at design school and decided to room together to save on expenses. She mentioned that Elisa had given her some tips on girly stuff—how to dress, makeup, that kind of thing. Seemed like Marsha had a kind of hero worship for Elisa."

I overlooked the 'girly' reference. "And what happens when your hero turns out to have feet of clay?"

"Meaning what?"

"Meaning when you look up to someone, take them as a role model, and then they betray you, it can leave a bitter taste in your mouth." I gave him the Elisa-Marsha-Alan story, then added, "Love triangles have led to murder before, and Marsha is not entirely stable."

"Yeah. She told us about the breakdown when we questioned her. But not about the boyfriend and Elisa. Damn it, we should've gotten that out of her." He shook his head and stared down at his hands for a few seconds. "That's the kind of thing that Liz would've gotten." His voice was low, mournful. "People just opened up to her." Then he seemed to realize what he'd said, grabbed his empty beer bottle, and stood up. "I think I will have another one. How about you?"

"Look, Wukowski, why don't we get something to eat first? I'm past the age of getting shit-faced from drinking on an empty stomach."

"You're right," he told me with a rueful glance at the empty bottle. "How about Ma's? I could go for an omelet."

"I'll drive. I'm parked right in front."

The Miata rated one raised eyebrow, but he managed to lever himself into the passenger seat. A breeze off of Lake Michigan had cooled the East side to about seventy, although it was probably at least ten degrees warmer inland. The infamous "lake effect" was a friend in the summer, but a bitter enemy in the winter, when it could dump fifteen inches of snow in downtown Milwaukee and leave the western suburbs with just a dusting. Tonight, we drove in silence, simply enjoying the cool air at the end of a hot summer day.

Ma Fischer's is an East side institution. In the 60s, it was a storefront with a U-shaped counter and two booths. The cook (also the owner) presided over a grill situated right behind the counter, flipping burgers, scrambling eggs and frying potatoes in plain sight of customers. George, the Greek owner, would serve a free meal to a homeless man at one end of the counter, while at the other sat one of Milwaukee's mayoral candidates. Ma's was always the last stop before home on a night of carousing. Now, it's expanded into a real restaurant, with its own parking lot, a kitchen that's separate from the dining room, and many tables and booths. Thankfully, the food is still good and plentiful. And George still feeds the homeless.

We took a booth and sipped coffee while we both waited for our late-in-the-day breakfasts to arrive. *In for a penny*, I thought. "You said at Ed's that your partner, Liz, was pretty good at getting information from people."

He didn't answer right away, but seemed to consider and reach a decision. Then he responded. "Right. She had the knack. Like you, Angie." I raised my cup in a silent acknowledgement of his compliment. "She would've found out about the Elisa-Alan business, too. Maybe it's a woman thing." He held up his hand to stop me from interrupting. "That's not meant in a bad way. But there are differences between the sexes, and not just physical."

He looked at me, and I nodded and said, "Go on."

"Well, I've observed that women seem to get a lot more information during questioning than men do."

The waitress set our plates down and we started to arrange our meals—salt, pepper, jam, utensils, all the little things one does to prepare to eat. As I spread boysenberry jam on my toast, I noted, "Could be that people feel less threatened with a woman. Could also be that you come across a little hard-nosed, Wukowski."

"You think?" He started to laugh, a deep rumble that didn't quite burst out but escaped in short gasps, as if he were uncomfortable with a real belly laugh. "I know you'll find this hard to believe, but I've heard that before. It's not just me, though," he said as he punctuated his speech with his fork, "'cause Iggy's one of the friendliest guys you'll ever meet, easy to talk to, and he doesn't get the response, either."

"Well, then the solution's easy enough. The department should assign a woman partner to every team."

His face changed to the guarded look that I was used to. I stared at him, really looked and analyzed. This wasn't his "usual" face, I decided. The laugh lines that radiated upward from his eyes and mouth were deeper, more habitual, than the frown lines in his forehead and the downturn of his lips. *Wukowski's not a perennial badass*, I decided. *It's a recent veneer, one that threatens to overwhelm the real Wukowski, but it hasn't yet.*

God help me, I wanted to reclaim him. It might be a hopeless, helpless emotion, but something in me wanted to see that other Wukowski do more than just break the surface for a quick gulp of air every once in a while. To really escape the riptide of his emotions, he needed to talk. I wondered if he'd done more than the obligatory session with the department's shrink after Liz White's death. He quirked an eyebrow and I realized that I was still staring at him, lost in thought.

"Sorry, my brain goes off on me like that sometimes. Where were we? Oh, yeah, women partners." I started to cut one of my breakfast sausages into small bites. "Of course, there aren't enough women detectives or officers to make that practical, are there?"

"Nope."

"How about sensitivity training? Maybe they can train you guys to conduct questioning like women would. Do they do any of that?"

"Nope."

"Think it would be worthwhile?"

"Nope."

I started to hum "Do Not Forsake Me," the theme from the Gary Cooper classic western, *High Noon*. He caught the reference and his lips turned up slightly. "See, Wukowski, the thing about a conversation is that it has to be two-sided. Otherwise, it's just a monologue." I kept my tone light and teasing. It was a technique that had worked with my brooding teenage son. *Maybe*, I thought, *it will work with brooding middle-aged men, too.* "Even during interviews, you give a little to get a little. You open up in order to get the other person to open up. Tit for tat, as they say."

He nodded. "My ex-wife used to tell me that, too. But I never caught the sense of useless chatter. I just figure, if it's not important, don't say it."

"And if it is important, keep it to yourself?" I smiled, but inside I was deadly serious.

"Busted," he said, shaking his head. "You nailed me."

"You know, this is a skill that can be learned, Wukowski. You're not inarticulate. You just have to get over thinking that every word from your lips must be a pearl of wisdom. It's okay to talk piffle, sometimes. For instance, what's the last movie you saw in the theater?"

"*Gladiator.*"

"Russell Crowe in a toga." I groaned.

We talked piffle for the rest of the meal—Roman war tactics, heavenly images like the Elysian Fields in the movie, philosophies of the afterlife. It turned out that we were both believers, but not in the same sense. He saw heaven as a place of final justice, where all wrongs would be righted and the bad guys would get what's coming to them. A cop's heaven. I saw it as a place where all hurt would be healed and wrongs forgiven, where we would live in understanding and love. A mom's heaven.

"Take Jeffrey Dahmer," he challenged me. "He claimed to have found Jesus in jail. Is that enough for him to be forgiven? Do you want to spend eternity with him in heaven?"

The Dahmer case touched a raw nerve in much of the Milwaukee-area population, myself included. To have a serial killer, cannibal and necrophiliac living in the midst of the city, less than five miles from my condo, was horrifying. I spent a few restless nights during the heyday of the Dahmer arrest and trial.

"First of all," I answered his challenge, "I don't know if Dahmer was sincere in his jailhouse conversion or not. Either way, I'm not in a position to judge the outcome. A friend of mine is fond of saying, 'Don't try the case if you're not on the jury.' Well, we're not on the jury, thank God. I guess if I meet Jeffrey Dahmer in heaven, it will be because we both belong there." I saw a look in his eyes. "You think I'm too soft, don't you?"

"Maybe. But then again, maybe I'm too hard. All I know is that when the chips are down, you have to be able to do the hard things, and I worry that a woman's natural instincts for life are against her if deadly force is needed. When you don't have time to stop and think, to reason it out. When you have to act and consider the consequences later." A haunted, sad look passed over his face, followed quickly by his usual mask.

"Is that what you think happened to Liz? She hesitated when she should have shot?"

"Until we find the scum that killed her, we'll never know." He signaled to the waitress for more coffee. "This isn't something I usually talk about, Angie." He was telling me to back off.

I wasn't taking the hint. "Maybe you need to. It was a pretty awful thing to go through, more than you should have to handle on your own. Probably more than a person *can* handle on his own."

"So I should spill my guts to some department shrink, who'll write me up as unfit for duty?"

"There are private resources. And it might make you more fit, not less."

"I don't know how we got into all this talk about me. I really wanted to talk about you, about your involvement in the Belloni investigation."

"Yes?"

"Look, you won't like this, but I have to say it. This isn't a job for a private investigator or a woman. It's a job for the police. It's murder, for Christ's sake, murder! What if you do get lucky? What if your investigative skills uncover something that someone doesn't want known? He's already killed once, killing again will be easier than the first time. You won't be able to talk your way out, Angie, you'll either kill or be killed. Are you ready for that?"

"I guess I should be flattered that you think so highly of my investigative skills, Wukowski. But I don't understand why you think I'd put myself in danger. I'm just collecting data, I'm not going down a dark alley at midnight."

"Those two notes say otherwise. They say that someone is worried about what you'll find out. They say that you're standing in the entrance to the alley. Give it up, Angie. Let Bart Matthews take whatever you have and make a case that Tony wasn't the only one with a motive. Our evidence isn't good enough to convict. He'll get off."

"And his wife and kids will spend their whole lives as the family of the guy who got off for murdering Elisa Morano. Being stared at and whispered about. Hearing taunts on the playground. I heard them as a kid, Wukowski—Mafia princess—and my dad was never arraigned for murder."

He slammed his palms on the table, making the dishes rattle and jump, and shouted, "You'd be alive, damn it! Isn't your life worth it?"

The other diners, the wait staff, the busboys all stopped dead in their tracks. Conversations stalled as everyone in the room turned to look at us. The hostess signaled to the kitchen, and George, the owner, bustled over. "What? What? You gotta problem? The food? The waitress?" he asked in his Greek-American syntax.

Wukowski raised his hands, palms forward, and started to apologize. "Sorry, I didn't mean to create a scene. We were having a disagreement, that's all. I lost my temper. I'm sorry. We're leaving."

George pocketed the check. "It's on me. No arguments." I gathered my purse and briefcase while Wukowski left a hefty tip on the table. As I walked out, embarrassed by the attention and longing to get to the car, I heard George pull Wukowski aside. "Women, they can be very irritating, no? But it does no good to lose your temper. You are the man, you must be in control of yourself. No?"

I smiled all the way to the car.

We drove in silence back to Ed's Tap, where Wukowski had left his Jeep.

"I'll see you at the funeral tomorrow?" he asked.

"Yes." As he started to extract himself from the Miata, I put a hand on his arm. "And thanks, Wukowski, for caring." For a moment, I thought he was going to say something more, but he just waved and got into the Jeep.

I drove home and parked in my spot underground, feeling slightly uneasy as I walked up the parking garage stairs to the lobby. I thought about Wukowski's challenge. *What would I do if confronted by a murderous killer? Would I be able to respond with deadly force?* I didn't know.

Chapter 20

Value is the most invincible and impalpable of ghosts, and comes and goes unthought of while the visible and dense matter remains as it was.

—W. Stanley Jevons

The alarm clock woke me from a horrendous dream, in which I was making love with my ex-husband and, worse, enjoying it. *God,* I thought, *how hard up do you have to be to dream about being in bed with Bozo?* Even my morning run didn't help expunge the memory of that dream. As I pounded the pavement, I thought about my love life, or lack thereof. I hadn't been exactly celibate since my divorce, but neither had I been profligate. I mentally ticked off on one hand the men I'd been with. Being choosy meant that I sometimes went a while between men. Was that why I dreamed about Bozo? Because of frustration? *Screw it,* I thought. *It probably has nothing to do with sex.* After all, according to Freud, all kinds of non-sexual dreams had sexual meanings, so probably sexual dreams are really related to grocery shopping or gardening.

At six-thirty, sharp, I tapped on the door of AAAA Auctioneers, Starbucks carrier in one hand and my briefcase and purse in the other. I'd deliberately dressed down this morning, hoping to appeal to the no-

nonsense tone that Larry projected on yesterday's call. My black jeans, white tee and running shoes were aimed at making Larry think of me as a real working person, not a glamour girl. The roller shade on the door flapped up and I heard the door lock click open.

"You better be Angelina, 'cause I want my coffee," he growled, motioning me in.

"That's me. Call me Angie," I answered as I looked him over. He was tall, really tall—at least six-foot-six—and skinny, really skinny—about one-eighty. I was about eye-height to his belt buckle and didn't want to appear to stare at his crotch, so I craned my neck back to look him in the eyes. "Is there someplace we can sit and talk, Larry?"

He grabbed the coffee carrier and walked to the back of the shop, calling, "This way. Watch where you walk."

The place was a mess. I had to scoot sideways through narrow aisles of boxes, display cases and tables loaded with goods. It reminded me of rainy summer days as a child spent exploring Papa's attic, dusty and mysterious, with treasures just waiting to be discovered. It also made me feel itchy and dirty. I would have to shower again before attending Elisa's funeral.

Larry set the coffees on a small card table in the back room of the shop and motioned me to a folding chair. At least when we were both seated, I didn't feel like a midget. I uncapped my coffee and took a sip as I looked him over. He wore khaki pants and a short-sleeved plaid sport shirt, with a paisley tie open at the neck. Did the man dress in the dark, or simply put on whatever was next in the closet?

I raised my eyes to his face to avoid the plaid-paisley combo and was pleasantly surprised. Dark brown hair, a little sparse, but he made no attempt at comb-over camouflage; green eyes, with crinkles radiating from the corners in an upward pattern, indicating good humor;

unremarkable mouth, enclosed within those parentheses that some call dimples but which don't really dent the cheeks so much as crease them. About forty-five. *Not bad*, I thought, *except for the clothes.*

"Finished?" he asked me.

I laughed, trying not to spray coffee. "Sorry, it's an occupational hazard."

"I don't have a lot of time. The shop's a mess since my assistant—who was also my wife—walked out on me three months ago. I'm trying to see clients, price and arrange stock and keep the shop open single-handed. So if we're gonna do this, we better get to it."

I laid the printout from the web on the table between us, and told Larry about Marcy and Hank Wagner. Larry's recent break-up made me wonder if his sympathies would lie with Hank. I needn't have worried.

"So the rat cleaned out their accounts and left, and she's trying to raise the kids alone?" he asked.

"That's about the size of it. If I could just get a handle on where he's at, there's a chance that I can recover some of their assets. I'm hoping I can flush him out of hiding with the Mego game. But I need to know how to auction it so that he has to reveal himself. A PayPal account or a cashier's check won't do it. I need an address, a phone number, something that will lead me to him. Any ideas?"

"Well, an auctioneer wants to know if the bidder will keep the item for himself or wants it for resale. That determines the value. Someone who wants the item for himself sets a private value on it. Someone who wants to eventually sell it sets a common value on it. Sounds like you think this Hank will want to collect it and won't be as concerned about the common value."

"That's right."

"So you want to advertise this item, which you don't really possess, collect bids and investigate the bidders, just to see if one of them is Hank?" I nodded. "Sure hope you're never after me, Angie." He slurped his coffee and thought for a moment as he swallowed, his Adam's apple prominent in his thin neck. "The thing is, no reputable auctioneer is going to advertise something that doesn't exist. It would be unethical. But I guess you could place ads yourself. I don't deal in this stuff, but there must be magazines that cater to the Trekkies. And they have conventions."

He continued to ponder the options. "Or you can put it on sale through eBay. I'd use a Trading Assistant, a local company that offers to do all the work for you. They can collect all the info on the bids for you to investigate. Maybe even trace the bidders through their internet logins or servers. Or go down the list of bidders one by one, pretending that each one was the winner. Guess you'll have to come up with a reason why you can't deliver the goods, though. Seems like a lot of work for what might not turn out to be any gain." His green eyes stared at me, waiting.

"It does. I need to rethink my strategy, Larry. But I appreciate your help and your time." As I turned to leave, a thought struck me. "You're looking for help in the shop?" He nodded. "Does it have to be someone with auction experience?"

"Right now, I'd hire Attila the Hun if he could ring up sales and straighten up this mess."

"I might have a candidate. Marcy Wagner. I know she's got office experience and she's worked in retail. Shall I tell her to call for an interview?"

"Why not?" He handed me a card and locked the shop door behind me.

I headed for home, to shower, change and attend Elisa's funeral.

Chapter 21

A funeral is not death, any more than baptism is birth or marriage union. All three are the clumsy devices, coming now too late, now too early, by which Society would register the quick motions of man.

—E.M. Forster

It used to be that only dark colors were considered appropriate for funeral wear. Now, anything goes. I've seen mourners exiting church in bright yellow dresses, or tee shirts and jeans. Frankly, I don't care much about what colors people wear, but respect for the solemnity of the occasion should warrant wearing a nice set of clothes. If the best you own is jeans, I guess that's okay.

I showered and donned a plain gray linen-blend shift and matching short-sleeved jacket. Black pumps and purse completed my rather restrained look, but I tucked a hand-painted scarf, all dreamy blues and greens, into my bag. *Later*, I thought, *I could remove the jacket, tie the scarf around my neck, and go about my business, not looking like I'd just attended a funeral.*

The service was slated for eleven at the Church of the Gesu. Known locally simply as Gesu, the 1890s French Gothic stone structure sits in the midst of the Marquette University campus on Wisconsin Avenue. Parking is fierce there, so I slid the Miata into a paid lot and walked five blocks to the church. The day was fine, and during the short stroll, I tried to reassure myself that it would be years before people would be walking to my funeral. Of course, Elisa's age denied the security of that belief.

Gesu's twin spires and huge rose window are reminiscent of Chartres. It boasts both an upper and lower church. The upper church is the more formal, with tall vaulted ceilings, stained glass windows and booming organ. It's usually only open on Sundays and Holy Days. The lower church is where daily Masses are celebrated and confessions are heard. I attended daily Mass here as a Catholic schoolgirl at the now-defunct Gesu Grade School. Back then, the lower church seemed big to me. Now, the low ceiling and lack of outside light made it seem dark and small. A slight sense of unease rumbled in my tummy. I hoped I wouldn't disgrace myself with stomach borborygmi during a silent part of the proceedings.

As I entered the lower sanctuary, I automatically dipped the first two fingers of my right hand into the holy water font and crossed myself, then stopped abruptly. Does one ever really escape childhood's religious training?

Mrs. Morano had evidently opted out of the traditional parish vigil with its rosary for the deceased. I signed the guest book at the back of the church, took a bulletin and holy card with Elisa's picture on it, and moved into the main aisle of the church, its old wooden pews flanking me on both sides. An informal receiving line had formed up front, with Mrs. Morano greeting mourners and accepting their condolences.

As I slowly walked forward, the smells of incense, burning candles, and altar flowers sparked my memories of lining up with my classmates, boys on the left and girls on the right, hands folded and eyes downcast, to receive communion. In front of the first row of pews was a bank of candles, which one could light in prayer. One weekday morning, Lena Martin's waist-length brown hair caught on fire as she piously waited and prayed in front of the candles. Sister Mary Benedicta, a fat little nun, shrieked as she ran up to us, shouting, "Fire, fire," and beating at poor Lena, who had no idea of the peril she was in. After that, the candles were moved to the sides of the church. It was my fondest memory of Catholic Mass, and I smiled as I recalled Lena trying to escape Sister's hands and whispering (for we never spoke out loud in church) "S'ter, I didn't do anything!"

Then I was next in line, murmuring words of sympathy to Mrs. Morano, holding her right hand between both of mine. "I didn't want my attending to upset you, but Detective Wukowski assured me that it would be all right."

She dabbed at her eyes with a tissue. "I'm glad that you could come. Elisa had so many friends. Just look at all the beautiful flowers." She gestured to several small arrangements on the chancel steps, and one extremely large and lovely bouquet of lilies.

Did she think I was a friend of Elisa's, or was she just mouthing the words that the bereaved seem to use? The departed (never 'dead one') is always a person of many friends, someone who cared about people, someone universally loved. I just nodded, and moved away to examine the funeral flowers. A small green plant from Mrs. Lembke. A bouquet of white roses and pink carnations with a card signed, "In memory of our friendship, Marsha Cantwell." No Alan. A standing spray of multi-colored flowers with a "Love, Richard" card. A vase of fresh daisies, cheerful in the dark church, from The Belloni Family. But the huge arrangement of lilies took pride of place, with a card signed, "Death leaves a heartache no one can heal; Love leaves a memory no one can steal—The Dunwoodie Agency." *What a lovely remembrance for her mother*, I thought. Then I turned back and surveyed the church.

Detectives Ignowski and Wukowski sat in the back, on the Mary (right) side of the church. I kept my arm at my side, but waggled my fingers in acknowledgement of their presence. Iggy nodded, Wukowski made no response, but it didn't bother me. They probably didn't want anyone to know they were back there.

Marsha Cantwell and Alan McGuire sat about ten pews from the front, also on the Mary side. Their knees were angled towards each other, but their bodies were turned slightly away from each other. Alan held Marsha's right hand in his left, and patted it absently while he apparently pondered deep thoughts. *That's no way to console a girlfriend or to reassure her that the person in the casket wasn't your real love*, I thought. I gave their living arrangements another two months, at best, before Marsha moved out. They both wore black business suits and white shirts. Obviously, attending the funeral service was only an interruption to the corporate day.

I started down a side aisle, planning to speak to them, when the Dunwoodies entered the church, Bobbie Russell ambling behind them. Jane wore a gray pinstriped coatdress and black pumps, and carried a black bag over her arm à la Queen Elizabeth. John, dressed in a man's all-purpose navy suit, white shirt and deep maroon tie, supported her elbow. They each dipped their fingers in holy water and crossed themselves, and as they genuflected and seated themselves on the Joseph (left) side, I noted the lacy black chapel veil on Jane's head. A little round doily, it was a reminder of the time when women and girls were required to cover their heads in church. Nowadays, it was all but extinct in the U.S. Leave it to Jane to maintain the old tradition. John lowered the kneeler and they sank forward in prayer, Jane covering her face with her hands. John sat back down after only a few seconds, but Jane continued in what seemed like fervent prayer. Neither of them approached Mrs. Morano.

Bobbie stood in the narthex, or foyer, of the church, his gaze and his head moving up and down as he surveyed the altars, statues, carved wooden confessionals, lit candles, and other minutiae that constitute a proper Roman Catholic setting. I quietly walked to the back and greeted him.

"Hi, Bobbie. Good to see you."

He put an arm around my shoulders and gave me a little squeeze. "You, too, Angie." Then he shook his well-coiffed head. "This kind of thing gives me the creeps."

"What? Funerals, or churches?"

"Both."

I nodded in semi-agreement. My stomach made a small rumbling noise. "Excuse me," I said as I patted myself slightly. "I'm surprised that Jane closed the office and brought you along."

"She insisted. Said it was a mark of respect for a fallen comrade." His eyes twinkled when he added, "I got quite a lecture when I asked her if she meant 'fallen' in the theological or the martial sense."

"You bad man!" I whispered and gave his arm a little punch.

"Who's the fellow looking daggers at me?" he asked, pointing with his chin towards the last pews.

"Must be Detective Wukowski. He's always scowling."

"Seems personal, Angie. You sure he doesn't have a thing for you?"

"A 'love thing'? I hardly think so." Of course, I had to explain the phrase, and we both had a hard time controlling the giggles. Jane Dunwoodie glared at us from her pew, stiff with disapproval.

"Guess I'd better find a seat and settle down," Bobbie told me. "Join me?"

"Can't," I said. "I'm actually on duty."

"Ahhh. Let me know if there's anything I can do to help." He headed up the center aisle and sat in the pew behind Jane and John, the very picture of good-looking young American manhood.

"Angie, I ain't late, am I? I had to park all the way over by the liberry." Mrs. Lembke bustled in, dressed all in black and with a small black hat, festooned with black sequins, bobbing on her gray head.

"No, you're not late, Mrs. Lembke. People are still extending their condolences, but I think it's time for the Mass to start."

"Doggone shame for someone to die so young," she said with a shake of her head, causing the black sequins to shimmer and send little showers of reflected light on her face and mighty bosom. "Let's get a pew, my ankles are awful swollen today."

"Which side do you prefer?"

"Mary," she said, and moved forward to sit directly behind Mrs. Morano.

"I think this pew is reserved for family," I told her as I leaned in. "I'm going to sit further back."

"Nah, there ain't no more. Look around." She surveyed the church. "This is it. Elisa's mother'll feel better with someone close behind her. You go ahead."

I nodded and sat about halfway back, behind the others, with the exception of the police. It gave me a good vantage point for observation.

A single solemnly tolling bell marked the start of the services. The priest, dressed in black cope over his white robe, proceeded to the back of the church to meet the pallbearers and coffin. He sprinkled it with holy water, intoning, "Out of the depths have I cried unto Thee, O Lord: Lord hear my voice."

Mrs. Morano started to sniffle as the pallbearers carried the coffin into the sanctuary, stopping just before they reached the steps to the altar. There, they set it in position, walked around to the side aisle, and sat with Mrs. Morano. Apparently, Mrs. Lembke was right. There was no other family present.

The coffin was a beautiful cherry wood, closed, and covered with a blanket of white roses. Mrs. Lembke glanced over her shoulder at me, eyes wide. Mentally, I toted up the dollars. How did Mrs. Morano come by that much cash?

The Mass proceeded, its ritual soothing, allowing me to think and observe. Marsha seemed focused on the readings and prayers, unaware of Alan. Mrs. Lembke's head bobbed in agreement with the words of Paul, "For the Lord himself will come down from heaven, with a loud command, with the voice of the archangel and with the trumpet call of God, and the dead in Christ will rise first," sending little sparkles around the pews.

The pallbearers, all young men, probably former MIAD friends, were stoic. Jane Dunwoodie wept several times, almost in concert with Mrs. Morano, and I felt sure that she was remembering her own daughter's burial. John handed her a clean hankie from the breast pocket of his suit, put his arm around her and pulled her close. I could hear little shushing sounds that he made to her. Bobbie sat, interested, as if at a play or concert.

Bobbie, Alan and I were the only ones present who did not receive communion. Even Iggy and Wukowski came forward. *Interesting*, I thought. *If the killer is present, he or she must have already received absolution for the murder.* I searched their faces, but saw no extraordinary emotion, only the downcast eyes and prayerfully folded hands that I expected.

As the Mass drew to a close, the priest walked twice around the casket, once to sprinkle it with holy water and once to pass incense over it. Then he prayed. "May the angels lead you into paradise: may the martyrs receive you at your coming, and lead you into the holy city, Jerusalem. May the choir of angels receive you, and with Lazarus, who once was poor, may you have everlasting rest." Shakespeare did it better in *Hamlet*.

The pallbearers filed out of the church with the coffin, followed by the priest and acolytes, Mrs. Morano, and the rest of us. The funeral directors efficiently loaded their cargo into the hearse, and circulated among us to find out who was planning to go to the gravesite. It seemed it would only be Mrs. Morano, the pallbearers and funeral home crew, and the police. What a sad ending to a sad morning. But it was noon, and the day was bright and sunny. That's a consolation, I always think, when I see a funeral cortege pass by.

Iggy sidled over to me and asked, "Can you meet us for lunch? One o'clock. Ma's."

"I'm not sure that Wukowski and I will be welcome there," I told him.

"How come?"

"Ask him," I said. "Look, why don't you come over to my condo? I'll make some sandwiches and we can talk in privacy." Then I turned to Mrs. Lembke. "Need a lift to your car?"

"Do I! My puppies are killin' me."

"I'm parked pretty close. It'll just take a minute." I walked quickly to my car, then drove back to pick her up. We talked about the funeral and what it must have cost. "Elisa had some money in an account. Maybe Mrs. Morano was able to use that. Or maybe Elisa had life insurance," I speculated.

"Could be," Mrs. Lembke nodded. Her black hat now rested on her ample thighs. "She was the kinda girl who would look out for herself that way. I'm glad for her mother's sake. But didja see the eye shadow she was wearin'? To her own daughter's funeral? I ask ya!"

"Gee, I didn't notice. Anything else strike you as odd?"

"Just that woman across from me, the one with the chapel veil on." She snorted. "If you ain't gonna wear a proper hat, don't wear none at all, I say."

"Right," I agreed. "Did you see her do something else strange?"

"Well, ya know when they recite the *Dies Irae*—I always think it's kinda mean to carry on at a funeral about how 'the doomed no more can flee from the fires of misery.' At least in the old days, when it was in Latin, ya didn't know all the words. Well, anyways, when the priest started in, she really turned on the waterworks. I thought, lady, didja know Elisa that good, to be that worried about her sins and all?"

"I noticed the crying, too, but I think it's because her little girl died when she was only five years old, and Mrs. Morano's pain got to her. I'll tell you this, if any of my children died before me, I'd never be able to attend a funeral again."

"You're right. I din't know about that. It just goes to show ya."

We were at the lot where her car was parked. I got out and came around the passenger side to help her out and promised to call her when I had any news to share. As I waited for her to start her car and leave the lot, I thought of the poem by Ernest Dowson, who, like Elisa Morano, died young, at the age of thirty-two.

They are not long, the weeping and the laughter,
Love and desire and hate:
I think they have no portion in us after
We pass the gate.
They are not long, the days of wine and roses:
Out of a misty dream
Our path emerges for a while, then closes
Within a dream.

Chapter 22

Success is a consequence and must not be a goal.

—Gustave Flaubert

As I unlocked the door to the condo, I heard the vacuum cleaner whooshing in the back bedroom. *Odd that Lela would be here on a Wednesday*, I thought. She generally cleans at the end of the week, although we keep it flexible to accommodate her acting engagements. I put my purse in the hall closet and walked into the master suite, where Lela was dancing while pushing the upright vacuum, earphones in place, singing along to Marvin Gaye's *Sexual Healing*. I walked around the bed, where I'd be in her line of vision. She switched off the vacuum, pressed a button on her MP3 player and tugged the little plugs from her ears.

"Angie, I didn't expect to see you today. I hope it's okay I came in to clean, I know I was just here on Saturday and it's only Wednesday, but you don't have to pay me full price. I just wanted to get you done because—" she jumped up and down, and then grabbed me in a bear hug, lifting my feet off the floor— "I got a part in the Rep's new production." She stopped, gazing straight at my face, waiting for my reaction.

"Omigod, Lela, that's fantastic. Come into the kitchen and tell me all about it. I have to make sandwiches for a couple of police detectives, who are meeting me here at one." I waved her to a stool at the kitchen counter while I made coffee and set out cold cuts, cheese and bread. "Now, tell me all."

"Well, I got the call from my agent on Monday. I've auditioned for them a couple of times, but nothing ever came through before. Seems the director saw me in that bit part I did for *Broadway Baby* last year, and he thought I'd be perfect for their production of *Night Must Fall*. I read for them on Monday, and they called me yesterday to sign the contract. I'm going to play the old lady's nurse." She hugged herself and then waggled her long, expressive fingers at me. "It's only a few lines, Angie, but it's THE REP!"

I poured us each a glass of Reisling, handed one to Lela, and raised mine in a toast. "To Lela, on the occasion of the first of many parts with the Milwaukee Repertory Theater." We clinked glasses and sipped. "After this, who knows? Chicago, New York, Los Angeles."

Lela laughed, the sound deep and rich. "Let's not get carried away, girl. They don't pay enough to make the rent. I'll still be cleaning for you, just earlier in the week."

"The artist's life is not an easy one," I commiserated. "But I'm glad you'll still be here, even if it is selfish of me."

She leaned across the counter, a wicked gleam in her eye, and demanded, "Tell Lela 'bout Saturday and ole Kevin."

I gave her the unvarnished story of the beautiful Saturday night—"You sent him home alone? You crazy, girl!"—and how Kevin had appeared on Monday—"Now you talkin'. 'Bout time you get something goin', Angie."—followed by the fizzle of the fireworks that night—"Good Lord Almighty, what that man thinkin'? He need some lessons, for sure."

"For sure," I agreed. "But not from me." I sighed. "He keeps calling, but I see the caller ID and I don't answer. I wait until the next day, when I know he's at work, and leave him a voice mail at home telling him how busy I am with the Belloni case and how sorry I am to keep missing him. I know it's cowardly, Lela, but I don't know how to tell a guy he's bad in bed. I'm trying to think of other excuses to let him down."

"Angie, the man needs help and he doesn't even know it! Why not tell him the truth? You might be the one to save him from himself. And to save a sister from his fumbling."

"Yeah. Well, exactly how would you phrase it, Lela?"

She rested her chin in her hand, her index finger tapping her cheek, her eyes lifted to the ceiling for inspiration. "Hmmm. Let's see. How about—Kevin, you bad in bed. You think you a stud, but you a dud that just went thud. You ain't the man, you a flash in the pan. Honey, you not hot, you can't find the spot. Baby, you out of luck when it comes to…"

"Stop," I begged, holding my sides. We were laughing so hard that both of us grabbed napkins to wipe the tears away. I was dabbing at my face when the doorbell rang. "Oh, no, it's Iggy and Wukowski. They're early."

"Iggy and Wukowski?"

"The police detectives assigned to the Morano murder case."

"'Scuse me, I'll just finish cleaning the master bath and then I'm outta here."

I opened the door, still dabbing at my eyes with the napkin, and motioned the two men inside. "I'm not quite ready, I got into a conversation with my cleaner, Lela. But it won't take too long. Come on through to the kitchen."

Iggy gave me a serious look. "You crying over Elisa, Angie?"

"No, of course not." I examined myself in the hallway mirror. My mascara was smudged around my lower lids and a little had run down my right cheek, leaving a brownish trail. Very attractive. "The raccoon look is in, didn't you know?" I teased them as I wet the napkin with saliva (a mother's handiest cleaning tool) and rubbed at the marks. "Lela and I were just being silly. Laughing too hard. You know." Iggy nodded, but Wukowski simply stared, impassive.

As we reached the kitchen, I asked, "Coffee? Wine? Soft drink?" They both opted for coffee, so I left them to it as I gathered salad fixings from the fridge. "It won't take long to toss a salad."

Wukowski set his coffee cup down and took the large wooden salad bowl from my hands. "I'll make the salad, you set the table." He washed his hands, then split a clove of garlic and rubbed it on the bowl. Watching him rip lettuce into manageable pieces, I decided he was competent, so I did as he suggested and laid the table in the dining room. Soon, we were seated and crunching the very tasty salad that Wukowski had assembled. I didn't remember putting oranges or walnuts out, but they certainly combined nicely with the lettuce and onions, all topped by his vinegar-and-oil dressing. Yummy.

Before our conversation could start, Lela appeared in the doorway. "I'm off, Angie. I'll call you about next week."

Wukowski grabbed the napkin from his lap and rose. *Shades of Papa*, I thought. Iggy took a moment, then followed suit.

"Lela, this is Detective Ignowski and Detective Wukowski. Gentlemen, this is Lela Jones, my friend and sometime cleaner, soon to be a star with the Milwaukee Rep."

"The Rep? Big time," Wukowski noted.

"Well, Angie exaggerates just a little. I got a small part in the next production. But who knows?" she responded.

"Who knows, indeed?" he answered.

Nice of him, I thought.

I walked around the table and hugged Lela. "Call me, let me know how rehearsals are going."

"Rehearsals. With the Rep," she whispered in my ear. I could feel her tiny shiver of excitement. How sweet that first taste of success is. Then she whispered, "That Woo-man, he's pretty cute. You know what the nuns say, when God closes a door, He opens a window. Go, girl." She gave me a wolfish grin and waved as she left the room.

We sat back down. "So, how did things go at the gravesite?" I asked.

"Typical," Wukowski answered. "The priest prayed, her mother cried."

Iggy gave him a look that said, Jerk. "It was pitiful, Angie. Even the pallbearers left after they got the casket to the grave. Just Mrs. Morano, the priest, the funeral director, and us. I sure hope there's more to mourn me when the time comes."

"Of course there will be, Iggy." I helped myself to more salad and built a sandwich—turkey, Swiss, lettuce and thousand island dressing on rye bread. "I know it's speaking ill of the dead, but honestly, she was buried alone, except for her mother, because she lived for herself alone. What goes around, comes around." I took a bite of my sandwich.

"'Do not be deceived, God cannot be mocked. A man reaps what he sows,'" Wukowski intoned, then bit into his ham, Colby, sweet pickles and mustard on rye.

I nodded and chewed.

"Newton's third law," Iggy added. Both Wukowski and I stopped chewing and stared at him. "Hey, I'm no dummy. I read," he protested.

"What a eulogy," I said. "Well, the funeral didn't tell me much. What about you two?"

Wukowski leaned forward. "You read the cards on the flowers?"

I nodded.

"What'd you think of the lilies? Pretty spectacular, wouldn't you say?"

"They were lovely. And the card was, too. But, of course, a business would send more than just a small bouquet. After all, Jane Dunwoodie would want the agency to look good."

"Maybe," he mused. "But what about the tears?"

I told them the story of Jane and John's little girl, adding, "Any mother would break down at a child's funeral, if she'd been through that."

"Elisa wasn't a child, except in the sense that we're all someone's child."

"Okay, but don't you think that Jane would relate to Mrs. Morano and remember her own grief, too?"

"Maybe," he repeated. "But I think a little judicious nosing into the affairs of Dunwoodie wouldn't hurt." I opened my mouth to argue, but he added, "You ought to be glad. It gets us away from Tony, doesn't it?"

He was right, I ought to be glad of that. So I shut up and ate my lunch, sipping my unfinished glass of wine while the men drank their coffee and talked about the latest Brewers loss. It felt quite cozy, sitting at the table, sharing a meal with the two of them, almost like a wife, husband, and hubby's friend. "'O, that way madness lies,'" I told myself. They left, and I stacked the dishes in the dishwasher and stored the salad in the fridge for later. I wouldn't let hassles with the cook spoil my enjoyment of the leftovers.

***

The funeral had unsettled me. And the investigation was at a point of uncertainty. I wasn't sure which way to turn, what to look for next. I'd uncovered enough dirt on Elisa to cast doubt on the circumstantial evidence against Tony, which was what Bart wanted. But what *I* wanted was to see the killer named and tried and sentenced. I wanted justice. For Elisa, for her mother, for the Belloni family. Did that make me crazy? Did I want to confront the letter-writer? To put myself in harm's way? Something in me shouted—leave it, let it lie, walk away! Something in me whispered—don't be a coward, do your duty, finish what you started.

I paced the living room, aware of the beauty that I'd struggled to create for myself after my divorce—the special-order furniture, the custom draperies, the art works and *gingillo*—knick-knacks—that I'd spent hours and days locating and placing. And there, scattered among the books in the wall of carpenter-built shelving, the pictures—young David and Emily, their weddings, their children. I hugged the framed photo of my grandchildren, taken last Christmas as they stood in front of Papa's fireplace and sang "O Little Town of Bethlehem," their mouths rounded into perfect little ovals. It was my life, and it was precious to me.

Isn't Gracie's life precious, too? I asked myself. *And her children's, and the new baby's, not even born? Can you walk away from them, tell them you've gone as far as you care to? Can you?*

No, I sighed. *No.* I replaced the photo on the shelf and made myself a cup of tea. When it was ready, I sat on the couch, my back to the view, and called the Belloni house.

Tony answered. "Angie?"

Caller ID. It's a good thing. Unless you're the one whose call they don't want to take. Kevin flashed in front of me, but I shoved the image down. One dirty job at a time. "Hi, Tony. Yes, it's me. Angie. How are you holding up?"

"Not so good, Angie." His voice was strained. "The press is camped outside the house again, and I can't get a damned thing done at work. They even followed us to Gracie's OB appointment today. You'd think we were Princess Di, the way they act."

"It won't last, Tony. It's just because today was Elisa's funeral. They're trying to get footage for the nightly news. Stay inside and lay low." I paused. "How's everything with Gracie? Only three weeks to her due date, right?"

"Right. And I'm here to tell ya, this is the last one. No matter what the church says. They might have Gracie scared, but I just don't buy that birth-control-is-a-sin stuff, do you?"

"I'm not the right person to ask, Tony. I walked away from the whole Catholic thing years ago."

"Yeah?" He sounded surprised. "Well, I'm not turning my back on holy mother church, but I made up my mind—no more babies. You know what it costs to send one kid to college? And I got five!" A short silence, then, "Course, jail would solve both problems, wouldn't it? No more sex, so no more babies. And no way to educate the ones I got."

"Now, just stop right there, Tony. That's no way to think or talk. What if Gracie heard you? You need to be strong for her, keep a positive attitude. The charges won't stick. They can't, because you're innocent. Right?"

"Right. But innocent men have gone to jail before, Angie."

"Not this time." *Please God*, I thought, *make it true.* "Now, I want to talk with you and Gracie but I don't really want to run the journalists' gauntlet again. Is there another landline phone in the house that she can pick up?"

"Sure thing. Hang on and I'll get her. And thanks, Angie, for everything. I know you think I'm scum, but for my family, I thank you."

I heard him set the handset down and walk away. In the background, the sounds of TV and children's laughter. *Cartoons?* I wondered. I sipped my tea and waited, impressed despite myself by Tony's humility and the strength it took any man, much less an Italian man, to say those words.

Then Gracie and Tony were on the line. "Hi, Angie. How are you?" Gracie sounded tired, normal for any woman in the last month of pregnancy.

"I'm good, kiddo. How about you? That little one letting you get any rest at night?"

"Not much." She chuckled. "Last night in bed, I had my belly up against Tony's back, and the baby kicked so hard, it even woke Tony up."

"Only fair," I said, and heard them both laugh.

"I was at the funeral today." Dead silence. "The flowers you sent were lovely. I'm sure her mother appreciated the thought."

"Yeah, well, Bart thought we should do it. As a gesture of respect, know what I mean? Not because of any fond feelings." Tony's voice was anxious, trying to convince Gracie.

"Exactly," I concurred. "A sign of respect, that was how I interpreted it. I wanted to let you know, and also find out how Gracie is feeling."

"Like a giant medicine ball is attached to my ribs. What I wouldn't give to take a deep breath again. Not to mention, get a night's sleep. Why do babies always want to do the breaststroke as soon as you lie down?"

Simultaneously, Tony and I both said, "Not much longer, Gracie."

She just sighed, a long, quavering breath. "Right."

"You both hang in there. The investigation is moving ahead and I have no doubt that Tony will walk out of the courtroom a free man." We said our good-byes and I hung up.

***

I was stumped. I admit it. No idea where to go or who to see next. So I had another cup of tea and read over my interview notes, hoping to spot something that I'd missed so far. *The man at the dumpster,* I mused. *I could ring doorbells in the building and try to locate him.* But what would that do, ultimately? If he hadn't seen Tony sitting in the car, so much the better. If he had, and I jogged his memory and he brought it to the police, Bart would have my hide. *Better to leave it,* I decided.

Murder wasn't my area of expertise. My business centered on locating lost, stolen or hidden assets, things that could be found using straightforward records investigation. I'd managed to find plenty of people with plenty of reasons to want Elisa dead. Motive, I'd read, is always the least reliable of the infamous murder triumvirate—means, opportunity, motive. I needed to find out who had the means and the opportunity to kill Elisa. I took a sip of now lukewarm tea and grimaced, sure that I was miles behind Iggy and Wukowski on this road. *But they haven't arrested anyone yet,* I told myself, *even if they have done the means-opportunity work. They don't understand the motives like you do.*

I whipped out the table that I'd developed, opened my laptop, and started to revise, eliminating Mrs. Lembke and Bobbie Russell due to lack of motive, and Richard Llewellyn due to lack of opportunity. I would focus on the rest, arbitrarily filling in blanks based on my best guess. Intuition is highly underrated. There's usually fact hiding beneath it.

There were an awful lot of unknowns floating around in that table. No wonder everything seemed so nebulous. The easiest way to fill in the blanks was to talk Bart into letting me share information with Wukowski and Iggy. Tit for tat. Or rather, motive for means and opportunity.

I called Bart's office. Bertha answered. "Law Offices of Bartholomew Matthews."

"Bertha, it's Angie."

"Jah? You are leaving your home?"

"No, I'm not calling to check in. I need to talk with Bart."

"He is engaged."

Since the only way to Bart was past Bertha. I had to grovel. "I know it's an imposition, but I need his okay to talk with the police about the Belloni case. I wouldn't want to do anything without your agreement." The word 'your' was intentional. If Bertha didn't feel in charge, she'd stonewall me all afternoon. "Is there any chance I can get fifteen minutes of his time? It's important, or I wouldn't bother you."

She let me dangle for a few seconds, then said, "I will check. Hold, please." Bertha must have been in a classical mood that morning, when she set up the radio station for listeners on hold. A Strauss waltz played almost to the end before she came back on the line. "I will transfer you now."

"Thanks, Bertha."

Clicking, followed by Bart. "Angie, how are things?"

"Pretty good, Bart. I want to fill you in on the funeral service." I gave him the low-down on the mourners and mentioned the extremely expensive casket and blanket of white roses. "It didn't seem to me that Mrs. Morano has that kind of cash, Bart. I'm wondering if she was able to get funds from Elisa's accounts or if there was life insurance."

"Could be. But I don't see how we can find out, unless you ask her. Would she open up to you?"

194

"I'd say yes. She doesn't seem to really understand the situation. I think it's more than just a mother's grief. I honestly don't think she's too smart. Cunning, maybe. But not smart." I didn't like myself too much for the next statement. "I can probably use that to our advantage."

"Then what are you waiting for?" Bart's internal scruples were obviously not as sharp-edged as mine.

"There was a nice bouquet from the Belloni family. I talked to Gracie and Tony this afternoon. They told me you advised them to send the flowers."

"Right. I thought it would look cold and maybe suspicious if there wasn't any sign of sympathy. Gracie sound okay about it?"

"Actually, she did. Tony made a point of saying the flowers were a mark of respect, not affection. He's trying to mend fences."

"Good thing, too. The weasel."

"Bart!" I was shocked. Cynical Bart, condemning Tony for a little action on the side? It didn't seem in character.

"Know why I'm still unmarried, Angie? Not because I'm fat. Not because nobody will have me. Believe me, there are women who would jump at the chance." He took a drag on his ever-present cigarette. "It's because I've seen enough of cheating spouses and failed marriages and the misery they cause the kids, and I'm realistic enough to know I wouldn't be any better than Tony. I'm a single guy who plays around, not a married guy who made a promise and broke it. It seems better that way. Am I right?"

"As long as you're not breaking promises to all those women who are lined up, ready to hop into your bed or into marriage with you."

He started to laugh, but it became a hacking cough. I waited until he finally recovered and said, "Angie, you're a pistol." Puff-exhale. "I have a client in twenty minutes. I don't think you called just to tell me about the funeral. So what's up?"

It wasn't easy to convince Bart that an exchange of information with the police would benefit Tony's case. I had to do a lot of tap-dancing before he agreed. But when I ran down the chart and convinced him that only the legal power of the police or the D.A. would force the "suspects" to answer means-opportunity questions, he stopped fighting and started to set up parameters. By the time we said our good-byes, I had Bart's permission to work with Iggy and Wukowski on the unknowns in the chart, and to share the known information I had, with one exception—Anthony Belloni and the Belloni family were off-limits in the discussion with the police. Now all I had to do was convince Iggy and Wukowski.

I spent the afternoon online, checking gun registration records, kicking myself for not thinking of it before. Put it down to my lack of criminal investigation experience. I pay a pretty penny to several national database companies for access to information that the average citizen can't get. Imagine my surprise to find handgun registrations for Jane and John Dunwoodie, Gracie Belloni and Alan McGuire. Oh, and Anthony Belloni—no surprise there. That meant that anyone on my chart, including Marsha—through Alan—had access to a gun.

The coroner's report stated that the bullet that killed Elisa was a 9mm cartridge. Each of the men, and Jane Dunwoodie, had a gun registration for at least one 9mm weapon. Not surprising, since the 9mm is the most purchased weapon in the U.S. Gracie Belloni was registered as owning a .22 handgun. But I had to suppose she had access to her husband's weapon. It didn't narrow down my suspect list, but now I could approach Iggy and Wukowski with slightly more confidence. I had means and motive. They had opportunity. Time to dicker.

I insist on absolute honesty in personal relationships, but in my business, I deal mostly with people who are trying to get out of their moral and legal obligations. I've been known to use a little misdirection—a much nicer word than 'lying'—and feminine wiles—no, not sex!—to get what I want. The way I see it, women are penalized for their gender often enough. Why not use it to our advantage when the opportunity arises?

Iggy might be the easier target, but it was Wukowski I'd need to convince. I dialed his number.

"Detective Wukowski," he answered on the third ring.

"Angie Bonaparte. Long time, no talk." He made a sound between a grunt and a chuckle. "Look, Wukowski, I have Bart Matthews' okay to meet with you and Iggy and exchange some information."

"Really? That desperate, huh?"

Big dumb cluck. He was right, though. I hate that. I made my voice all tender and girly. "I just don't know where to go with this anymore. I thought if we got together and talked about the suspects, you and Iggy might spot something I missed."

"Not much in it for us, though."

Damn the man. "Oh, I don't know. I have a lot of notes from my interviews. People seem to open up to me. You said so, yourself."

"That doesn't mean crap, Angie. Everybody and his uncle might have reasons to hate Elisa, but that doesn't mean they did it. Sounds like worthless information, to me."

Blast it! I would have to play my poor-poor-pitiful-me card. I will not go so low as to get weepy, under any circumstances. "Well, maybe you're right. I feel like I'm in way over my head." I heard a small gulp. Was it working? "I'm only on this case to help Gracie. The baby's due in less than a month, you know." He cleared his throat. "I can't blame you and Iggy, I know I've been in your way."

The bastard broke out into a full-fledged laugh. "Angie, just how far were you going to take this little charade?"

"Wukowski, you sonofa…"

"Hold on, woman. You were the one trying to scam me, right?"

I wanted so badly to slam the phone down. *Why did I let him get under my skin like that?* With anyone else, I would've just laughed right back and said I thought it was worth a try. *Keep your perspective*, I told myself. *This is professional, not personal.*

"What gave me away?" I asked.

"You did, Angie. The woman you are. Only a fool would think that act was real. Or someone who didn't know you." His voice was silky and low.

I started to flush. Was he coming on to me? Should I use it to get my way? My inner referee threw down a penalty flag and shouted, "Unfair use of personal tactics in the business arena." Okay, okay. I backed up ten yards and started over.

"Look, I'm sorry for the act. But I was sincere about wanting to get together and share our findings. If you don't think it's useful, I understand."

"Oh, I'm sure it will be useful." I heard typing. "Looks like Iggy and I are free tomorrow morning, say ten o'clock?"

"Perfect. My office? I have a meeting at eleven-thirty so I want to stay close." Not true, but I would schedule something now, just to make it true. Anything to avoid those smelly, desperation-soaked interrogation rooms at police headquarters.

"Sure thing. See you then."

I heard his laugh, low and soft, as he hung up, and I smiled. A worthy opponent.

***

True to my promise to myself, I called Bobbie Russell at Dunwoodie's and arranged to meet at eleven-thirty the next day. "How was Jane after the funeral?" I asked him.

"Really broken up. John had to take her home and call the doctor. He explained to me about their little girl. Tough. Really tough."

"The worst," I agreed. "Bobbie, I wonder if you can check something for me. I need to know what was on John and Jane's calendars, on the night Elisa was killed."

"Holy…you think one of them did it?"

"Not really. I'm just trying to fill in some gaps. I never thought to ask Jane or John, when I interviewed them, where they were that night. If I bring it up now, they'll have the same reaction you did."

"Who could blame them?"

"So I was wondering if you could take a peek at their calendars, before they get back to the office."

"I don't know, Angie. It might be unethical."

"I just want to eliminate them as suspects." He didn't answer. "Of course," I continued, "I can ask the police detectives. But if they never thought to ask the Dunwoodies, either, then my question might lead them in the wrong direction."

"Hmmm." A few seconds pause. "Okay, let me see what's there, then I'll decide if I can tell you." I heard the sounds of keyboard clicking, then he was back. "Looks like Jane was at a seven o'clock meeting of the RCCLU, and John was at a Rotary dinner."

"What's the RCCLU?" I asked.

"Roman Catholic Civil Liberties Union. You know, the right-wing group that's always denouncing something."

"Any idea how long the meeting lasted?"

"She blocked out two hours."

"Where do they meet?"

"It says 'Da Vinci Room, Italian Community Center.' But last month, it was at the Archbishop Cousins Center. The month before, O'Herlihy's Tavern. Quite a variety. Everything but your local gay bar or Protestant church."

His comment made me wonder. "Bobbie, does Jane know you're gay?"

"Just like in the Service, she never asked, I never told."

"It might be illegal, but I bet she'd fire you if she found out. Watch yourself, okay?"

"I'm getting ready to move on, anyway. One of my friends needs some help with his business and he's offering me a much better salary than Dunwoodie's. I plan to give notice on Friday."

"Good luck. By the way, where was the Rotary dinner that John attended?"

"Let's see. Would you believe, the Marconi Room at the ICC? Right next door to Jane's meeting. Convenient. They probably drove together."

"Thanks, Bobbie. You've been a big help. I still want to take you to lunch tomorrow. Maybe La Scala at the ICC?"

"Angie, you bad girl, what have you got up your sleeve?"

"Me?" My voice dripped with innocence. "Not a thing. Unless some of the waitstaff happened to be working the night that Elisa died. In that case, I might want to talk with them."

"Oy vey, as my friend would say."

"Jewish?"

"Only a very small part of him."

We were laughing as we hung up.

***

The receiver barely touched the cradle before the phone rang again. Caller ID showed me the name—Schroeder K. I took a deep breath and blew it out, told myself not to be a baby, and answered. "Hi, Kevin."

"Hi, Angie. Gee, I thought I'd get your voice mail again."

"Nope, it's the real me. I'm working from home this afternoon."

"The Morano case is keeping you really busy?"

"Today was the funeral. I attended and then I had lunch with the police detectives."

"Was that Wukowski guy one of them?"

"Afraid so." An uncomfortable moment of silence passed. "He told me that they don't think you have any connection with the case. He came as close to apologizing as I suspect he ever does."

"Some men have a real hard time verbalizing their feelings."

Some women, too, I thought. *Like me. Like now.*

"Anyway, Angie, I hate to say this on the phone, but you're so tied up now and it might be weeks before we can get together, and I wouldn't want you to go on thinking..." He cleared his throat. "Here's the thing, Angie. I think you're a wonderful and sexy woman. But you're just not the woman for me."

What? WHAT? Kevin was breaking up with me? After all my agonizing over how to break it off? No way! No freaking way!

"I see," I responded in a neutral tone. My voice hardly quavered at all. "You pursue me for weeks, you finally get me in bed, and then you decide I'm not the one? Is that what you're telling me, Kevin?"

"Please, Angie, don't make this harder than it has to be. You're a great person. I respect and value you and I hope we can be friends."

The kiss of death—I hope we can be friends. All that remained was to decide whether the conversation would end with polite good wishes or hateful words. I chose the former, although I wanted like hell to say the latter. But first, I had to have my say. "I'm afraid that friendship is not an option, Kevin. You see, I don't seduce my friends. I don't sleep with my friends. I know the difference between someone who's a potential lover and someone who's a friend. Friends don't treat each other the way you treated me."

"Come on, Angie," he whined.

I wanted—oh, so much—to use just one of Lela's funny lines, to tell him he was a lousy lover and I'd been avoiding him ever since the night we had sex. But now it was too late. He'd only think it was spite. "I don't think we have anything else to say, do we?"

"I guess not. But I want you to know, this isn't about you—"

"—it's about me," I interrupted. That chestnut is used by men the world over to deflate the anger balloon that their actions have blown up. Couldn't he come up with a more original line? I covered the phone so he wouldn't hear me breathe deeply. I didn't want him to think I was about to cry. "Look,I guess I should thank you for calling and telling me. At least we both know where we stand."

"Right. That's what I thought, too."

We wished each other well and ended the conversation. I must have looked like a maniac, pacing in my living room, fists clenched, muttering and occasionally bursting into crazy laughter at the irony of life. How dare he break up with me before I could break up with him? How dare he get his words in before I could say mine? Arghh! I needed to go to the gym and pound something.

202

Chapter 23

*The true fulfillment of reason as a faculty is found when it can embrace
the truth simply and without labor in the light of single intuition.*
—Thomas Merton

I slept well that night, a result of the combined effects of the gym, my
steam shower and resignation to the inevitable fact that life makes fools
of all of us at times. At least I no longer had to fret over Kevin. As Darcy
said to Elizabeth in *Pride and Prejudice*, "That chapter is definitely
closed."

Thursday dawned bright and sunny. I dressed in a sleeveless black
silk-blend shift that enhanced my curves with artfully placed seaming,
and topped it off with a scarf of red poppies on a black background,
fastened at the neckline. A hint of red toenails peeked through my black
open-toed pumps. *Perfect ensemble for a lunch at La Scala with a gorgeous
man*, I thought, as I assessed myself in the mirror. But first, I would
meet with Iggy and Wukowski. I added a little more mascara, grabbed
my black clutch and briefcase, and headed for the Miata and the office.

The detectives arrived promptly at ten. I'd already done my email
and had one voice mail, from Marcy Wagner. She left a message that
she'd met with Larry at AAAA Auctioneers and they agreed to a

temporary work assignment, part-time for now and full-time after the beginning of the school year. "What a scarecrow!" she said on the message. "But he seems nice and he sure needs the help. And he's offering me enough that I can quit my other two jobs and spend more time with the kids." I hoped it would work out for her. She sure needed the help, too.

Iggy accepted a cup of the coffee that I offered. Wukowski surprised me by brewing a cup of Susan's herbal tea from her stock next to the coffee pot. I sipped at my Starbucks skim latte and glanced at the means-motive-opportunity worksheet that I'd been reviewing when they arrived.

Wukowski gave me a sardonic grin. "Table of suspects?" he asked.

"Smile if you want to, Wukowski," I said. "I'm the kind of person who makes lists. It helps keep me on track."

"Okay, let's see what you've got."

I handed copies to both men and waited as they perused them. I felt slightly smug about my entries in the Means and Motives columns. Their copies did not include the Belloni family, per Bart's instructions. They did include my notes on the various gun registrations and the Dunwoodies' meetings on the night of the murder.

Wukowski finished reading first and sipped his tea while he waited for Iggy.

"Not bad, Angie," Iggy noted after a few minutes. "Not bad at all."

I looked at Wukowski. "I don't see Tony or Gracie on this list," he noted, his tone flat.

"I'm starting with the premise that they're not guilty of the murder. Tony's involvement with Elisa looks bad, but there's no real evidence that places him at the scene that night. Right?" I waited, hoping they would agree, hoping that no one had seen Tony in the parking lot.

"Right," Iggy said.

"Besides," I continued, "the only way I could get Bart to agree to this exchange was to promise to keep the Belloni information confidential. I'm sure you understand."

"This is the damnedest thing I've ever done in my career," Wukowski shook his head, "spilling our guts to the defense lawyer's investigator. I hope the captain never finds out."

"Don't worry, Ted," said Iggy, "I'll never tell. And neither will Angie."

I wanted to get their information before Wukowski could raise any further objections. "I've talked to a lot of the people who knew Elisa. I even interviewed her former boyfriend, who now lives in Texas, via phone. The chart only shows you the ones I think are possibilities, based on access or motive." Wukowski started to argue, but I cut him off. "Excluding Tony and Gracie. That's not open to discussion." He clamped his lips shut. "It's interesting that these four—John and Jane Dunwoodie, Marsha Cantwell and Alan McGuire—are all either registered for handguns or have access to them. I know, because I own one, that a 9mm is not too much for even a small woman to handle, with a little practice." Iggy nodded. Wukowski raised one eyebrow. "Yes, Wukowski, I own a registered handgun, a 9mm Beretta 92FS. And I know how to use it."

"Shooting at a target is a lot different from shooting at a person, Angie." His voice was low, just above a whisper.

"Of course," I acknowledged. "All I'm saying is that I can handle a gun under controlled circumstances. As far as real danger goes, I agree that I'm untested. But that's not the point here. The point I'm making is that any of these people might have the means and the motive. As far as opportunity goes, you're the ones who can ask that question."

Iggy piped in. "I see you already eliminated the Dunwoodies."

"Not on the strength of their dinner alibis. Did you check with some of the others at those meetings? Maybe one or both of the Dunwoodies never showed up. Or ducked out early. I've investigated enough cheating spouses to know that business meetings are a favorite excuse to get out of the house at night."

"You're right," Wukowski agreed with me, for once. "We haven't tried to validate the Dunwoodies' alibis yet. But my take on it is that if one of them was the killer, they either had to be in collusion or they did it together. It's barely possible for one of them to leave their meeting, rush to Elisa's, kill her and get back to the ICC before the other one's meeting let out. But it's not likely."

"Okay," I said, "then let's look at Alan and Marcia. Any alibi for either of them?"

Iggy checked his notes before he answered. "Nope. Marsha says she stayed at the office, working late on a big project. The security guard's log shows she clocked out at ten-thirteen. He says she worked late a lot that week and the log backs him up. He doesn't remember the specific night. So she could have faked the entry the next day. She could've even stayed late that night, but left the building by a back door and come back after killing Elisa. Alan claims that he was home alone, until Marsha got in around ten-forty. No phone calls, no one at the door. He watched some design show on HGTV. When she got in, he went to bed. He heard her in the shower, but then he fell asleep. They share quarters, but they're not involved sexually." He paused. "At the present time." He looked up. "No way to validate."

If I tell them what my instinct is saying, will they discount it? It was important to me to be perceived as professional, not some lady detective who was only good for digging up marital dirt. They'd been straight with me so far, so I plunged in. "What does your instinct tell you? I mean…" I hesitated, then went on. "Look, don't ask me why. I just can't see Alan or Marsha in that room, shooting or stabbing Elisa." I stuck out my chin. "And don't crack jokes about female intuition."

Iggy started to snicker. Then he looked at my face and held up his hands, palms forward. "No, no, don't get me wrong, Angie. I'm not laughing at you. It's Ted." Wukowski reddened. "C'mon, Ted," Iggy said, turning to his partner, "you're always talking about your gut says this and your gut says that. Isn't that intuition?"

"Yeah, well…" Wukowski muttered, his eyes cast down. "I'm usually right, aren't I?"

"Correct," Iggy affirmed. "Darned near one hundred percent."

I looked from one to the other. Wukowski intuitive? I'll be darned! And Iggy confirming it? Actually relying on it? *Incredibile*, as Papa would say. I decided to put him out of his misery. "Okay, given that we both have gut instincts, what's yours telling you about Marsha and Alan?"

"Not guilty," he said, looking me straight in the eyes. "Not involved."

"And the Dunwoodies?"

"There's something there, I just don't know what. I can't put my finger on it." He flipped back through his notebook. "When I interviewed her, she said that Elisa deserved to die. Let me find it." He scanned the pages, then stopped. "Here. Here's what she said. 'The family is the most sacred of God's creations, Detective. Anyone who threatens the family threatens God's order in the world. I can't feel sorry for her. God took vengeance on her for her sins.'" He looked up. "Pretty nasty, huh?"

"It just doesn't jibe with her behavior at the funeral, though. The flowers, the card, the tears, her having to go home afterwards." I shook my head. "I don't get it. I don't understand. Is she that cunning? Or that crazy?"

"No way to tell," Iggy chimed in. "But we can do a little digging, see if she disappeared from the RCCLU meeting before nine."

I told them about my lunch plans with Bobbie and our reservations at La Scala. "The staff there knows me, and Papa was a big contributor to the building campaign. They might open up to me more than they would to the police."

"Yeah," Iggy said. "See what you can find out. We can always go back later and talk to anyone who won't cooperate with you, put some official muscle behind it."

"Be careful, Angie." Wukowski rose and looked down at me. "Be careful."

"Your gut telling you something, Wukowski?" I asked flippantly.

"Maybe." He shut his notebook and tucked it into his breast pocket. "I want you to call me after lunch. Check in. Okay?"

Great, I thought, *now I have two wardens—Bertha and Wukowski.* Of the two, I knew who I preferred, and he didn't have a German accent.

Chapter 24

Do not let a flattering woman coax and wheedle you and deceive you; she is after your barn.

—Hesiod

The maître d' seated us at a table in the center of the dining room. I took this as an indication that we were worth seeing. Bobbie certainly was, in his designer suit, shirt and tie. I hoped I was up to standard, too. We ordered—salade niçoise and iced tea for me, pasta alfredo for Bobbie. While we waited, I glanced around the room. "See anyone you know?" I asked Bobbie.

"Other than some politicians and celebrities, no."

"I meant, anyone you know personally?"

"That dark-haired waiter, over in the corner, looks familiar. I think I've seen him at a bar or two."

"Excellent. Now we just need to find a way to talk to him without causing a commotion."

"No problem." Bobbie left the table and ambled toward the vestibule, as if heading for the men's room. I watched covertly, but didn't see any sign that he'd made contact with the waiter. A minute later, the waiter went into the kitchen area. Bobbie returned to the table before the waiter returned.

"Would you believe the guy's name is Guy? Can you imagine going through life as 'gay Guy?'" He shook his head. "Some parents are incredibly cruel."

"In all fairness, Bobbie, they didn't know their son would be gay."

"Even so." Our meals arrived and we began to eat. "Guy worked the private rooms on the night of the RCCLU meeting. He remembers, because he had to listen to some of the speaker's ranting and raving, and he was pretty offended. Seems it was a gay-bashing night."

"Does he remember anything about Jane?"

"Her hair. He joked about the helmet hairdo."

"How about John?"

Bobbie shook his head. "Not offhand, but maybe if you show him a picture."

"I need to interview him. Do you think he'd meet me?"

Bobbie extracted a Dunwoodie business card from his pocket and handed it to me. "Said he'd meet you tonight after work, in the parking lot of the War Memorial Center, ten o'clock. He's pulling a long shift to cover for a friend. His cell phone number's on the back of the card, in case you can't make it."

I tucked the card into my purse with a smile. Paraphrasing Jackie Gleason, I growled, "Bobbie, you're the greatest," as I lifted my iced tea glass in a salute to his skill.

He fluttered his eyelashes at me. "Aww, Ralph," he kidded me.

***

The web is a great tool for investigators and scammers. The information you need to impersonate someone else is so available. When I got back to the office after lunch, I ran a few searches and then called the local RCCLU office.

210

"Good afternoon. Roman Catholic Civil Liberties Union. This is Mrs. Erna Staunchley. How may I help you?"

Her voice was so cheerful that it made my teeth ache. And that name—Mrs. Staunchley! Staunchly what? Against everything that was not orthodox RC, if she was in agreement with the official web site.

I channeled Southern. "Mrs. Staunchley, my name is Susie Williams," I drawled. "I'm new to the Milwaukee area. My husband and I just moved here from Atlanta."

"Oh, my," she said, "did they warn you about the winters?"

"Did they!" I responded. "I guess I'll have to go shopping for snow boots and a down coat." She giggled. "But the reason I'm calling is that Arvil Minton, from the Atlanta office, told me to be sure to get in touch with you all. I was just about to join the Georgia branch when Billy got his job transfer."

"Well, Mrs. Williams, we'd love to enlist you in the cause right here in Wisconsin. Shall I send you the enrollment form and calendar of events?" I gave her the address of my private box and made a note to tell them to expect a letter addressed to "Mrs. Billy Williams." She fed right into my plans with her next question. "Mrs. Williams, I know that our local president, George Wilfred, would love to talk with you. Can I give him your number?"

"I hope y'all won't be offended, Mrs. Staunchley, but I would prefer to look over the materials first. And since I'm in a position to make a sizable donation should I find that your goals are in line, I'd also like to talk with one or two of your members. A gal can't be too careful with her money, now can she?"

"How true." She sounded distracted. Probably making big red notes on her phone pad—DONATION!

"So could y'all just give me a couple of names to call? Maybe someone who attends meetings regularly, who'd be current on all the plans and goals? I just hate to sound suspicious, but Billy and I worked hard to get where we are and we don't want to throw it away. After all, as I told Arvil, six figures is a substantial sum."

I could hear her gulp. "You're so right, Mrs. Williams." She gave me three names and numbers, including Jane Dunwoodie's, and we parted with my promise to call "Georgie" as soon as I'd reviewed the materials. If the waiter, Guy, couldn't confirm whether Jane had an ironclad alibi, perhaps the RCCLU meeting attendees might. I couldn't think of a way to approach them, though. Maybe Wukowski and Iggy would have to handle that task.

***

I returned to the office and ran some checks on the Dunwoodies. The Dunwoodie Agency information was limited, due to its being a privately held LLC. But they had to file with the regulatory agencies, so I submitted online requests for information and paid the fees using my VISA. I also requested credit reports, which turned up the interesting fact that John had an offshore asset protection trust (OAPT) account, in his name only. In Belize. Red warning lights started to buzz and rotate in my head. While an OAPT can be a legitimate means of protecting those with deep pockets from frivolous lawsuits, it can also signal an attempt to hide income, or even a plan to cut and run. None of those options seemed likely, but I'd been fooled before and I wasn't about to take him at face value.

Additional web searches produced the profile of a good citizen and family man—born 1952 to Jonah (a butcher) and Sally (a housewife); graduate of Marquette High School, a local Jesuit all-boys secondary school affiliated with Marquette University; undergrad degree, 1975, from UW-Madison; MBA, 1982, from Northwestern; married to Jane in 1980 (query—did she support him while he finished the MBA?); son John, Jr. born 1983; daughter Mary Elizabeth born 1985; daughter Lily born 1987 and deceased in 1992; started the Dunwoodie agency in 1986, after working for an investment firm since college. The agency did about twelve million in business annually. John was a member of Rotary and Toastmasters and on the board of his church. He and Jane sponsored numerous children's charity events. Mr. Upstanding.

Jane was next. Born 1956 to Rafael (a high school teacher) and Matilda (a domestic worker) Jenkins. Graduate of St. Joan Antida, an all-girls Roman Catholic secondary school; 1978 undergrad degree in Religious Studies from St. Mary's College, Indiana; then a gap until her marriage to John in 1980—note to myself to investigate further; births of children; involvement with mostly Catholic charities; member of society boards and committees; joined RCCLU in 1992. Numerous quotes critical of Milwaukee Archbishop Rembert Weakland, a "notorious liberal," in the Milwaukee papers. Then in 2003, the year their remaining daughter turned eighteen and presumably went off to college, Jane joined the agency as a partner and administrator. Portrait of a truly insular upbringing, resulting in a textbook reactionary conservative (my prejudice, I admit it).

There didn't seem a lot in those bios to indicate any level of lawlessness. Quite the contrary, in fact. I printed the records and stored them in my briefcase, with copies in my filing cabinet. Then I sighed, wishing Susan were at her desk. I needed to pick her brain on the financials. I went home, to grab a light supper and a power nap.

***

Bobbie'd given me a lot of flak about meeting Guy at ten at night in an empty parking lot. He insisted on accompanying me, for safety and to assure that Guy would talk to me. I promised to meet him at nine-thirty, at Ma Fischer's. He was there, sitting at a booth and chatting with George, when I walked in. I slid into the seat opposite him and greeted George, who waggled his index finger at me and told me, "No fighting tonight, okay?"

"Okay," I solemnly promised. "Can I get a cup of coffee, George?"

"Sure thing." He brought me a cup, filled Bobbie's and left us.

I took a swallow and looked Bobbie over. He was dressed from top to toe (I peeked under the table) in black—black silk turtleneck, black trousers, black socks and Nikes. I wasn't about to question what was underneath. "When we leave, are you going to pull a black cap over your hair and smear black greasepaint on your cheeks?" I asked.

He blushed slightly. "Too much?"

"Not if you're planning to steal the jeweled dagger from the Topkapi Palace," I responded drily, then sipped my coffee.

"Okay, maybe I went a little overboard," he admitted. "I was just trying to get into character."

"Bobbie," I said, shaking my head, "we're going to talk to a waiter. This isn't a heist. It isn't national security. It's just an interview." I stared at him for a moment. "If Guy thinks this is a big deal, it might scare him off. I don't want him to get the idea that there's anything dangerous in this. So let's keep it casual, okay?"

"Got it. Casual. Nothing dangerous." He nodded as he spoke. I could tell he was talking to himself. Bobbie was obviously in an actor mentality tonight, and I was his director. *Amateurs*, I thought.

The parking lot of the Milwaukee Art Museum / War Memorial Center was empty when I pulled in and parked under a tall light fixture, which cast an orange glow, giving Bobbie a goblin-like appearance. I was pretty sure it didn't enhance my looks, either, but I wanted Guy to see us and I wanted to be able to see his face while we talked.

He pulled into the lot at ten after ten, in a Honda that belched blue smoke. I decided to offer him some money for talking to us.

Bobbie made the introductions. "Guy, this is the private eye I told you about, and my friend, Angie." I was touched. "She wants to find out whether Jane or John Dunwoodie left their meetings for more time than just a bathroom stop."

Guy's eyes traveled the perimeter of the lot. His handclasp was sweaty, despite the cool breeze off the Lake. *Nervous,* I thought. *I wonder why.*

When he spoke, he stammered slightly. "I, uh, I'm not sure. I thought about it after we talked, Bobbie, and now, uh, now I'm not sure."

I leaned slightly forward and pitched my voice low and soft. "Guy, did something happen? You seem a little nervous."

"Well, after you left today, John Dunwoodie came in for lunch. With a couple of clients." He stopped and looked around the lot again. "He remembered me. Asked me if I wasn't the same waiter who'd served at the Rotary dinner."

"Do you think he was just making small talk?"

"Nooo." He hesitated for several seconds. "Look, I don't know how to describe it exactly, but he spooked me. I could feel his eyes on me, every time I turned around. When I came out of the kitchen with an order, he'd be staring at the door." He turned to Bobbie and whispered in a little-boy-scared-of-the-monster-in-the-closet voice, "He's not a nice man, Bobbie. I'm afraid. Why are you asking me questions about him? What did he do?"

I gently laid my hand on Guy's arm and spoke in my best mommy voice, reassuring and confident, relating the Elisa story. "Guy, if there was no time when either John or Jane left their meetings, then you have nothing to be worried about. But if they did leave for more than just a bathroom stop, you need to tell us. It's the only way you'll be safe."

"Ohmigod," he interjected, practically hyperventilating. "I *am* in danger!"

"So John left the meeting?"

"No," he said. "His wife did. Right after they finished the main course. I was hanging around in the hallway to serve the coffee. I didn't want to go in there and stand. They'd been ranting all night about filthy disgusting homos and saying how we aren't fit to live with normal people. How our sins are the worst. How we all need to be reprogrammed. Stuff like that."

"God," I murmured.

He nodded. "Yeah. Really nasty. Well, I was wheeling the coffee cart in when I saw Mrs. Dunwoodie scuttle off down a side hallway, like she didn't want to be seen. I cleared the dinner plates and served dessert and coffee before she returned."

"How long do you think that took?"

He scrunched up his face. "Let's see. Eight people, probably fifteen minutes. No, wait. I remember I had to get someone a packet of pink sweetener because they couldn't use the blue, and it took me a while to locate. Yeah, about twenty minutes."

"And John was in his meeting all that time?"

"I think so. But I can't really remember. I was upset about the RCCLU meeting and all the crap they were spouting. I didn't really pay attention to people in the Rotary room, just went through the motions." He paused. "Now what? What do I do to stay out of their way?" He gave Bobbie a pleading look. "I've been beat up before, but nobody ever tried to kill me. I'm no hero. I just want to be safe."

Bobbie, bless him, put an arm around Guy's shoulders. "No worries, mate," he said in a terrible Australian accent. "I'll put you up until this is resolved. There's no reason for anyone to look for you at my place, right?"

Guy's face relaxed and he looked as eager as a puppy waiting to be picked up and petted. "Right," he answered. "I'll just get my stuff and…"

"No need, Guy. I can lend you anything you need. We're about the same size." He added with a smile, "My friend's in the rag business. I've got a closet you wouldn't believe!"

Guy turned back to me. "I still have to go to work, though. I can't afford to take time off without pay."

"Are you scheduled for tomorrow?"

"No," he answered.

"Okay, let me check with some of my friends. They might want to finance a short vacation for you." His eyes lit up. "Of course," I continued, "you'll have to agree to tell this to the police."

"Police?" he practically squeaked.

Again, Bobbie came to the rescue. "It'll be okay. See, there's these two cops, Ignowski and Wukowski, investigating the Morano homicide. I met them. Wukowski's kind of gruff, but he seems fair. Ignowski's the nice one. I bet Angie can set it up so Ignowski talks to you, right?" He looked at me and nodded slightly.

"Right. Absolutely. I'll see to it," I promised. Inside, I groaned. How was I supposed to make sure that Iggy did the interview? Tell Wukowski that he came across too hard-assed for poor, scared, gay Guy? Oh, lord, now I was doing it—gay Guy.

Bobbie gently led Guy back to his car and they rattled off together in a cloud of blue smoke. I went home to condo, sweet condo and checked in with Bertha, then left a message for Iggy on his voice mail at the homicide unit. A nice soak in the whirlpool tub and a glass of Riesling later, I settled into bed, but sleep wouldn't come. So I pulled out my laptop and typed up my latest notes on the case. Feeling righteous, I opened the Sue Grafton that I'd started only eight days ago. Was it only eight days since Elisa's murder? It seemed like months, not days. Soon, I was deep into the story and wondering how Kinsey would ever solve *her* latest case. As usual, it ended in a heart-pounding confrontation with the killer, with Kinsey managing to escape death by a hair's breadth. I thumped the book closed, turned off the light and snuggled under the sheets. *Good thing I don't have cases like that*, I thought.

Chapter 25

Love is whatever you can still betray...Betrayal can only happen if you love.

—John le Carré

The phone rang at seven-thirty the next morning. I hadn't fallen asleep until after one the night before, so I was feeling pretty put out with the caller. "Hello," I growled.

"Angie, it's Wukowski."

"Geez, Wukowski, you always call people this early?"

"Sorry. You left a message last night for Iggy. It sounded urgent."

"Not really. I just had some information on Jane Dunwoodie to tell him." I frantically pulled a robe on and padded into the kitchen for a cup of coffee. I needed caffeine, and badly, if I was going to think straight enough to avoid a confrontation. "Hang on a minute, Wukowski," I told him, "I'm getting a cup of java and I'll be right with you." He started to sputter, but I set the cordless phone on the counter, waited for the coffeemaker to brew, and slugged some creamer into my cup. I took a deep draught and felt the hit. Ahhh, my drug of choice was not only effective, but legal. "Okay, I'm back."

"Look, Angie, I'm up to my eyebrows in alligators this morning.

Iggy got admitted to St. Joe's last night—burst appendix."

"Burst? That's bad, he could be in for a rough time."

"Yeah, I've been bugging him for two weeks now to see the doctor, but he just kept popping antacids and telling me he was fine." I heard him take a slurp of something at the same time I grabbed another swallow. "So last night, or rather three this morning, I got a call from Marianne, very upset, that they just wheeled Iggy into surgery. Her mom was with the kids, so I drove over to sit with her. He came out about forty minutes ago. I'm sorry I called so early, I didn't even look at the clock."

"Hey, don't worry about it. He'll be okay, right?"

"Most likely." A slight pause. "They had to 'lavage the peritoneum'— wash the sewage out of his gut—and they've got him on big-time antibiotics and painkillers. They keep saying 'if all goes well,' like all might not go well, and Marianne just looks at them and turns whiter than white. When I left, she was sitting by his bed, praying the rosary. I don't know what to do."

I heard a clunk, as if he'd slammed his cup or something else onto his desk. *He must be feeling pretty helpless,* I thought, *and I know how angry that can make a person who's normally in control.* An inspiration occurred. "Listen, Wukowski, my Aunt Terrie's a semi-retired nun. She has a lot of clout at St. Joe's and the other local Catholic hospitals. And she's good people. Why don't I call her and ask her to go over for a visit with Marianne? She can talk to the nurses and the administrator, get Marianne out of the room for a meal, do the small things that help. She's great at that."

"God, Angie, that would be wonderful. You're a lifesaver."

"Give me ten minutes to talk to Terry and twenty minutes to shower and dress. Then I'll call you back."

"Wait," he said, then paused for a count of ten. "I suddenly realized

I'm starving. Why don't we get some breakfast? My treat. You can tell me your news about Jane Dunwoodie."

We made arrangements to meet at Ma's in an hour. Wukowski insisted, said we had to mend fences with George and prove we could act like civilized people. I snorted, but agreed, and at eight-forty I was sliding into the booth that Wukowski had already claimed. He looked tired, but his shirt was unwrinkled and his face was shaven. I commented, as I signaled for coffee, "You look pretty put-together for a guy who's been up half the night."

"I learned a long time ago to keep a clean shirt and an electric razor in my desk drawer. I've pulled so many all-nighters that I've lost track." He took a long swallow of coffee. "It's one reason why my wife walked out. She told me once that a woman needs a lot more security than I could ever offer. She was sick of worrying about me, waiting for a call to rush to the hospital or the captain at the door in the middle of the night." He shook his head. "Can't say I blame her."

That was a lot more inner Wukowski than I ever thought I'd hear. Coming face to face with mortality, especially the mortality of a friend your own age, can trigger a lot of angst. I just nodded and sipped, waiting to see if he wanted to dump any more baggage. But he sat back, grabbed the menu, and said, "Let's order," in a no-nonsense voice, so I figured the moment had passed.

After we gave the waitress our identical orders—eggs, hash browns, sausage, toast—Wukowski took a notebook and pen from his inner suit coat pocket. "So, what did you call Iggy about?"

I already decided that, with Iggy laid up, I'd have to confide in Wukowski and hope for the best. I filled him in on the web searches and gave him a copy of my notes on the Dunwoodies. Then I dropped my little bomb. "Bobbie Russell, from the Dunwoodie agency, looked at their calendars for the night in question. They both had supper meetings at the Italian Community Center—Jane in one room, John in another."

"Yeah, I had that in my notes." He peered at me. "Sometimes the cops get it right, you know."

"A lot of the time," I assured him. He looked me over pretty sharply, to see if I was razzing him or not, but seemed to accept my sincerity.

"Here's the thing, Wukowski. Bobbie and I had lunch at the Italian Community Center yesterday and we talked to a waiter who was working the banquet rooms that night. Guy by the name of Guy, if you can believe it." He smiled slightly. "So Guy told us that on the night Elisa was killed, when Jane was at her RCCLU meeting, he saw her leave the building."

"No shit! He saw her go outside, get in her car?"

"Well, no. He saw her sneak down a hallway and she didn't return to the meeting for about twenty minutes. It was toward the end of the meal."

"Twenty minutes. Tight, but just enough time to do the deed, if she was extremely lucky and efficient."

"That's what I thought, too."

"I need to talk to this … to Guy."

"Okay. I can arrange that. But I'd like to be there."

"No can do, Angie. It might taint his testimony."

"You might not get any testimony without me." He raised one eyebrow as I explained about John's behavior at the restaurant yesterday and how skittish Guy seemed. "He wasn't happy when we told him he'd need to talk to the police. Bobbie and I kind of promised him that we'd set up an interview with Iggy."

"Hey," he protested, "I can play the good cop if I want to."

"Sure you can, Wukowski. But I still think you need me there, just to reassure Guy. I don't think he'll talk to you otherwise." I didn't tell Wukowski that Guy had been reluctant to talk to me without Bobbie being present. I wanted to be in on this discussion and I thought I could manage Guy, whether Bobbie was there or not. "He's scared, Wukowski. Apparently he's been the victim of gay bashing in the past."

Wukowski's head snapped back slightly and the right-hand corner of his mouth raised. "Gay Guy?"

"I know. Awful, isn't it?"

"Just awful," he responded, in a lisping parody of the male homosexual stereotype. But he didn't say it in a way that seemed mean, just sadly funny.

"Stop it," I told him, grinning, but trying not to.

"You're right," he said. But we were both smiling. "So, how do I get in touch with Guy?"

"He's staying at Bobbie's place for now. We thought it would be better, given John's interest, if Guy didn't go back to his apartment. Bobbie offered to put him up until the case is resolved."

"He working today?"

"Well, that's another thing. He's scared and he wants to lie low, but he can't afford to take time off without pay. So I thought I'd call Bart and see if there might be funds available to allow Guy to take some vacation time."

"Are you nuts?" His voice was a whispered shout. "You do that and the prosecution can claim that you bought the witness. And so can the Dunwoodie defense, should it come to that. No way, Angie. No freakin' way."

I was angry that he called me nuts, but I kept my own voice low and even, concerned that George would kick us out if we started another ruckus in the restaurant. "What do you suggest then?"

"We'll take his statement and put him up in a hotel until we can verify it."

"That doesn't solve the problem of his living expenses, Wukowski. The guy still has to pay his rent and utilities, even if the Department's footing the bill for his room and board for a few days. And he seems to be living hand to mouth."

"Sorry, Angie, but if you pay him, you blow any chance of building a case based, even in part, on his testimony. And that's the bottom line. The perp will walk."

"There must be a way. Doesn't the Department have any kind of special fund for things like this?"

"*Nada*," he answered, forking eggs and sausage into his mouth.

I took a bite of toast and chewed, pondering the impasse. "Okay, how about this. Guy thinks he's in danger because of serving at the RCCLU meeting and seeing Jane leave. What if the gay community would put up some money to help him out? That way, there wouldn't be any advantage for Guy to exonerate Tony, so Bart will be happy. And there wouldn't be any advantage for Guy to finger Jane, so the prosecution will be happy. And Guy will feel safe, so he'll be happy."

"You always work this hard to make everyone happy?" he asked.

"Not always, Wukowski," I said with a wicked grin, and couldn't resist adding, "but when I do…"

He smiled his killer smile, the one that was seldom seen. "I can only imagine," he muttered. Somehow, as we talked, we both managed to clean our plates. The waitress cleared away and refilled our coffee cups, then set the check on the table. Wukowski grabbed it. "My treat, remember?"

I nodded. "Fine by me. Thanks."

"So," he said, "what else you got?"

"Nothing else at the moment. But you notice on that printout I gave you, that John has an offshore account. I'm going to ask Susan, my office mate, to check into it, see if she can find out how much is going there and how often."

"Good." He pulled a page from his briefcase and passed it to me. "Since we're being so open and aboveboard with each other," he said as I took it.

It was a rap sheet. For Jane Dunwoodie. My shock must have shown, because he told me to close my mouth and read.

At the age of seventeen, Jane was arrested and detained overnight for a knife attack on a gynecologist, on the sidewalk outside his home. He was known in the city for being willing to perform abortions. He suffered a cut tendon in his hand when he defended himself.

I looked up at Wukowski. "Why didn't this show up when I did the legal searches on her?"

"She was seventeen. The doctor wasn't badly hurt. Her family paid big money to the doc to forestall litigation and the DA agreed to drop the charges and seal the records because she was underage."

"Some justice," I commented. Then it hit me. "A knife, Wukowski, she used a knife. And Elisa was badly mutilated by stabbing."

"Yeah, but it wasn't a knife that killed her. It was a bullet. The knife was used after."

His matter-of-fact delivery brought me up short. I visualized the photos in the police report. Nasty, and very personal. "If Jane Dunwoodie was capable at that young age of taking matters into her own hands, what would she do now if someone offended against her personal standards? She's twenty-two years older and life has kicked her around. She's involved in a group that openly advocates violence against those who don't 'respect marriage' or fail to 'uphold the sanctity of human life.'" I let the sarcasm drip as I quoted from the RCCLU web site statements.

He took the paper from my grasp and put it into his briefcase. "I can't let you keep that. And you didn't see it from me." I nodded. "The real question, Angie, is what did Elisa do that would set Jane off? As far as I can find out, and I dug deep, she never had a baby or an abortion. She wasn't gay or bi. Why would Jane want to attack or kill her?"

An idea began to form. Wukowski had trusted me with the rap sheet. By now, I trusted him enough to share my surmises. "What if John and Elisa were making it? And Jane found out?"

"No go. I talked to a neighbor who's known them for years and used to be close to Jane, until Jane objected to the neighbor's plan to terminate life support for her mother. Seems that John has had a string of chippies over the years. Jane just looks the other way, as long as he comes home to her. It's a classic case of dutiful wife syndrome."

My heart did a little flip-flop. *Was I undutiful when I kicked my philandering spouse out? So be it. There was no way I would deal with that nonsense year after year.*

Getting back to the matter at hand, I asked, "What if Elisa wasn't a chippie? What if John was serious about her? What if he asked for a divorce so he could marry Elisa? What if that's what the OAPT was all about, an escape fund?"

Wukowski whistled, long and low. "That'd put the cat among the canaries, all right." He leaned across the table, hands clasped earnestly in front of him. "But how do we find out, Angie? How do we prove it?"

My heart flip-flopped again, but this time in joyful recognition that Wukowski saw me as an equal, a partner. "No clue," I responded. "I'll have to think on it."

Wukowski paid the bill and followed me to my car, where I perched myself on the front fender and called Bobbie's place from my cell phone. Bobbie answered, sounding very chipper. "Morning, Bobbie," I said, as Wukowski, facing me, leaned close to hear the other side of the conversation.

It took me about five seconds to realize that I hadn't responded to Bobbie's next statement, hadn't even heard it. All I heard was my heartbeat pounding in my ears. My world narrowed down to the feel of Wukowski's suit coat on my bare arm, his breath on my cheek. I gulped, gave Wukowski a little push, and stood up. "Hold on a minute, Bobbie," I said into the phone, then held it to my side. "Give a girl a little room, would you, Wukowski?" He just grinned in response and gave me a one-handed wave, as if to say, "Be my guest." *Cheeky,* I thought. *But adorable. Damn it.*

"Sorry, Bobbie, bad reception. What was that you said?"

"I said, I went into the office today and gave Jane my two weeks' notice, just like I planned. The little bitch told me to pack up and leave. And she stood there and watched every single thing I put in my box of stuff to bring home. Can you believe it?"

"Gosh, Bobbie, I forgot that you told me you were giving notice on Friday. I hope she at least promised you a severance check in lieu of pay. You're entitled, you know."

"Don't worry, I called John on his cell phone and he promised to take care of it. But I ask you, what is that woman thinking? Who's going to answer the phone and brew the coffee and run the reports and make copies and mail stuff out? Not Mrs. Dunwoodie, you can bet your sweet little ass!"

I smiled at his description of his job duties. Shades of the fifties female secretary. "Well, whoever they get to fill in, at least you'll be better off." I asked if Wukowski and I could drop by to talk with Guy. Wukowski started to protest, but I turned my back on him and got directions to Bobbie's place, near the University of Wisconsin–Milwaukee. Then I hung up and informed Wukowski that unless he wanted to question Guy at the police station—and good luck getting any information from Guy if he did—I would be there. He glared at me, got into his Jeep and followed me as I drove off in the Miata.

Bobbie lived in a converted carriage house at the back of a large mansion on Lake Drive. He was on the patio, sipping a cup of tea and reading the *Journal Sentinel*, when we arrived. He laid the paper on the patio table and rose to greet us, dressed in a tank top and cut-offs that were way too short. I hoped to God he was wearing underwear, because if he was going commando, I'd see a lot more of Bobbie than I wanted to when he sat down.

I kept my gaze determinedly at eye level while Bobbie shook hands with Wukowski, then gave me a big bear hug, and gestured us to padded chairs. I sat with my back to the sun, forcing Wukowksi to face it and squint, despite his sunglasses.

"Well, boys and girls," Bobbie said, "I'm now officially free of Dunwoodie's, and believe me when I say, I'm a happy camper." He poured us each a cuppa from a ceramic carafe, then lifted his in a toast. "To freedom," he said.

"To freedom," Wukowski and I solemnly intoned, and we took a sip.

"Mr. Russell," Wukowski began, but Bobbie interrupted him.

"Call me Bobbie," he said.

"Bobbie, I need to talk with Guy, um." He thumbed his notebook pages. "I don't think I have his last name."

"It's Daly, D-A-L-Y." He started to chuckle. "When we got home last night, I offered him a drink. I'm afraid he had a little too much. He told me his name is Irish, and it means 'assembles frequently.' Then he told me just how frequently. Right before he passed out." Bobbie sipped his tea. "Ahh, the don't-give-a-damn days of my youth. Being a man of greater maturity and in a settled relationship, I, of course, escaped the morning-after megrims. But Guy is having a long shower."

Bobbie gave us a tour and short lecture on the history of the main house, once the province of a brewery king's son and family. The stone "cottage" that Bobbie rented was originally a stables for eight horses, then a six-car garage, with sleeping rooms for the groom/chauffer up above. Today, it housed three cars, one Bobbie's, with ample room for the paraphernalia that a large estate requires—riding mower and snowblower, snowplow blade, work bench, cupboards.

Upstairs, we viewed a totally renovated kitchen, all gleaming stainless and granite; a living room filled with the kind of soft, squishy leather furniture that you sink into and can't get back out of; and two bedrooms, one decidedly sybaritic, with a large *en suite* bathroom that contained a double occupancy whirlpool tub. A picture flashed through my mind of Wukowski and me in that tub, covered in bubbles, hands sliding across wet bodies.

Damn it to hell! I turned and walked back into the living room, calling over my shoulder, "Really great place, Bobbie." Seconds later, the door to the other bathroom opened, and Guy emerged.

To say he looked rough would be an understatement. His eyes practically glowed red in a complexion of sickly yellow. He hadn't shaved. I glanced at his hands. *Too shaky,* I supposed, *for even a safety razor.* Bobbie's borrowed short-sleeved polo shirt and khaki shorts hung on Guy. We made a little parade through the living room and into the kitchen—Guy, me, Wukowski and Bobbie. Wukowski started to introduce himself, but Guy cut him off with a raised hand and a "Just a minute. Please." while he poured himself a cup of coffee and topped it with a large slug of brandy. He stirred it and downed the entire cup in a long series of swallows, never stopping for air. Then he set the cup on the kitchen counter, placed his palms flat on either side, closed his eyes and waited. Presently, a long "Ahhhh," emerged, his eyes opened, and he looked at us. "You were saying?" he asked Wukowski.

"Bad case of the jim-jams?" Wukowski responded, his voice sympathetic.

"Man, you cannot know. You just cannot know. My host—" he nodded toward Bobbie—"is generous with his liquor." Bobbie gave him a tip of the imaginary hat. "And I was pretty upset by the whole murder story and John Dunwoodie's staring me down at the restaurant." He shook his head, then regretted it.

Bobbie moved to the refrigerator, poured a tall glass of water from the dispenser, extracted some pills from a cupboard, and placed them all on the counter in front of Guy, who knocked them back like a trouper. "Thanks, man," Guy said.

Wukowski explained that he would need a statement from Guy concerning Jane Dunwoodie's movements on the night in question. I could see that the officialese made Guy nervous. His eyes darted around the kitchen, as if searching for an escape route.

"Guy," I said, "just tell Detective Wukowski what you told us last night in the parking lot."

"What if they find out? That John Dunwoodie is one scary dude. You didn't see the way he was watching me."

"Actually, Guy," Wukowski told him, "if they find out you've spoken with the police, you're home free. Once we have your statement, there's no reason for them to want to prevent you from talking about what you saw. So really, it makes you safer." I had to hand it to Wukowski, it sounded entirely reasonable and he delivered it in a voice that was reassuring and confident. But it was all BS. Bobbie had one eyebrow raised as he caught my eye. He knew it, too.

The statement would only be the first step. If a case was built against Jane Dunwoodie, Guy would have to testify and there would be all the reason in the world to try to prevent that. But one step at a time. First, Wukowski needed the statement.

He and Guy settled in the living room, Wukowski in a big comfy club chair and Guy half reclining on the couch with an arm across his forehead as he spoke. Bobbie and I perched on bar stools at the kitchen counter, within eyesight and earshot, but not obvious participants.

Guy didn't have anything new to add to what he'd told Bobbie and me last night. Wukowski tried several approaches to jog Guy's memory about John Dunwoodie, to no avail. All Guy had focused on that night was the rhetoric in the RCCLU meeting and seeing Jane scurry down the corridor. I had to admire the way that Wukowski handled the questioning—strong when he wanted Guy to buck up and stop sniveling, tender when he sensed that Guy had reached his limits. Very professional. Very manipulative. I noted it for future reference.

Bobbie and I spoke in an undertone about the possibility of Guy getting some financial support from the gay community, to allow him to take time off work. "I'd set up something through the Belloni attorney, Bobbie," I told him, "but Wukowski thinks it would taint Guy's testimony, like we were paying him to say things."

"I can see how that would look," he answered. "Let me do some checking and see what I can come up with." He leaned close to me. "He spilled his guts last night. He's a mess, Angie. His apartment's just a rest stop between lovers. His job barely pays the bills. He has too damn many lovers—this isn't the seventies, you can't have unprotected sex with multiple partners without consequences. And not for publication, but Guy needs a job with health care. Now."

Bobbie didn't explain further, and I didn't ask, but the specter of HIV sat with us at the kitchen bar. I looked over my shoulder at Wukowski and Guy. Gay Guy. Pitiful Guy. Dying Guy? Jane Dunwoodie would say, serves him right. But don't we all face that ghost, every time we have sex? Even protection isn't foolproof. And surely we are all fools for love—or lust—now and then. Perhaps my own relatively conservative count of lovers was only due to fear or suspicion. Perhaps Guy's was the result of being willing to take a chance, to trust. Or perhaps it was simply biological. Regardless, my Catholic upbringing had taught me that "… in the same way you judge others, you will be judged." Jane Dunwoodie might want justice, but I sure as hell wanted—needed—mercy more.

I waggled my fingers at Wukowski, gave Bobbie a big hug, and left for the office.

Chapter 26

A fool's paradise is a wise man's hell!

—Thomas Fuller

Susan was in the office when I arrived. "Coffee?" she asked.

"I'm way over the limit," I answered. "I had breakfast at Ma's with Wukowski, then another cup at Bobbie Russell's place."

"Do tell." She leaned forward, chin in hands, ready to dish. "Is his place as gorgeous as he is?"

"Just about. I'd kill for a whirlpool like the one in the master suite." I blushed slightly as I recalled my thoughts about me and Wukowski in the tub together. "Listen, Susan, I need some help and it has to be undercover." I handed her the printout I'd made of the Dunwoodie assets and pointed to the OAPT. "Any chance you can find out how much is in the account and how regular the payments are?"

She shook her head. "Very unethical, Angie. I could lose my license."

"How would they know?"

"Most of these accounts are tagged. If you query them, the owner is notified."

"Crap." I put my purse in my desk drawer and opened my laptop. "Strictly off the record, then, is there anything you can tell me that you've picked up from working for Jane?"

"Hmm. Let's see." She pulled out a flash drive and inserted it into her computer. "Mrs. Ellingsworth asked Jane for a lot of financial stuff when we were updating her account this week. Seems that one of Mrs. E's grandchildren is engaged to the daughter of a big competitor, and the kid is trying to get Mrs. E to change over to his fiancée's firm. So Mrs. E told Jane that she needed to run a financial analysis of both agencies." Susan smiled, widely. "I thought Jane would pee her pants, but she gave us all kinds of statements on the agency."

As she spoke, Susan quickly scanned documents on her monitor. "Bingo. Here's the OAPT. Balance of almost one-and-a-half mil. Marked as "retirement account" for the Dunwoodies. Looks like they put in about 100K a year."

"Is that a lot, for their income level?"

"With their other investments in the US, it's a pretty big chunk. More than forty percent of what they take out of the agency, all told."

"Apparently the OAPT is not a hidden asset, though. They're reporting it and Jane is aware of it?" Susan nodded. "Too bad," I said, "it would mean a lot if John was stashing funds undercover."

"Sorry to disappoint you, Angie, but it looks like it's on the up and up." She paused. "But this is odd."

"What?"

"Two days after Elisa's death, the agency made a payment to Mrs. Morano. One hundred big ones."

"A hundred thousand dollars?" As Susan nodded, my heart started pounding in my chest. *At last*, I thought, *a paper trail. Something to take to the police. Something official.* Then the logical side of my brain kicked in. "Susan, is there any reason you can think of for the agency to make a payment like that?"

"Nooo." It was very tentative.

"Sure?" I asked.

"Well, I'm just wondering if there was an account under her name. From what you've told me, her mother didn't have much. Maybe she needed money in a hurry for the funeral and the Dunwoodies advanced it to her." She looked up from her screen. "But it seems odd that they'd front that large an amount. Even a lavish funeral wouldn't approach that, not for someone like Elisa."

"It's time I paid another condolence call on Mrs. Morano," I told her. "Keep looking, would you? See if you can locate Elisa's account and determine its balance." I gave her the info on Elisa's 401K and hightailed it out the door and down to the car.

***

The Mrs. Morano who responded to my knock at her apartment door was not the same woman I'd interviewed prior to the funeral. Her hair was styled, her make-up in place, and her well-fitted white capris and boatneck navy cotton top showed off her slim figure. Even her toenails were painted, I noticed as I took in her white sandals. Very put together.

"Mrs. Morano, it's Angie Bonaparte. I hope you don't mind my dropping in like this, I was down the street on an assignment and thought I'd stop and see how you're doing."

"Just great," she responded with a big smile, as she took the chain off the door and motioned me in. The room was full of packing boxes. "Excuse the mess," she said. "I'm getting ready to move."

"Really?" I seated myself without waiting for an invitation. The scratchy upholstery dug into the bare skin on the backs of my thighs, knees and calves. I angled my legs away from the seat in order to minimize contact. "I hope it's a move to a nice place," I said.

"Honey, it's a move to paradise." She paced the small clearing in the middle of the room, her arms and hands fluttering as she gestured and spoke. "Ever hear of a place called Belize?"

I remembered that the Dunwoodies' OAPT was established in Belize, but pleaded ignorance, knowing from her manic behavior that she'd be happy to enlighten me.

"It's a little country down there near Mexico. Lotsa beaches and sun. Great tourist spot."

"So you're taking a vacation?"

"No, I'm moving." She punctuated the words by tapping her taloned fingernails on the tops of boxes. "Moving. Can you believe it? The job just dropped into my lap."

"Wow. A job in Belize. How did you ever hear about it?"

"Jane Dunwoodie, she's the one who set me up." She stopped pacing for a moment and gave me a sheepish look from lowered lids, her chin down. "I was wrong about her, Angie. She's been real nice to me since Elisa died. Even paid up on Elisa's insurance policy ahead of time, so I could take care of the funeral expenses. She said they wanted everything to be nice for the funeral and for me afterwards. So even though I won't need to work for a few years—who knew that Elisa would take out a policy for that much?—Jane decided to see if some of their acquaintances in Belize might need help. Just so I could get away for a while."

She looked around the room, spotted her purse, and extracted a pack of Luckies from it. "D'you mind?" I shook my head and she lit up and kept talking, gesturing wildly with the hand that held the cigarette. I hoped all of the flying ashes were dead.

"So, I leave in three days. All this junk's going into temporary storage. Jane set it up for me. I'm just taking my summer clothes and my photo album." She pointed to a pitiful little pile on the couch. "There's a nice little villa waiting for me, a timeshare with a maid, can you believe it? And a part-time job at a local insurance agency. They speak English there, did you know that?" I shook my head again and let her continue. "I don't even have to start right away, Jane set it up so I'd have some vacation time." She took a deep drag on the cigarette. "I tell ya, Angie, I was wrong about her, way wrong."

"Well, that's great news, Mrs. Morano. I hope you'll really like it there and I hope your new life turns out fine. I'm glad Mrs. Dunwoodie is taking care of all the paperwork for you. That can be a real hassle, signing all the documents after a death."

"Yeah, Jane's taking care of everything. I haven't had to lift a finger, not even to sign stuff. Except her check, of course." She giggled a little.

Hitting the bottle this early? I wondered.

I repeated my wishes for her happiness and made my escape, glad to be out of the miasma of smoke and the sense of impending disaster. Something was very, very wrong. No insurance agency in the world would hand over money without the receiver signing papers for it. What was really going on here?

I sat in the Miata, closed my eyes, and let images roll on the screen of my mind. My first interview with Jane Dunwoodie, aggressive, cold, sure that Elisa got what was coming to her. Her children's pictures on her desk. Jane as a long-haired girl, knife raised to attack a man on a sidewalk. The RCCLU meeting, scary enough to make Guy sweat and shake. Elisa's funeral, with Jane and Mrs. Morano rivaling each other for tears.

My eyes popped open. I'd attributed Jane's tears to remembrance of her own daughter's funeral. But it seemed that she hadn't exhibited that kind of behavior at other times. Instead, she'd channeled her grief into rage and attacks on those who disagreed with her strong opinions. So why the tears over Elisa? Guilt, maybe? And the money, the villa in Belize, the job—reparation?

Chapter 27

We must repay goodness and wickedness: but why exactly to the person who has done us a good or a wicked turn?

—Friedrich Nietzsche

I used my cell phone to call the RCCLU office. Mrs. Staunchley's cheery voice greeted me. "Mrs. Staunchley, can you put me in touch with a priest who belongs to your organization?" I asked. "I'm writing an article for the *Herald-Citizen* and I want to be sure that my facts are correct."

"Well…" she hesitated. "I'm not sure if Father Tom will have time. Maybe our director can help you?"

"I'd love to set up an interview with your director, but, for now, I'm in need of clarification on some theological points. And I don't want to talk to one of those *liberals*." I made the word as nasty as I could.

"My, no. That would not be helpful." I heard some papers rustling and I waited. It only took her a couple of seconds to decide and to locate the information. "Father Tom Merrill is the RCCLU advisor. He's an instructor at St. Francis." She gave me his number at the archdiocesan seminary. I thanked her and quickly disconnected before she could try to set up an interview or ask for my name.

My Catholic upbringing had taught me one thing. A priest will not divulge what is told to him in confession. *However,* I wondered, *what about something that might be mentioned or alluded to outside of confession?* I figured it couldn't hurt to ask. And I also figured it couldn't hurt to have a police officer do the asking. So I called Wukowski and filled him in.

"Good work, Angie. But I don't know, I can't see this priest being willing to talk to us." I waited in silence. "I guess we can try. Let's just drive over there and try to find him. If I call first, he's more likely to stall or put us off with official statements."

St. Francis De Sales Seminary is the oldest seminary in continuous existence in the United States. The grounds account for a large part of the city of St. Francis, a suburb just to the south of Milwaukee. I drove through a canopy of maples and parked in the drive in front of Henni Hall, the main building on the campus. Its colonnaded front and towering dome made a strong statement of permanence.

Wukowski exited the police sedan as I got out of the Miata. I noticed his chin drop slightly and imagined that, behind his dark sunglasses, he was ogling my legs in my short summer shift dress. *And on church grounds, you naughty boy!* I thought.

As we entered the building, he spoke to me in an undertone. "Let me do the talking." I nodded.

There was no listing in the entryway for the RCCLU, but Wukowski cornered a young seminarian, who told us where we could find Father Tom Merrill. In a move to economize, the archdiocese had closed other administrative buildings and relocated to empty floors at St. Francis. Father Tom had a small office on the second floor, barely as large as my walk-in closet. The door was open, probably for air circulation, since there didn't seem to be any air conditioning working.

Wukowski stuck his head in and said, "Father Thomas Merrill?"

The man at the desk nodded and motioned us in. Wukowski flipped open his badge wallet and displayed his badge. I angled around to read it. "W.T. Wukowski." No first name. Then I turned back to the priest and introduced myself as simply Angie Bonaparte, expecting that he'd think I was also with the MPD.

He didn't ask. "It'll make the room hotter than blazes," he said, "but perhaps we should close the door."

The small room contained Father's desk and chair, three walls of bookcases, a couple of filing cabinets and one visitor chair. Wukowski dragged another chair into the room from the hallway, where they were lined up along the wall, as if waiting for miscreant students to fill them. As he closed the door and we took our seats, I studied the priest.

He wasn't what I expected. I guess I thought that an advisor to a group like the RCCLU would be an old, crotchety, hidebound iconoclast. This man was about forty-five, tall, dressed in a black cassock. His light brown hair was adorably curly, a halo of short ringlets that encircled his face. It was hair that a woman would love to run her fingers through. *What a waste*, I thought.

Wukowski explained that he was part of the investigation into the murder of Elisa Morano. Father Tom's face seemed to relax and he exhaled and smiled slightly. *Odd reaction*, I thought. Then his words made the reaction clear. "Thank God, I thought it was another abuse case." The Milwaukee archdiocese had its share.

"Murder is a relief then, Father?" Wukowski asked, no emotion in his tone. But the very question was offensive, and Father Tom snapped to attention.

"Of course not, Detective. I apologize if it came across that way. It was just a gut reaction." His eyes squinched in puzzlement and he ran a hand through his curly hair. "How can I help you? I'm afraid I didn't know Ms. Morano or Mr. Belloni, although I've read about the case in the papers and seen it on the TV news. In fact," he paused and looked at me, "aren't you the investigator?"

"That's right, Father. Detective Wukowski and I have a joint interest in some aspects of the case, and he's been kind enough to let me tag along so that I don't have to bother you later with more questions."

He nodded. "Unconventional, but if the police don't mind, I don't. However, as I stated, I have no involvement in the case."

"Father, we understand that you advise a group called—" he paused and flipped open his notebook, even though he knew the name as well as I did—"the Roman Catholic Civil Liberties Union, or RCCLU."

Father Tom sighed. "Yes, I have that dubious distinction." I raised an eyebrow and he smiled at me. Cute smile. Cute hair. And I was pretty sure from the vibes that this was not a gay priest. "You see, Detective, Ms. Bonaparte, the archdiocese feels it's best to have a calming influence on groups that might otherwise be an embarrassment. To work with them in order to mediate their behavior. Last year, I chaired a seminar on the ethics of abortion to save the mother's life, and I guess that led to my being selected to act as their spiritual and theological advisor." He shook his head as if asking himself how he got into this situation. "It's not that I disagree with their positions on matters like abortion and gay marriage. It's just that some of them are fairly radical in the way they approach the issues." He looked at me. "We're not all fanatics."

"Were you at the dinner at the Italian Community Center last week?" Wukowski's voice was flat and unemotional.

"No, I couldn't attend. I had a prior commitment that night. Did something happen?"

"Not at the dinner itself, Father. We're just trying to ascertain the movements of some of the attendees."

"I see. Well, I'm afraid I can't help you there."

"I hope you'll keep this conversation confidential, Father, so as not to impede the progress of our investigation." Wukowski closed his notebook and started to rise.

I couldn't let it rest there, so I jumped in with both feet. "Father, if someone came to you and confessed to murder, and you knew that an innocent person was likely to be convicted for the crime, what would you do?"

He rested his elbows on his desk chair arms, steepled his fingers under his chin, and closed his eyes briefly. When he opened them, there was a glint that I hadn't seen before. "Ms. Bonaparte, I am prevented as a priest from disclosing anything learned by me in confession." He reached for a large tome on his desk, opened it to a bookmarked page, and began to read:

Regarding the sins revealed to him in sacramental confession, the priest is bound to inviolable secrecy. From this obligation he cannot be excused either to save his own life or good name, to save the life of another, to further the ends of human justice, or to avert any public calamity. No law can compel him to divulge the sins confessed to him, or any oath which he takes—e.g., as a witness in court. He cannot reveal them either directly—i.e., by repeating them in so many words—or indirectly—i.e., by any sign or action, or by giving information based on what he knows through confession. The only possible release from the obligation of secrecy is the permission to speak of the sins given freely and formally by the penitent himself. Furthermore, by a decree of the Holy Office

(18 Nov., 1682), confessors are forbidden, even where there would be no revelation direct or indirect, to make any use of the knowledge obtained in confession that would displease the penitent, even though the non-use would occasion him greater displeasure.

He looked up, saw Wukowski scribbling furiously in his notebook, and told him that he would make a copy of the page for his use.

He closed the book with a thud and set it back on the corner of his desk. "So you see," he said, "I cannot disclose anything told me under the seal of confession."

"Father," I persisted, "I seem to recall that part of the process is the penitent's requirement to atone. In other words, if someone harms another, and they confess having done the harm, don't they have to make reparation?"

"They are expected to do penance, but it is not required. The confession of sin and sincere regret are required for absolution. But the Church holds that satisfaction—what you call reparation—is due to God, and if the penitent does not satisfy God's justice on earth, he or she will satisfy it after death, usually in purgatory. So there is no requirement for a penitent to make reparation to the one harmed nor is there a requirement to do penance. But it's certainly recommended and strongly encouraged as a matter of justice and to save one from, as they say, doing hard time." His eyes twinkled and he looked at Wukowski as he spoke those last words. Then he rose, picked up the book, and excused himself to make a copy of the page.

When he returned with copies for both Wukowski and myself—a nice touch, which I appreciated—I sprung my final question. "Father, do you ever require a penance that involves reparation to the one offended as well as penance to satisfy God? Is that appropriate?"

He lowered his eyes and compressed his lips as he thought. Then he seemed to reach a decision, and looked me square in the eyes. "As I said, neither reparation nor satisfaction is required to receive absolution. All that is required is confession and contrition. And there may be cases where making human reparation would actually cause more harm than good. So the confessor would be very careful if he asked the penitent to make human reparation."

"What about justice, Father?" Wukowski interrupted. "Doesn't God care about that?"

"Of course, Detective. And no matter how it may seem to you, God always achieves justice, in one way or another. Let's take a case where a man commits adultery with another man's wife. The other man doesn't know about it. No one is hurt physically or emotionally. But the spiritual life of the adulterers is corrupted. So the adulterous man goes to confession, repents and is granted absolution. He even does penance, which means he's not only forgiven, but he doesn't rack up any time in purgatory for his act." He paused. "Doesn't seem fair, does it? Doesn't seem like justice has been served."

"Exactly," Wukowski agreed.

"If his confessor required him to make amends to the man he wronged, how would he do it? Tit-for-tat would seem to indicate that he should offer his own wife to the guy, but certainly God wouldn't approve of that! Maybe he should pay him money. Let's see, what's the going rate for one night of passion with another man's wife? And don't forget that to make amends, he would have to make the guy aware of the wife's betrayal, causing him extreme emotional pain. So we have to add in a payment for that." He raised his hands and shrugged in the classic Gallic posture of bewilderment. "Frankly, I don't know how to measure the cost or determine the method or amount to pay back, do you?"

By now, I was practically tap dancing with suppressed emotion. "Father, let's talk about a simpler case. Say someone steals from another person. Takes something valuable. If the thief confesses and is contrite, wouldn't he need to return what he stole?"

"Not to receive absolution, Ms. Bonaparte. But it would certainly go a long way toward easing his conscience and keeping him on the right track in the future."

"Okay, so he decides to return what he stole. What if he can't do it without letting the other person know that he took the item? In other words, he has to ruin his own reputation and maybe face criminal charges for the theft. Maybe do jail time. Would you, as his confessor, recommend that he go ahead, knowing it might expose him to the world and possibly affect his family?" I could feel a little buzz of excitement from Wukowski as he tensed slightly. He knew, as I did, that I was talking about the murder and not a theoretical case of theft.

Father Tom sat down at his desk and began to tap on his keyboard. After a moment, he cleared his throat slightly and read. "This is what the Catholic Encyclopedia has to say, in part, about restitution:

The grounds on which restitution becomes obligatory are either the possession of something belonging to another, or the causing of unjust damage to the property or reputation of another. These are called by divines the roots of restitution, for it is due on one of those two grounds if it is due at all.

The deliberate causing of unjust damage to the property, reputation, or other strict rights of another imposes on him who does the damage the obligation of making restitution for it, as we have seen. For, although in this case there is no possession of what belongs to another, still the wronged person has not what in justice he should have, and that through the unjust action of him who did the damage. The latter therefore has unjustly taken away what belonged to the former, and he must restore to him something which is equivalent to the loss which he has suffered and which will balance it, so that equality between them may be restored.

He looked up from the monitor. "I would tell the person to make restitution as far as possible without causing more harm to others. If restitution cannot be made without causing harm, I would recommend that the person simply accept forgiveness, do penance and move on, with the intention of doing right in the future."

Wukowski shook his head. "That's not fair, Father. Not just."

"Detective Wukowski, I wish I could say that all things would be made fair and just and right in this world, but I can't. All I can offer is that they will be made fair, just and right, in God's way and in God's time."

We heard a quiet knock at the door. Father Tom checked his watch, told us that it was an appointment he needed to keep, and ushered us out with assurances that he was available to talk further about anything that was not under the seal of the confessional. As he shook my hand, he said, "You're a Catholic, Ms. Bonaparte?"

"Not anymore."

He nodded in understanding. "Do you have a spiritual advisor?"

"No," I replied.

"Please feel free to call me if you should want to talk further." I raised an eyebrow and he laughed. "Believe me," he said, "I enjoy the company of an attractive woman, but that's not part of my offer." He leaned a little closer to me. "Perhaps it's time to come home, Angie."

"Perhaps, Father. But as Angela Carter said, 'Home is where the heart is and hence a movable feast.' I think my heart and my feast have moved on. But I'll think about it."

Wukowski and I left the building in silence. When we got to the cars, I motioned to the Miata and we sat in the sun for a brief confab. "You noticed that he had bookmarked the page about the seal of the confessional?" I commented.

"Seems Father Tom has been reading up recently on what's allowed and what's not allowed concerning matters told in confession."

I turned to him and grasped his arm with my hand in excitement. "Jane confessed to killing Elisa. I just know it, Wukowski."

"Yeah," he nodded. "I think you're right." He gently disengaged my hand and turned to stare out the windshield at the beautiful grounds. "But we'll never bring it to the DA without proof. And you heard the man, he'll never tell by work or deed or inference what she confessed." He sighed and rubbed his forehead. "I have a bad feeling about this one, Angie. It might be number four."

"Number four?"

He continued to stare straight ahead, avoiding eye contact. "Most murders are easy to solve. The perp is stupid or strung out or too emotional to cover their tracks. The evidence or the motive is strong. You ask, they confess." His hands, placed awkwardly on his knees, tensed and his knuckles whitened. "I've been a cop for twenty-two years. I made detective fifteen years ago. Three times since then, I've had cases that didn't fit the mold. Cases where some smart guy—or gal—set up a homicide with such precision and planning that there didn't seem any way to bring them to justice. It eats at you, Angie."

I wanted to put my arms around the big lug and hug him, but I knew consolation wasn't what he needed. He needed justice. It was his reason for living, it was what he'd talked about and agonized over ever since Elisa Morano's murder. I couldn't give him justice, but I could listen, let him talk out his frustration and anger ... if he would. "So, what happened in those three cases, Wukowski. Did the bad guys walk?"

His shoulders hunched up as he tensed again, then he let out a breath and turned to me. In the little car, our knees and arms were just inches apart and his breath fanned my face. He closed his eyes and started to talk, almost as if he were visualizing the evidence. "Maloney, he claimed to be disabled from an industrial accident. The insurance investigator caught him on film, lifting a big table saw out of the back of his pickup. Two days later, the investigator is missing and Maloney has no idea what might have happened to the guy." He opened his eyes, reached over and took my left hand in both of his. Looking down, as if he'd never seen my hand before and was infinitely fascinated by it, he continued. "We never found any physical evidence to link him to the disappearance, but we did get a conviction on the fraud charges."

He started to caress my fingers, one at a time, running his thumb up and down each finger while he gently held my hand in his. I could barely breathe. "Then there was Sue Chappel. Remember her? The woman whose baby was killed in an attempted carjacking?" His voice turned into a low rumble, as he moved up to my wrist, turning my hand over and massaging the pulse point. "We never even suspected that she wanted to eliminate the baby and live the free and easy single life again. But the accomplice, the carjacker, was caught on a security tape from a building across the street. He sang like one of the Three Tenors when we charged him."

He released me and ran both his hands up and down my bare arms, still looking down. "Then there was Liz." His voice broke and he pulled me into his arms.

The stick shift jammed me in the knee, but I tightened my embrace and rubbed his back. "God, Wukowski," I whispered, "I'm so sorry."

"Angie," he murmured in my ear.

Wait a minute! Was that his lips on my earlobe? Oh, yeah. And then, little nibbles from his teeth that sent heat to areas further south. His hands caressed the nape of my neck and started to move down my dress, making circles through the cloth, as if he were trying to memorize the topography of my back. *This isn't wise*, I told myself. *Shut up and enjoy!* I responded. I flung my legs over the shifter and rested them on his thighs. He leaned further into me, pressing me into the seat back.

As my dress rode up and his right hand followed suit, I heard a clear "Harrumph" and opened my eyes to see an elderly priest observing us from the sidewalk. Feeling like a guilty teenager caught necking in the cloakroom at a CYO dance, I pushed Wukowski away, retrieved my limbs and straightened my dress. "Sorry, Father," I murmured to the priest.

Wukowski's head snapped around and a deep red darkened his neck and face. He hastily opened the passenger door of the Miata and climbed out, then slammed the door and leaned over to kiss me quickly on the cheek. "I'll call you at your office. Okay?"

"Definitely okay," I answered.

Chapter 28

Virtue consists, not in abstaining from vice, but in not desiring it.
—George Bernard Shaw

The message on my office voice mail was short and sweet. "Angie, it's Tony. Baby number five is here, little Angelina. Eight pounds, two ounces. Twenty-one inches long. Gracie's doing fine. We're at St. Mary's, so stop by if you have time today. If not, Mama and baby will probably come home tomorrow. They don't keep them in the hospital for long anymore." Click.

Angelina. Named after me? No, it couldn't be. I barely knew them. And Angelina is a fairly common Italian name. Probably the baby was named after an older relative. A *nonna* or a *bisnonna*. My watch read three-thirty. Time to do some baby shopping!

What does a couple with four children need when number five arrives? Of course, they already had plenty of clothing, crib linens and toys. They didn't need a car seat, a stroller, a carrier.

I decided to stop concentrating on the baby and to focus on Gracie and Tony. What do new parents need, regardless of the number of their previous offspring? Sleep. Privacy. Time together. I made a few calls, then stopped at the local drug store for a greeting card, slipped three of my business cards into it, and signed it 'Love, Angie.'

Gracie was snoozing when I entered her room. I sat down in the hospital recliner. Its wipe-off surface felt sticky on my bare thighs and, as I shifted slightly, her eyes popped open. "Gracie, how are you feeling?" I asked.

"Fine. But tired. You know."

I nodded. "I still remember. How's that little angel?"

"Oh, Angie, she's just beautiful. Dark curly hair, long eyelashes. Did you see her in the nursery?"

"Not yet. I decided to stop and see you first. Want to take a stroll?" I helped her get out of bed, only too aware from her careful movements that the stitches probably were pulling. We walked slowly, arm in arm, down the hallway to the nursery, where the babies were lined up in their little plastic bassinets. Baby Angelina was indeed adorable, small wisps of dark hair peeking out from her pink knitted cap. "Oh, Gracie, she's a beauty all right."

"We named her after you, Angie."

I sucked in a breath and turned to Gracie, feeling tears well up suddenly. "No kidding?" She nodded. "I'm so honored." I wanted to ask why, but Gracie beat me to it.

"Angie, when I wanted to just give up and run away, you gave me hope. I don't know if things will ever be the same between me and Tony, but I know from knowing you, from seeing what you've done with your life, that I can handle it if they're not." She clasped my arm. "And I really believe you're the one who'll get to the bottom of this business with Elisa and clear Tony's name."

I hugged her and we stood there, both of us a little weepy and emotional over the new life that lay in front of us.

When we got back to the room, I handed her the greeting card. "I didn't know what you and Tony would need or want, so if any of this isn't right, just say so. You won't hurt my feelings!"

She opened the greeting card and the three business cards slid out and onto the bed sheet. The first was for a paid suite at the Pfister, any weekend they cared to make the reservation. The second was for my services as a babysitter for that weekend, with the notation, "Children and Grandchildren References Available." And the third was for a couple's massage at a local spa.

"Oh, Angie, it's wonderful," Gracie said as she reached over to hug me. "Thank you so much."

"You're so welcome," I told her. "Just one thing, when you take that weekend, be really careful about baby number six, okay?" I grinned.

"No way! No effing way!" Gracie exclaimed, then put her hands up to her cheeks as she realized the pseudo-cuss word that came out of her mouth. "I'm sorry, I think I've been spending too much time with Tony."

As we laughed and talked new mommy and baby stuff, my mind circled around the Morano case. There had to be a way to prove Tony innocent. *This would not be Wukowski's number four,* I vowed. *No effing way!*

***

Bobbie was home when I called. "I need to pick your brain," I told him. "Can we meet for a drink?"

"Yes, yes, yes. Anything to get me away from Guy for a while." He sounded desperate as he whispered into the phone. "He's so *needy!*" His voice rose, so I assumed Guy had entered the area. "Let's meet at Ed's Tap. It'll be private this early in the day." Some mumbling in the background, then Bobbie's voice. "No, it's a business acquaintance. She might have a job lead for me. I'm afraid you can't come. Just order a pizza and hole up for a while. I'll be home by eight." Then, "See you there, Ms. Engel."

Engel? I had to look it up. Engel—German for 'angel.' Imagine, a guy with looks and brains! *Too bad he's gay,* I thought. Then I remembered Wukowski and I pushed all else aside for a moment, reveling in the memory of his hands and his lips and his teeth—and he'd only gotten to my ears, neck and back. *What would he be like in bed?* Then and there, I was determined to find out, caution be damned!

Bobbie was waiting at the bar as I entered. I boosted myself onto a stool and looked at him. I still wore my yellow linen shift, the one he'd seen me in that morning. He, however, had changed from his dangerously cut-off cut-offs into a tan knit polo shirt, bright blue linen slacks, and sockless slip-on moccasins. Very trendy, on-the-river clothing. I felt slightly mussed and unfresh.

I ordered a glass of the usual.

Bobbie leaned close and almost whispered, "What's up? You said you needed to pick my brain, such as it is. What do you need to know?"

"Bobbie, it seems that the Dunwoodie Agency has paid big money to Mrs. Morano, Elisa's mother, as part of an insurance settlement. Did they cover you when you were an employee?"

"Well, not for free, but they offered me a good break on a term policy premium."

"What was the face amount on the policy?"

"Fifty K. Enough for a nice send-off and enough left over to pay my Visa bill." He laughed. "Was Elisa's payout the same?"

"Nope. It was double. Maybe because she'd been there longer."

"I don't think so, Angie. She hadn't worked there a year, and Jane told me specifically that all benefits would be reviewed at the end of my first year. Except salary, that was at six months."

"Hmm. So why pay Mrs. Morano a hundred thousand, without her signing any papers, mind you? And why set her up with a job and a villa in Belize?"

"Sounds like someone is paying hush money, doesn't it?"

"It sure does. And I'd give a lot to know why."

"No idea. But Angie—" he leaned over and put his well-manicured hand on my arm— "why don't we just verify that the payment wasn't really for insurance?"

"How do we do that, Bobbie?"

"I'll bet you money that they never changed the security code. Jane was always misplacing her keys, so she had one of those digital keypad locks installed on the back door. I used to open up for them, so I had to have the code." He raised one eyebrow. "You game?"

I set the wine glass on the bar and faced him. "What's the worst that can happen? We get caught and charged with breaking and entering. I lose my license and my business. I have to get a job in a library, or live on my investments like the rich ladies do."

"Sounds good to me, girlfriend."

I nodded. "Let's go."

As we drove, I thought about a cover story, just in case we were found inside the agency. "Any legitimate reason why we might be in there, Bobbie?"

"Well, it just happens that I left my gold money clip in my desk. I was sooo upset when Jane booted me out the door." He pulled the clip out of his pocket, put all but ten dollars in the glove compartment, and waved it at me. "It has sentimental value. See there, it's engraved—To Bobbie, Love Stan. Of course, I haven't seen or heard from Stan in years, but a fella's got to have his gold money clip, right?"

"Right."

"And little Miss Jane was so mean to me, I didn't want to call and ask her for it. So I simply decided to walk in and take it. It may not be the best story the cops have ever heard, but I don't think they'll prosecute, do you?"

"Doubtful. But first thing we do when we get inside, if we get inside, is shove that clip in the back of your former desk drawer, under some papers. That way, you can claim that you overlooked it in the trauma of being fired."

It was six o'clock when I parked a block from the agency, in an unsecured lot. We took up places in a building across from Dunwoodie's, one that housed a lot of independent businesses. From the lobby doors, we watched and waited. No one came in or left across the street. One light burned in the reception area. It seemed to be deserted.

At seven o'clock, as we walked down the alleyway to the back door, Bobbie grabbed my hand. "Was that a stakeout, Angie?"

"Kind of. Usually they take a lot longer and are a lot more boring."

"Wow. I find that hard to believe. My heart's pumping." He fanned his face with one hand.

"Calm down, Dick Tracy. We need cool heads."

"Right." He took a deep breath, then another. "I'm okay now."

"Good." We stood outside the back door to the agency. It was a steel door with a digital lock, the kind where you depress the little black buttons for each number. "Now or never," I told him, and gestured toward the lock. "It's not too late to back out."

He cast a scornful glance at me and punched in six numbers on the keypad. A little green light lit up, he turned the doorknob, and we were in.

I grasped Bobbie's arm and motioned for quiet. We stood, silent, waiting. "Where's the alarm panel?" I whispered to him.

He opened an access door and punched in the same combination of numbers that he used on the back door. The panel flashed "Alarm Disabled." We both breathed a deep sigh.

"Stay here while I check out the offices," I whispered in his ear. "If you hear anything, run like crazy." I handed him the car keys.

"No way, Angie. We're in this together." He followed me down the hallway. The bathroom on the left was empty, as was the mail / copy room directly across from it. Bobbie tsk'd under his breath at the piles of boxes in there. "Either they haven't hired a secretary, or she's not up to the job," he whispered.

John's office was next. I slowly eased the door open and looked. It was absolutely pristine. No sign of work anywhere. "He's never here during working hours, why would he be here after?" Bobbie whispered. I moved on, to the door to Jane's office. Here, the scene was entirely different. Stacks of files littered the credenza and desk top. "Jane's never been this messy," Bobbie told me. "She's losing it!"

The reception area faced the street. Its big plate glass windows were barred with steel grates that retracted during the day. Now, they were firmly in place and locked. "Looks like we're alone," I told Bobbie.

He pulled the desk drawer open. It was squeaky clean, except for one pen and a memo pad.

"Slip the money clip in the back," I said, "and let's nose around in Jane's office."

We stood in the organized mess. "Where do we start?" I asked Bobbie.

"It might take us hours to find paper. Let's check the computer." He sat down at Jane's desk, flipped a switch on her monitor and started to type. "She never powers off," he told me. "She just locks it. Let's see if my old login still works." Some keying, then he shook his head. "I've been disabled. But maybe there's still a way. I've seen Jane do this a million times. Her login's 'JaneD.' Original, huh? And her password is four letters, all typed using the right hand, that much I know."

"Try 'John'."

He keyed it in. "Nope."

"Can't be 'Jane,' that uses the left hand, too." I remembered my conversation with Susan about Jane's children. "Try 'Lily.' L-I-L-Y."

"Bingo. We're in." I scooted around the desk and stood behind Bobbie, looking over his shoulder. He started an unfamiliar program. "It's agency software," he told me. "Helps us manage clients and accounts." I watched as he typed 'Morano' into a box and pressed Enter. Suddenly, the screen flashed and a message appeared—'Access Denied.'

"Shit. This program is always burping, and it's slower than slow. Let's try again." Again he entered 'Morano,' but this time, the screen flashed and a page appeared. "I was always telling Jane to update the software, but of course she didn't listen. At least we're in. It'll save us searching through all those boxes. Here's Elisa's 401K. Let's see what else she had."

"Wait," I told him. "Can you print a summary of that for me, and any transactions in the last year?"

"Sure thing." He pressed a few more keys and the printer started to hum. "We'll have to wait, though. The memory on this box isn't adequate to manage more than one thing at a time."

It seemed as if enough time passed for a medieval monk to manually copy the information using a quill pen, but in reality it probably only took three minutes for the pages to print. I scooped them up and looked around for an envelope.

Bobbie pulled a folder from the desktop and handed it to me. "It's an empty," he said. "She reuses them. What next?" he asked.

"Did Elisa have life insurance?"

He moved the mouse, clicked, and the screen altered. "No such account," it read. "Guess not," Bobbie told me.

"Not even a closed account?"

"No. That's odd." He half turned to look at me as I gazed over his shoulder. "Even a closed or inactive account should show up, Angie. It looks like Elisa never had coverage through Dunwoodie."

"Print the screen for me, Bobbie." He obliged and we waited as the printer hummed again. "Why would the Dunwoodies pay Mrs. Morano for a non-existent policy?"

"Hush money," he answered. "Payola to keep her quiet."

"I don't think so. She seemed genuine when she told me about it being an insurance policy payout. I think she believed it. But they were lying to her."

"One of them was lying," he corrected me. "Who paid her?"

"Jane." Goose bumps rose on my bare arms, even though the office was stuffy. "Any other accounts for Elisa?"

"No. Just the 401K."

"Okay, let's log off, wipe down and leave." I pulled a single-use packet of Shout laundry treatment from my purse. "Works great on fingerprints and skin oil," I told Bobbie. He logged out, I wiped off the keyboard, mouse and power button on the monitor. For good measure, I addressed the printer control panel, although I didn't think I'd touched it. Then I followed Bobbie down the hall. After he retrieved his money clip, I cleaned the desk drawer, where he'd pulled it open. "It won't matter if they find your prints inside the drawer. Those could be old. We just want to be sure you didn't superimpose them on something that the new secretary touched after you left."

"You're one smart lady, Angie," he told me. "I would never have thought of that. But why wait till now to wipe down? We could've done it as we went."

"That wouldn't mesh with the story of the money clip. It would make us look guilty if we got caught in the act."

"Ahh." He tapped his head with one finger.

We retraced our steps down the hallway, me using the Shout towelette on each doorknob as we went. We were at the mailroom / copy room when I heard the clicking at the back door. "Someone's pressing the door keys," I told Bobbie. "We're busted. Remember the plan."

I lifted my shift dress up over my hips, folded the papers in half and shoved them into the back of my underpants, tossing the empty folder into the mailroom mess and cursing the day I'd given up briefs for thongs. Bobbie's eyes grew big, but he said nothing as I yanked the dress down. "Okay?" I asked him. He glanced behind me and shook his head. "Cover my butt," I told him.

It would have been bad enough to be confronted by police or private security, but we had some hope of convincing them that we were, if not innocent, at least not malicious. When the door slammed open and Jane Dunwoodie stood there, pointing a 9MM Beretta at us, I felt my heart plummet to my knees. No way was she going to buy the money clip story. But we had to try.

"Jane, sweetie," Bobbie sprang into action. "I hope you don't mind that I came back for my money clip." He pulled it from his pants pocket, acting nonchalant, as if staring down the barrel of a pistol was an everyday occurrence for him. "I forgot it in the desk drawer. It was a gift."

"Really." She bit the word off, disdain dripping from each syllable. "And the computer access—were you trying to find the money clip by asking the computer?"

"I don't understand," Bobbie answered, turning to me as if confused. He slipped the money clip back into his pocket and put an arm around my shoulders. "Angie and I were just down the block having a drink. I offered to buy, but then I realized that I had no cash. That's when it dawned on me where I'd left the clip. I asked her to walk over with me to get it."

"You lying faggot." Jane spit venom with each word. "I was working at home, by coincidence doing a remote access for the Morano account, when I got a message that it was in use. John was watching a ball game in the den, so it couldn't be him. That leaves you and your snooping friend. You were in here, looking at the account." It was a statement, not a question.

The "Access Denied" message that we got when Bobbie first tried to open the page flashed in front of me. Jane must have closed down at home and rushed right over. She might be mean, but she wasn't dumb.

Bobbie opened his mouth to protest, but quickly shut it when Jane yelled "Enough! Get into the mail room," and motioned with the gun. We backed in, Bobbie in front of me, his hand still in his pants pocket as he nervously fingered the money clip.

"Mrs. Dunwoodie," he said, his voice nervously loud, "what good will it do to shoot us here, at the agency office? It won't change what happened to Elisa Morano. And the police are sure to find us."

"Right. But it'll be self-defense, won't it? I came in to clear up some work and caught you rifling my desk. Before I could call for help, you attacked me. I pulled my gun and shot you both. Who could blame me? I didn't even know who you were until after the event."

If I was going to die, I wanted answers. "Why did you kill Elisa Morano?"

"That bitch. That lying, cheating, conniving bitch!" She snarled the words, her lips drawn back from her teeth and spittle flying from her mouth. "She thought John would leave me for her. Can you imagine? She was nothing more than another piece of ass to him. He would never violate the vows of marriage for trash like her."

"Seems to me that he did just that when he slept with her," Bobbie interjected. I pushed a finger into his back, trying to tell him nonverbally not to aggravate her.

"Oh, he might have committed adultery. But leave me? And the children? Divorce me? I laughed in her face that night, when I met her at Tony's apartment." The hand holding the gun started to waver slightly. She grasped the weapon with both hands to steady it. "She said she wanted to talk…she called me things, ugly hateful things. I didn't mean to do it. I was angry, I lost control. Even Father Tom agreed, he told me it wasn't planned, that he could absolve me."

"Why the stabbing, Jane?" I asked in a quiet, calm voice.

She was practically sobbing. "When I shot her, when she fell and bled all over, when she lay there, still beautiful, even in death … I couldn't stand it. I grabbed a knife and stabbed her, wiped out her beauty. Her beauty was only outward. She had no spiritual beauty, she wasn't a godly woman." She stopped, seemed to come to her senses. "I tried to make amends. If you'd left it alone, no one would know. Her mother would be happy, living the good life I set up for her."

"But Elisa is dead, Jane. You can't make amends for that." My voice was hypnotic, like a mother reading a bedtime story, hoping that the child will drop off.

"I'm not going to jail," she said. "I have my husband, my children, my church to consider." Her voice dropped to a whisper. "I'm sorry." She sighted the gun.

As she spoke, I was groping behind me, my smaller frame hidden by Bobbie. My hands fastened on a bottle. It felt like a laundry detergent bottle. I twisted the top off. When Jane sighted, ready to shoot us, I swung the bottle sidearm, around Bobbie's body and straight at her.

Black powder. Choking. Gasping. Gun shots, ringing in my ears. Falling, Bobbie on top of me. Pain in my side. Bobbie whispering in my ear, "Hold on, Angie. Hold on. The police are on the way." Sirens. Shouts. Running. More sirens. *Wukowski? No, that can't be right.* Spiraling down a dark black hole.

Chapter 29

How many desolate creatures on the earth have learnt the simple dues of
fellowship and social comfort, in a hospital.
                              —Elizabeth Barrett Browning

The room was light green. Sun was shining on my face. Wukowski leaned over me, holding my right hand. "How you feeling, beautiful?" His voice was low, intimate.

"Awful." My throat was dry and hurt like the devil. So did my left side and my head. "What happened?"

"Remember tossing the copier toner at Jane?"

So that's what the black powder was that filled the room!

"She fired wild. You took a bullet in the side. Went right through. You'll have to get used to explaining the scar if you wear a bikini."

"Bobbie?" I panicked and tried to sit up.

Wukowski pushed me gently back against the pillows. "He's okay. Quite the hero, as a matter of fact. He tried to cover you."

Tears welled up in my eyes as I recalled him on top of me, telling me to hold on. "Jane?" I asked.

"In custody. Look, I have to go. They only allowed me three minutes, but I knew you wouldn't rest until you heard what happened." He carefully placed my hand on the bed clothes, as if it were made of finest porcelain.

"Wait," I croaked. He stopped. "Were you there? Why do I remember you being there?"

"Yeah, I was there, but not in time."

"How?"

"Bobbie Russell is one smart guy. While he was pretending to finger the money clip in his pocket, he was really dialing 9-1-1 on one of those super skinny cell phones that look like a credit card. The dispatcher got the whole conversation between you, Bobbie and Jane—'Mrs. Dunwoodie, at the agency, Elisa Morano, what good will it do to shoot us?' She figured it out and sent a squad, then contacted me as the detective in charge of the Morano case." His face tightened into a mask. "I thought for sure that you were a goner, Angie. I thought I was too late again."

I started to retch and a nurse suddenly appeared with one of those little kidney-shaped plastic basins. *Why are they shaped that way?* I wondered, as I spit up bile. *Does it catch the vomit better?* When she laid me back down and wiped my face with a cool cloth, Wukowski was gone.

The next time I woke, Papa was leaning over the bed, watching me. "Hi, Papa," I said in my froggy voice.

"Angelina, you took twenty years off my life, and I don't have that much to give." His voice quivered with emotion.

"I'm sorry, Papa" I mumbled.

Aunt Terry stood behind him. "Pasquale, stop haranguing her. I bet she hurts all over. You can yell at her later, when she's home. For now, just say you love her and let her get some rest."

"*Ti amo, cara figlia,*" he said as he kissed my forehead. I love you, dearest daughter.

"*Ti amo,* Papa," I said, tears and my sore throat making the words almost silent. Terry handed me a tissue, kissed me on the cheek, and said in an undertone, "Don't worry, he'll get over it."

It was dark when I woke again. A white-coated woman stood beside my bed, reading papers from an aluminum clipboard. "I'm Dr. Rodriguez. How are you feeling?"

"Like hell."

She nodded. "That's about what I expected. On a scale of one to ten, with ten the worst, how bad is your pain?"

"Which pain?"

"Start with the worst."

"My head feels like the top will blow off and it would be a relief if it did. That's about an eight."

"You hit the floor with a bang, they tell me. Mild concussion, causing headache and vomiting. It should subside within twenty-four hours of injury. I'll order Tylenol in your IV. What else?"

"My throat feels like it's been scraped raw."

"You inhaled a lot of copier toner and we were worried about your breathing. We had to intubate you briefly. It's irritating to the throat, but it keeps the airway open. This, too, shall pass. I wish I had something to give you to ease it, but it just takes time. What else?"

"Tell me about the bullet."

"It went through the fleshy part of the left side, near the waistline, and missed all internal organs. It exited the back with no complications. All we had to do was wash the wound out and stitch you up. Of course, you're on antibiotics to prevent infection. And you're getting mild narcotics in your IV drip." She flipped the chart closed. "You were damned lucky, Ms. Bonaparte."

"How long will I be in here?"

"We'll probably release you in a couple of days if there's no fever or other contraindication. Is there someone who can stay with you, or whom you can stay with? It's best if you're not alone, at first."

"Oh, God. Not Papa."

She smiled. "I've had several conversations with your dad. He's a lot like mine. Tough but tender. Must be the Latin temperament." She patted my arm. "Don't worry, he won't stay mad forever. And you have a couple of days to line up another caretaker."

The next morning, my throat was indeed better, although I still tended to croak. My head only pounded when I moved it. I begged the nurse for a cup of coffee and sipped at it carefully, savoring the caffeine. Things were looking up.

The door to my room eased open, and Gracie and Tony peeked in. "Angie," Gracie whispered, "is it okay if we come in for a minute?"

"Come, come," I motioned with my hand.

She was carrying little Angelina, all decked out in a pink onesie with little lacy bows on the feet. "Oh," I sighed, "can I hold her?"

Gracie laid her in the crook of my right arm. "Now you tell me if it hurts."

I gazed down at my namesake and smiled. "No, she makes it all better." I ran a finger along her smooth round cheek. "So soft."

"Angie, we can't stay," Tony said. "We're not supposed to be in here with the baby, but we wanted to see you before we took her home."

Home. Was it only yesterday that she was born? Had all this happened in just one day? I must have seemed confused, because Gracie got a concerned look on her face and gently extracted the baby from my arms. "We'll never be able to thank you enough for helping Tony," she said.

"All that I have is yours," he intoned in typical Italian male fashion.

"Really?"

A look of alarm passed over his face, but he sucked it up and said, "Really."

"Then if I can't find someone else to stay with when they release me, can I have a room at your place? Please? I don't want to go home with Papa."

Gracie grinned. "Are you sure? We'll have five little kids running around."

"Any amount of noise is better than an Italian father's wounded sensibility over his only daughter."

"Okay, then it's a deal. You call me and I'll be here to rescue you." Gracie patted my hand, Tony kissed me on both cheeks, and they slipped away with the baby.

It went on like that throughout the day. Visits from Papa and Terry, from my children, from Bart Matthews, all interspersed with nurses taking vitals and asking me silly questions about who the president was and what day it was.

About two o'clock that afternoon, Bobbie came in with a huge bouquet of yellow roses. He set the flowers on my bedside table and took my hand. "Does it hurt too much to kiss you?" he asked.

"No way." I lifted both arms to enfold him in an embrace. "You saved my life, Bobbie. How can I thank you?"

"Angie, you're kidding, right? If you hadn't thrown that bottle of toner, we'd both be dead meat."

"If you hadn't been smart enough to call the police on your cell phone and talk them through what was happening, all without alerting Jane Dunwoodie, we'd be dead meat anyway."

"So we're even," he said.

"Okay, we're even," I agreed. "You weren't hurt?"

"Just a little banged up from falling on the concrete floor. At least it had carpet, but it was that cheap industrial stuff and it ripped the skin right off my arms. But you, Angie. A bullet! I was never so scared in all my life when the police came in and I got up and saw you lying there, bleeding. Thank God for Wukowski. He just swooped you up and carried you right out to the ambulance. A knight in shining armor, that guy!"

"Really? I don't remember any of that." *Go on*, I thought, *tell me more*.

"Well," he continued, "when I got to the hospital emergency room, they were already calling for a surgeon and Wukowski was talking in that tight hard voice he gets. 'I want the best for her, not some resident who's been on duty for the past thirty-six hours. You understand?' I think he's got that 'love thing' for you, girl." He grinned.

"You think?"

He nodded. Then he looked around the room. "I should have brought you chocolates. This place looks like a florist's." He started to read the cards to me. "Daisies—Get Back on Your Feet, We Need You, from Marcy and Larry. Cinquefoil and honeysuckle—For My Beloved Daughter, Papa. A card, from Lela—Rest easy, I'll take care of things on the home front. A teddy bear, from Bart Matthews. Isn't that cute? Who knew he could be so sentimental? A family picture, nicely framed, with a card—We love you, get well soon, Your kids and grandkids. Oh, look, cards from Iggy and Marianne, and from the Bellonis. And someone named Judy sent the bouquet of white miniature mums. Worse Than a Dirty Diaper? on her card." He quirked an eyebrow, but I didn't have the energy to explain "Susan says she'll bring egg drop soup as soon as you can handle it. And a religious card from a Father Tom." Both brows shot up. "Nothing from Wukowski. Must be planning to deliver a get-well present in person."

I grimaced. "Bobbie, hand me a mirror. I need to see how bad I look." He rummaged in the bedside table and retrieved my purse, then handed me my compact. "Omigod." The face that looked back at me was not my face. It had a big purple bulge on the forehead and a black eye below it, nicely accented by the pallor of the skin elsewhere. The lips were puffy and chapped. The hair was matted. I set the mirror on the bed and started to cry. *It must be the meds*, I thought, *I never cry like this.*

Bobbie patted me on the shoulder and murmured, "Now, Angie, don't worry, it'll all be fine in a few days. Nothing's broken. You'll look normal before the week is out. Don't be upset. Everything will be fine." He kept that up for a while, handing me tissues as I bawled and discarding the used ones as I set them down. He brought me a cup of water and encouraged me to take sips. He was there. He was a friend.

When my crying jag ended, Bobbie asked, "Want me to do something with your hair?"

"Can you?"

He left the room and returned with dry shampoo, which he gently worked through my hair and scalp, using a towel to release the sweat and oil that fear had deposited. Then he wet a comb and carefully ran it through my short locks. There was enough residual styling gel to produce my usual spiky do. He handed me the mirror and I concentrated on the hair, avoiding looking at my face. "Thanks, Bobbie. That looks so much better."

The nurse came in with a tray. Liquids only—coffee, milk, jello, ice cream, chicken broth. Bobbie charmed her into bringing him a cup of coffee and he coaxed me into eating as he drained his cup. I could barely keep my eyelids open, so he pressed a kiss on my nose. "I'll leave the newspaper for later. We're celebrities, Angie! I'll be back in the morning. Call me if you need anything."

I dozed. I woke and read the news accounts, which stated that Jane was charged with second degree homicide and John as an accomplice after the fact. Both parents. I felt sorry for the children, but at least they were old enough now to function on their own.

I dozed. Five o'clock. No Wukowski. Another tray arrived. Soft foods—scrambled eggs, white bread, milk, tea. I forced myself to eat, but it stuck in the back of my throat. I couldn't get it down, not any more than I could swallow the bitterness of Jane Dunwoodie's senseless act.

I thought about all the people she hurt. Elisa, her life cut short, who would never have the chance to overcome her selfishness and find real love. Mrs. Morano, left alone, now probably deprived of the "insurance" settlement too. I would have to talk to Bart Matthews about that. Maybe he could help. Tony and Gracie Belloni and their children, their family problems exposed to the world. Guy, afraid for his life and in danger of losing his livelihood. Marsha Cantwell, Alan McGuire and Richard Llewellyn, all suspected of the killing and all carrying tainted memories of Elisa. And, of course, me and Bobbie, partners in investigation who almost became victims ourselves.

Why? For what? So a plain Jane could take vengeance on a beauty? So a 'righteous' woman could triumph and an adulterer be punished? So a marriage that was already a shambles could be preserved for the sake of religious rules? I dozed and dreamed, of a deep voice resounding from a mountaintop—Vengeance is mine, I will repay. Of a gentle voice, teaching—Forgive, and you will be forgiven. Of a crazy voice— She wasn't a godly woman.

I woke. Midnight. No visit from Wukowski. Either Bobbie was

wrong about the 'love thing,' or Wukowski was still too scared to take a chance. I was scared, too, damn it! Scared to be hurt. Scared of rejection. Scared of letting my guard down and getting sucker punched yet again. Scared that he just wasn't up to the challenge, the struggle, the flat-out denial of oneself for the sake of another which real, deep, lasting love requires. Scared that I wasn't, either. F. Scott Fitzgerald said, "Show me a hero and I will write you a tragedy." Wukowski and I were headed for tragedy, if the same were true for cowards.

Chapter 30

The main motive for "nonattachment" is a desire to escape from the pain of living, and above all from love, which, sexual or non-sexual, is hard work.

—George Orwell

When an unknown detective showed up in my hospital room the next day to take my statement, I knew what it meant. *Finito.* Done. Over before we started. *At least I have nothing to regret,* I told myself. No need to wish anything away because nothing ever happened. Just a few looks, some chemistry, a casual touch, a kiss. Just a sense that a real chance at happiness was running away as fast as it possibly could.

Whoa—way too melodramatic, girl. Way over the top. You'll be fine. You have a great life. You'll go back to it, get back in the groove, move on as if nothing ever happened. Because nothing had. Nothing had.

They discharged me on the third day. I spent one night with Papa and Terry, then went home to my condo, over their protests. I kept up a brave front with family and friends, working a few hours each day— my business doesn't run itself—and pretending all was fine. But at home, I let my calls go to voice mail, popped pain pills and slept.

I tried to talk myself out of the pit of self-pity that I descended into. So what if Wukowski was attractive? There were better-looking men out there. So what if he was funny, on occasion? I knew funnier guys. So what if he appealed to me like no one else had for years? So what if there was something special between us? No answer for those.

It was still dark, early in the morning of my fifth day out of the hospital, the sun not yet up over the horizon. I was curled up on one end of the couch, spooning Ben and Jerry's Chunky Monkey right from the carton into my mouth. My bruises had faded to a putrid yellow-green. After my morning shower, with my side still too sore to bend over, I didn't bother with underwear or socks, just slipped into a cotton nightie. I looked and felt like hell.

When I heard the front door lock snapping open, I yelled, "Papa, if that's you, please go home. Leave me alone. Just for a while. *Desidero essere solo.*" It sounded so much better when Garbo said it—I want to be alone. So sophisticated and self-sufficient. I sounded whiny. I didn't care.

A hand emerged from the hallway, holding a steaming cup from Starbucks. A man's hand. Wukowski's hand. My heart started to hammer and my mouth went dry.

Wukowski's face popped around the entryway. "Peace offering," he said.

I sat there, unsure of how I felt and what I wanted to do. I was both angry at him and glad he was there. I didn't want him to see me looking this way and I couldn't stop my eyes from feasting on the sight of him. I wanted to hug him and I wanted to kick his butt right out the door. I decided to play it cool. "Thanks," I said, as I took the cup and sipped from it. My hands were steady and my voice didn't break. So far, so good. "Who gave you the key?"

"Lela. Don't be mad at her, I forced it out of her by threatening a traffic ticket every time she pulled her car onto the street." He drew in a ragged breath. "I had to see you in person, Angie, and I was afraid you wouldn't open the door." Then he asked, "How you feeling, beautiful?" just as he had at the hospital.

I lost it. I slammed the cup down, coffee flying everywhere. I coughed and sputtered and cursed at him like a navvy, words I didn't even know I knew, words I won't repeat. "What the hell were you thinking?" and "You've got some balls, Wukowski!" and "You think you can waltz in and out of my life, without a word, without an explanation?" and "You are some piece of work, Wukowski!" and finally "These were the worst five days of my life."

"Mine, too," he said, simply, quietly. "Mine, too. I had to stay away, Angie, I had to face myself and decide what I wanted. I had to face Liz's ghost and figure out if I could care for a woman whose job puts her in danger. I had to decide if you were worth the fear and the pain. I had to decide if I was man enough."

"And?" I stood my ground, waiting. I was not going to make this easy for him. He either had to come to me with an open heart and an open mind, or walk away. No middle ground. No going back to the Angie of my marriage, the Angie who compromised herself away.

"I'm here, aren't I?" he asked, as he took a step toward me.

"That's not good enough," I said. "There are a lot of reasons why you might be here." I started to tick them off on my fingers. "One— You might want to get laid. Two—You might feel sorry for me, want to be sure I'm okay. Three—You might need information for the case against Jane and John. Four—You might feel guilty."

Before I could continue, he stepped up to me and put his hands on my shoulders. "Five—I might think I'm falling for you. Six—I might want to confirm it. And oh, yeah, back to One." His left hand moved, the fingers skimming my forehead where the goose egg had subsided to the size of a large marble, then cupping my chin as his thumb ran lightly over my fading black eye. Then it dropped to my waist and he asked, "Does it hurt?"

"Not at the moment," I answered, as my arms reached their own decision and encircled him.

His kisses were tentative at first, little nibbles, as if he were afraid to hurt me. His hands rested gently on my back. But as I let my hands move, as I explored his neck, his shoulders, the small of his back, I felt his hands start to move in those entrancing circles, down, down, until he whispered, "Angie, are you going commando?"

"Wukowski, I'm too sore to bend over to put on underwear."

"Works for me," he said.

Suddenly it dawned on me that I was about to make love with a man whose first name was a mystery to me. "Wukowski, I don't go to bed with strangers. What's your name?"

"I'll tell you in the morning," he answered.

"It is morning," I said.

"I mean tomorrow morning."

"Works for me." And it did. It did, indeed.

THE END

"The best way to thank an author is to write a review."— Anonymous
If you enjoyed this book, please consider posting a review on your favorite retailer's website.

Read on for an excerpt from the second Angelina Bonaparte mystery, *Cash Kills*.

Cash Kills—Chapter 1

Don't put your trust in money, but put your money in trust.

—Oliver Wendell Holmes

My office partner, Susan Neh, walked into our shared conference room, slowly pulled out a chair and, brows furrowed, sat facing me. "Angie, there's a woman here complaining that her parents had bank accounts worth millions and she doesn't want the money." Susan leaned across the table. "Can you imagine?"

"Maybe." I thought about the illegal ways that my papa probably accumulated wealth and how I would feel if I knew the details of my eventual inheritance. "What's her story?"

Susan opened her mouth, but abruptly shut it. "I think you should hear it from her directly. She's agreed to talk to you."

"I'm not sure that's legitimate, Susan, unless she wants to retain me."

"She might. I'm trying to convince her that she shouldn't ditch the money until she knows more. Come on, Angie, at least listen to her."

I pulled my five-foot-three frame up and checked myself in the small mirror that hung on the back of the door. A private investigator has to present a professional appearance in order to be hired. The days of tough guy Sam Spade have been replaced by the era of techno-geeks and corporate types. It's hard for a woman to be taken seriously. Clients expect a man. And for a fifty-something woman like me, it's twice as hard. So I ran my hands through my short spiky white hair, checked my teeth for lipstick and straightened my Donna Karan business suit. When we entered our common office, I grabbed a legal pad and pen from my desk and waited.

Susan and I share office space on Prospect Avenue, on Milwaukee's east side. I'm AB Investigations, she's Neh Accountants. The "s" on the end of both our firms can be misconstrued. We each run one-person companies.

Susan made the introductions. "Adriana Johnson, this is Angie Bonaparte." I smiled at the Sicilian pronunciation coming from my Japanese-American friend's mouth: Boe-nah-par-tay. I'd taught her well. Don't get me started on Napoleon. The little general was a French wannabe from Corsica, who ruined the name with his attempt to Gallicize it.

"Adriana, it's nice to meet you," I said. "Susan filled me in a little. Before we talk, I need to explain what a private investigator does and how it might affect this conversation. Then if you decide that you'd rather I wasn't privy to your information, I'll bow out with no hard feelings."

I assessed her as she nodded in response. She sat scrunched tight against one side of the client chair, taking up as little space as possible. The only way to describe her was nondescript: brown hair, light brown eyes, slightly olive complexion, slender, dressed head to foot in discount store beige. Bland and quiet. She hadn't moved or spoken since I entered the room.

I gave her a brief rundown on my services: tracking information and people. I explained that, under Wisconsin law, nothing she told me was private unless I was working for her attorney. In that case, whatever she shared with me would come under attorney-client privilege.

"May I please use your phone?" she said in a surprisingly sultry voice that contrasted sharply with her image. I handed her my cell phone and she placed a call. "Uncle Herman, this is Adriana." She pronounced it Ah-dreh-yah-nah. "I'm with the accountant you recommended. Yes, Susan Neh. She introduced me to a private investigator, whom I wish you to hire on my behalf. I understand that the investigator would then be covered by attorney-client privilege." She paused and listened, her face not showing any expression. Then she spoke again. "I mean no disrespect, Uncle Herman, but if you cannot accommodate me in this way, I will find someone who will." *Hmm, the mouse has teeth*, I thought. Then she handed the phone to me. "Ms. Bonaparte, this is my attorney, Herman Petrovitch. He was a friend of my parents and I've always called him Uncle. He'd like to speak with you."

I knew quite a few lawyers in the city, but I'd never heard of Herman Petrovitch. I took the phone. "Attorney Petrovitch, this is Angelina Bonaparte. I share office space with Susan Neh. She thought I might be able to help Ms. Johnson with her concerns about her inheritance."

When he spoke, his voice was rich and his accent middle-European. "I wish to retain you, Ms. Bonaparte. Anything which Adriana tells you must be kept confidential. I'm very concerned that when her inheritance is known, she might become the object of the press or even fortune hunters. She is a very good girl, but naïve in the ways of the world. I've told her that she can provide you with basic information, but I would like to meet with you personally once you and Adriana have talked. Is one hundred and fifty dollars an hour, plus expenses, acceptable?"

"That will be adequate, if I agree to pursue the matter, Attorney

Petrovitch." Actually, it was a bit more than my usual fee, but I wasn't going to argue with the attorney of a brand new millionaire. "I'll be in touch once we finish here." He gave me his address and phone number and rang off. I leaned back in my chair and waited.

Adriana's story began in the late nineties, in what was then Yugoslavia. She handed me three faded visas, for Jan, Ivona and Adrijana Jovanović. The visas were issued in 1994. Then she handed me citizenship papers for John, Yvonne and Adriana Johnson, issued in 1999. "My parents came to the U.S. near the end of the Bosnian War. I was four." That surprised me. I'd taken her for no older than twenty-one. "They wanted more than anything to be Americans, so we went to classes to learn English and Americanized our names. Uncle Herman settled here about three years earlier. He helped my parents get visas and citizenship by sponsoring us. He even helped Papa with money to start our little hardware store on the south side of Milwaukee. We felt comfortable there, among so many Poles and even some Serbs."

She paused. "Papa was a carpenter and mason in the old country. He could fix almost anything, even engines. So the store was a good fit for him. Mama helped out when I was in school. They sent me to parochial grade school, but there wasn't enough money for a Catholic high school, so I went to the public school then."

She leaned forward. "There was never enough money, Ms. Bonaparte. We rented a two-bedroom bungalow at the back of a two-house lot. My dresses were homemade or from the thrift shop. I didn't go to prom because it cost too much. Mama cut my hair at home. We never went on vacation. Our big treat was to rent a movie and watch it on our second-hand TV. I never owned a video game or a cell phone. When I graduated from high school and wanted to attend the university, there was no money then, either. So I got a job at a supermarket and helped my parents at the hardware store from time to time."

As she spoke, she twisted and clenched her hands and her voice got quieter. Then she paused and her gaze fell to her lap. "Last week, my parents died in a botched burglary attempt at the store. There was nothing stolen—the police think the robbers panicked and ran after they shot my parents. I would have been there, too, to help with inventory after closing, but I'd begged to be allowed to spend the weekend with a friend. The police have yet to find the ones responsible. Of course, in our little store, there was no recording equipment, and no one saw or heard a thing that night. A neighbor called the police when she got up to use the bathroom and noticed that the lights were still on in the front of the store. I buried my mother and father two days ago." The account was given without emotion, flat, as if she'd recited it so often that it no longer had impact.

"They always told me there wasn't enough. No matter what I wanted or asked for, there wasn't enough to have it or do it." Her jaw firmed. Tension radiated from her. "Yesterday, Uncle Herman showed me their will and their accounts. They had millions, Ms. Bonaparte." Her voice rose. "Millions. All those years of scrimping. All those years of not enough. I thought they loved me, that they would do anything for me, if they only had enough. And all that time, they did."

She stood and walked over to the window, her back to me and Susan. Her shoulders tensed and she remained there, stiff and unmoving, for several moments. Then she turned. "I told Uncle Herman that I didn't want the money, that if they never cared enough to give me the education I longed for and the nice things that others had, I didn't want their d-damned money!"

The mild profanity was obviously foreign to her. Susan moved forward in her chair, but I motioned her to stay still and let Adriana finish.

"How can I take it? I don't even know how they got it. We lived simply in the old country. We weren't rich there, either. And the store never produced that kind of income. I don't know what to do, but I know that I don't want ill-gotten money."

She'd wound down enough that I felt I could approach her without stifling her story. I stood and walked over to her and took her hand in mine. Hers was icy cold and I could feel the small tremors of her body. Her eyes were slightly unfocused. "Adriana—" I deliberately pronounced it the way she had on the phone, not the Americanized way that Susan used when she introduced us—"I think you're in a mild state of shock right now." I turned to Susan. "Would you brew us some of your fantastic tea? With plenty of sugar." She nodded and slipped out. "Susan makes the best tea, Adriana. No tea bags, she brews it from real tea leaves or herbs." As I soothed her, I led her to the conference room, sat her on an upholstered love seat and covered her legs with a throw. Susan came in with the tea and we watched while Adriana sipped and seemed to relax. When she set the cup down and leaned back, closing her eyes, I motioned to Susan to follow me from the room.

Susan and I met when we both worked for PI Jake Waterman. She conducted his financial investigations and I did his legwork—computer searches, tails, background checks. It didn't take Susan long to earn her CPA and go out on her own. Wisconsin requires that a person applying for a PI license be employed by a private investigator. I worked for Waterman long enough to learn the ropes—significantly shortened since I already had a degree in library science and understood the tenets of research. Then Susan and I decided to lessen expenses by sharing office space. Most of Susan's clientele are of Japanese descent, but lately, she's expanding her base and has made inroads into the Hmong and Vietnamese communities, as well as starting to get referrals for Caucasian clients.

Once in the outer office, I whispered, "Did you do the books for her parents' store?"

"Yes," Susan whispered back, "and there was no income there that would account for millions in the bank."

"Poor kid. Not only to lose her parents, but then to find out that they lived a lie all those years and lied to her, too."

We heard Adriana stir a bit and went back into the conference room. She was huddled under the throw, but her eyes seemed alert. I pulled a chair over and sat close, again taking one of her hands. This time, it was warm. I felt I could go a bit further.

"Adriana, what did your attorney tell you about the money? He must have some sort of explanation."

"He said that my papa had sworn him to secrecy, and that, as Papa's attorney, he couldn't tell me anything, even though Papa is dead now." She stopped, closing her eyes again. I mulled over the legality involving attorney-client privilege. Usually, an attorney cannot divulge information about a client, even after death, unless there was suspicion of fraud or intent to commit a crime. But in the case of wills, there was wiggle room, because the beneficiary had the right to understand the testator's intentions. However, that only applied if there was a dispute. Disputes over wills generally involved someone wanting more, not less. I needed to check my understanding before I met with Petrovitch.

I was ready to tiptoe back out when Adriana spoke. "If your papa and mama had behaved that way, would you want the money?"

"I honestly don't know," I replied. My father was a typical Sicilian father—protective, hard-working, and fairly chauvinistic about what his only daughter, and only child, should know. But to hide that much money while pretending that we didn't have enough for me to even go to college—no, no way would Papa do that to me. So how would I feel if I found that out? "If you don't accept the bequest, will you have enough to live on?" I asked her.

"Not for long. I have about three months' savings in the bank. And the store income has been steadily declining for years. I doubt I can salvage much from it, maybe a year's worth of living expenses, if I'm frugal. Of course, I've always been frugal, so that's not a burden that I've never carried before."

"We don't know if the money came from legitimate sources or not, so I think it's premature to decide to discard it. Let's take a small step back and consider options. If you decided to keep it, or some of it, what would you want to do? You mentioned college. Would that appeal to you now?"

Her eyes sparkled a little. "I've always felt that God intended me to be a nurse. But they said we couldn't afford the schooling." She stopped for a moment. "It's not too late, is it? People who are much older than I am go back to school."

"Yes, they do, and no, it's not too late, if that's what you want. So maybe keeping the money to finance your education and give you a start in life is not such a terrible thing, even if we're not sure yet where it came from." I smiled at her obvious excitement at that idea.

"Maybe not. Of course, I don't need that much. But there are lots of ways to put it to good use. I could talk with Father Matthieu at our church. He works with a lot of charities. He would know."

"Let's take it one step at a time, Adriana. First, are you still living in the same house?"

"Yes, but I've been staying with my friend, Jennifer, since my parents were killed."

"I think it might be time for a change of residence, at least until we know more about the money and about the persons who were involved in the killings."

"You think I'm in danger?" Her face, already pale, lost its remaining color.

"Probably not. But it won't hurt to be cautious, especially since nothing was taken in the burglary." She nodded. "What did Attorney Petrovitch tell you about drawing on the funds?"

"He said there's an account for living expenses and gave me a checkbook for it. He also said there are several other accounts for investments and things, that aren't so…um, liquid?"

Susan nodded. "That means that the investments aren't as easy to convert to cash in a hurry."

"I see," Adriana responded. "Well, there's a quarter million in the account I can draw on. I've never been that liquid in my whole life!"

We all giggled a bit. It was good to hear Adriana joke in the midst of her turmoil. It made me realize that she might be plain, but she had spunk. That would carry her far.

Now I needed to get her to a safe place. I called Anthony Belloni, aka Tony Baloney, a real estate mini-mogul who owed me big time for saving his butt when he was suspected of murdering his girlfriend, Elisa Morano. The dog had a wife and four kids, now five. I swallowed hard over working on his defense team—my own ex pulled the same shopping-around routine on me—but ultimately, Tony didn't deserve life in prison for infidelity. He agreed to rent a nice two-bedroom apartment to Adriana, furnished and ready to move in. The building manager would be waiting whenever we arrived.

While Adriana filled out paperwork for me, Susan and I conferred. She would start digging into the accounts that Attorney Petrovitch disclosed to Adriana. I would take Adriana to her parents' home to pick up whatever clothing and other belongings would fit in my Miata convertible. I didn't want Adriana to drive her own car, in case anyone had her under surveillance. My mind ticked over on ways to get from her home to Tony's apartment building with less chance of being followed. Paranoid? Maybe, but as the saying goes, just because you're paranoid, it doesn't mean there's nobody after you.

ABOUT THE AUTHOR

Nanci Rathbun is a lifelong reader of mysteries—historical, contemporary, futuristic, paranormal, hard-boiled, cozy … you can find them all on her bookshelves and in her ereaders. She brings logic and planning to her writing from a background as an IT project manager, and attention to characters and dialog from her second career as a Congregationalist minister. (Her books are not Christian fiction, but they contain no explicit sexual or violent scenes, and only the occasional mild curse word.)

Her first novel, *Truth Kills—An Angelina Bonaparte Mystery*, was published in 2013. *Cash Kills* is the second book in the series and was published in November of 2014. Both novels are available in paperback and ebook formats. Readers can enjoy the first chapters of each on her web site or on Goodreads. The third Angie novel has a working title of *Deception Kills*, with plans to publish in 2017.

A longtime Wisconsin resident, Nanci now makes her home in Colorado. No matter where she lives, she will always be a Packers fan.

Connect with me

My website, where you can find my blog:
https://nancirathbun.com/

Like and Follow me on Facebook:
www.facebook.com/Author-Nanci-Rathbun-162077650631803

Follow me on Twitter:
https://twitter.com/NanciRathbun

Friend or Follow me on Goodreads:
https://www.goodreads.com/author/show/7199317.Nanci_Rathbun

Check out my Pinterest boards:
https://www.pinterest.com/nancir50/

Made in the USA
Middletown, DE
23 September 2018